To Tina for believing in my work.
To Lucia for taking a chance on a newbie.
And to May for your wonderful counsel.
Thank you, ladies!

Alexandra Benedict

Too Great A Temptation

AVON BOOKS

An Imprint of HarperCollins*Publishers*

This is a work of fiction. Names, characters, places, and incidents are products of the author's imagination or are used fictitiously and are not to be construed as real. Any resemblance to actual events, locales, organizations, or persons, living or dead, is entirely coincidental.

AVON BOOKS
An Imprint of HarperCollins*Publishers*
10 East 53rd Street
New York, New York 10022-5299

Copyright © 2006 by Alexandra Benedikt
ISBN-13: 978-0-06-084794-4
ISBN-10: 0-06-084794-8
www.avonromance.com

First Avon Books paperback printing: November 2006

Avon Trademark Reg. U.S. Pat. Off. and in Other Countries, Marca Registrada, Hecho en U.S.A.
HarperCollins® is a registered trademark of HarperCollins Publishers Inc.

Printed in the U.S.A.

10 9 8 7 6 5 4 3 2 1

Prologue

England, 1819

The earth was sound asleep, lulled by a soft chorus of chirping crickets. Into the soothing surroundings intruded the distant hail of creaking wheels. Fast approaching, a rickety carriage jingled along the pebbled road, each squeak of the axle muffled only by the exuberant squeaks of the wench within.

"Why, ye wily devil." The doxy giggled in her drunken stupor, fumbling with the laces of her corset, trying to fasten the garment in mock gentility.

"Now, now, luv. Let's have none of that."

A robust hand brushed her gawky fingers away from her bosom. She dipped her head back in a peal of laughter, all but toppling off the hard set of thighs she was straddling.

Damian Westmore, the Duke of Wembury, dubbed the "Duke of Rogues" by his peers, was slumped back in his seat, mesmerized by the pair of plump breasts bobbing in rhythm to each lurch and wobble of the carriage. He was in no hurry to see the bountiful mounds tucked back into the shelter of the corset, and with a wicked grin, he cupped one heavy breast, raising the puckering nipple to the tip of his lips, and blew.

The wench giggled, then moaned with pleasure. In a lanky stroke, Damian licked the rosy bud, nipped, then licked again. She bucked in his lap, groaning, the sweet sounds of carnal hunger making him stiff and ready for her.

"Ride me," he growled.

Slipping her shaky hands beneath her skirt, the giddy wench grappled with the buttons of the duke's trousers.

And so the impassioned couple dallied in such a manner for the rest of the journey, insensible to the distraction their fervid voices inflicted on the poor coachman.

It was an hour later the screeching wheels—and voices—came to a whispered halt before the ancient dwelling.

A black leather boot kicked open the carriage door, and out stumbled the inebriated duke.

"Wait here," he gave the rough command to the driver, and then with a seductive growl, ordered the accommodating wench to do the same. "I'll be but a minute, sweet."

With a bubbling laugh, she collapsed against the

cushioned seat and rucked her skirt up over her knees. "Hurry back, Yer Grace."

His eyes went to those finely curved calves and glossed over firm, smooth thighs, as she lifted her skirt higher and higher.

Damian could feel the swelling in his groin again. He slammed the door shut to keep himself from pouncing back into the carriage.

"What a bird," he whispered with a devilish grin. But upon pivoting to confront the imposing main doors of the castle, he found his humor had quickly vanished. "Let's get this over with."

Stumbling up the stone steps, he rattled the handles. Locked. Blast it! He pounded on the mahogany entrance, cursing all the while at finding his own doors secured against him.

"Jenkins!" he bellowed for the butler.

One door opened. "Your Grace," came the stoic greeting, followed by a curt nod of obligatory respect.

Petulant after hammering on the door for some time, Damian demanded sharply: "Where is she, Jenkins?"

"In the parlor, Your Grace."

Damian stepped into the dark entranceway and slammed the door closed with the heel of his boot. "Take me to her."

Candle in hand, the old butler complied, and progressed through the stone-clad foyer and into the deserted corridor.

"What time is it?" snapped the duke, his deep blue eyes peeking into each of the desolate drawing rooms.

"It is shortly past nine o'clock."

"So where the devil is everyone?" And then the piercing table corner jabbed him in the thigh. "And why the hell is it so bloody dark in here!" he blasted, and promptly kicked the insolent table for having found itself in his direct path.

Jenkins, not the least perturbed by his master's display of temper, evenly answered both questions in sequence. "Her Grace has temporarily relieved some of the staff, and requested all but essential lights be extinguished."

"Well, I am the master of this castle." He pointed to his chest. "And *I* have not dismissed the staff nor ordered the house to be enshrouded in darkness. So fetch the servants back and light some infernal candles!"

"Yes, Your Grace."

The butler resumed his steady pace through the corridor, the fractious duke wavering in tow.

The servant soon paused before the sealed parlor door and proclaimed: "Her Grace has been expecting you."

Damian just bet the old nag was expecting him. Three days ago, his mother had dispatched a courier with a letter bidding him home *urgently*. He snorted. Urgent, his bleeding ass. He was accustomed to the woman's skullduggery, and this letter was just another one of her shams.

It seemed his mother had no other purpose in life but to disrupt his own. First had come the scathing lectures on propriety and responsibility and other such reprehensible nonsense. Then, when she'd learned of the hedonistic revelry reigning within the walls of his ancestral keep, she'd packed her bags, abandoned London, and moved back into the castle, forcing him to search for amusement elsewhere—which he found readily enough in the many dens of gamble and drink.

Now, unable to follow her son into the lairs of decadence, but still intent on reforming his immoral ways, his mother had resorted to luring him *out* of his havens through such feeble means as a fabricated crisis. Well, he'd not stand for it a moment longer. The next "urgent" letter to reach him would find its way into the nearest fire. He'd tolerate no more of the woman's interference, and he intended to tell her so that very night.

"Would you like me to announce you, Your Grace?"

"Not this time, Jenkins."

The butler gave a stiff nod and moved away from the door. "I am sorry, Your Grace." And with those cryptic words, he retreated down the corridor, the aura of candlelight receding with him and finally disappearing around the corner.

Damian stared down the shadowed passageway. "Babbling old fool."

A senile Jenkins was soon dismissed from his mind. There was still his mother to confront, and with a deep breath to help sharpen his befuddled senses, Damian flung open the parlor door.

Emily, the Dowager Duchess of Wembury, sat poised by the low-burning fire, her stern face aglow, her fingers knit tightly together in her lap. She spared her son a brief glance before her lethargic gaze returned to the snapping flames.

"At least you're appropriately dressed," she said.

Damian examined his attire, unable to recall what he was wearing. He noted he was arrayed in all black. Boots, breeches, greatcoat fluttering about his ankles. All black. And with his long ebony mane secured at the nape of his neck with a strip of leather cord, he appeared every inch the dark devil so many had termed him.

Eyes elevating to his mother, he realized for the first time that she, too, was adorned in sable black. He had seen her in such macabre garb only once before, when his father had died.

"What's happened?" he asked, some suspicion still enduring in his voice, for he had yet to determine whether this was a ruse of some kind.

"You haven't heard?" Her eyes abandoned the fire to concentrate on her son. "Here I thought grief had delayed your return. I am such a fool. So where have you been these last three days?"

He said nothing. That seemed answer enough.

The hollow sound of her laughter filled the dimly lit room. "A trollop has kept you well entertained, I see." She shook her head and returned her attention to the flickering flames. "I should have known. How could a man like you even mourn?"

Damian stepped deeper into the room. "Mourn?"

The newspaper spread out at his mother's feet went sailing through the air, landing at his.

Pirates Strike Again!

Damian stared at the bold headline, his vision blurring, his head beginning to throb.

"What the hell is going on?" he demanded, this time more passionately.

"A matter of little consequence to you, I'm sure. But my life is over—now that Adam is gone."

Upon hearing his younger brother's name, Damian went still, very still. The room appeared to be spinning. Shadows mixed with the soft orange glow of the fire and whirled before him in a maddening dance.

He brought his fists to his eyes and barked impatiently, "Where is Adam?"

"Dead."

His fists fell to his sides, and he looked at his mother in disbelief.

"He was sailing home with Tess," she recounted, her eyes still fixed to the hissing flames. "The ship was plundered by pirates. The vagrants took everything of value, bowed to the passengers in mock gratitude for their generous gift, and then aimed their cannons for the ship's hull. No one survived, save the captain's cabin boy, who clung to a piece of debris until he was rescued by a passing ship. The boy had time to relate the entire tale before a fever took his life."

Damian's dancing demons were back, clogging his vision, his mind. He brought his fingers to his temples in an attempt to slay them. But it did no good. They danced and laughed and chanted: *Adam is dead! Adam is dead!*

He closed his eyes, willing the racket in his head

to stop. Memories of Adam on his wedding day flashed through Damian's mind. It was the last time he had seen his brother. He remembered Adam now, all clad in his finery, that silly grin on his face as he prepared to marry his childhood love, Teresa. It had been the talk of the *ton* that the duke had arrived sober to the ceremony. But even he, impenitent sybarite that he was, would never blight the most important day of his brother's life. Damian had come to the event to support his sibling, for he loved his brother, more than he cared to admit. Two months had gone by since Adam and Tess had embarked on their wedding tour of Italy. And the couple was expected home within a matter of days.

His chest ached; his heart grew sore. Damian opened his eyes and connected with his mother's somber gaze.

"It's all my fault," she said.

"Yours?" He breathed raggedly. "How?"

"It was I who begged your brother's return. Adam wrote to say he and Tess would remain another month on the mainland. They were happy in Italy. But I was miserable. You were disappearing for days and weeks at a time. The stories reaching my ears of your dissolute ways were growing more obscene. So I wrote back to Adam, pleading for him to come home as planned. I had hoped he could reason with you again. He always managed to pull you away from your wretched habits, if only for a short time . . . but now he's gone."

The woman's apathetic features cracked. Her bottom lip quivered. Fat, soulful tears hung from her sooty lashes before dripping down her flushed cheeks.

"My son is gone." She choked on her words, her glossy eyes pinned intensely on her only living child. "Your father was a scoundrel, you are a villain, but Adam . . . he was the last noble thing in my life."

In that instant, every morsel of strength he had known his mother to possess crumbled before him. She sank to her knees and let out such a sorrowful sob, it echoed throughout the room, burning his ears. It was as though the walls themselves were wailing, the din was so great, and Damian found that even his hardened heart could splinter after all.

"Why?" she cried. "Why did it have to be Adam? Why could it not be you lying at the bottom of the sea?!"

And so she surrendered to her hysterics, crumpled onto the floor in a pool of black satin and lace.

Damian watched her for a time, knowing she would scorn any pitiful attempt on his part to comfort her. There was nothing he could do . . . except seek vengeance for his brother's death.

Softly, he walked out of the room.

Chapter 1

New York, 1821

Damian needed money. Lots of it. Ironic, really, that he, a duke, with his coffers of gold back home in England, should find himself a virtual beggar on the streets of New York. But when had fate ever been kind to him?

Wending through the bustling city port, the duke passed jeering sailors and vulgar wenches alike, making his way to the nearest gaming hell. A few coins in his pocket, he intended to amass a small fortune. And he could do it, too. Years of debauchery had prepared him for just such an endeavor. But unlike his former besotted self, he was sober now. With all his wits intact, Damian hoped to recoup as much of his wealth as he could. His ship was in dire need of repairs, and the crew would not follow him in exchange for bread crumbs. He needed blunt.

Damian came to a halt.

Neptune's Revenge.

It was aptly named, the shore house, for Damian, too, was seeking revenge at sea. And he was in desperate need of good luck. A shoddy hole christened after the wrathful sea king seemed the perfect place to find it.

But a nearby scuffle distracted the duke—and made the blood pound in his veins.

"Admit it, kid, you were cheatin'."

The horde, five in total, circled the so-called kid, a strapping young buck sporting a cheeky grin, who quipped, "Me cheat?" He snorted. "Sorry, Yanks. 'Fraid we Brits are just unbeatable."

Damian blinked.

The kid disappeared under a pummel of fists. Yet it was not the brutal thrashing that stirred the frantic rage in Damian's gut. It was the kid. He recognized the kid. It was Adam!

With a roar, Damian launched right into the fray and did a little pounding of his own. He had to save Adam! One thug staggered off with a bleeding nose, another stumbled away with a broken arm. But Damian soon lost the chance to trounce any more ruffians.

Shots rang out.

The kid was hit in the arm with a bullet.

Whistles blowing, pistols flailing, the authorities rounded up the lot of them. And it was then Damian looked down at the kid, curled in a dusty heap, and realized the boy was not Adam. He only looked like Adam.

Stunned by his visceral response, Damian could not say a word when the authorities snapped the shackles over his wrists. What the devil had come over him?

Carted off to the nearest gaol, Damian was tossed inside the brig, the kid his cellmate, and for three days he suffered imprisonment. Three miserable, dull days. And all the while he sat chained in the corner, brooding.

Woeful thoughts interrupted, Damian glanced down at the kid—Quincy was his name—groaning and stirring on the clump of hay. And try as he might to ignore the chap's distress, Damian could not.

Bloody hell. With each passing day, he grew more and more sentimental. A blubbering saphead, as his father would say. Teeth ground in disgust, Damian propped his manacled wrists under the lad's chest and pushed.

Quincy rolled over, hacking, and brought his forearm to his eyes to block the shaft of moonlight resting on his face. He was like a ghost, so pale and sluggish, and Damian could feel that galling worry creeping into his chest again.

"Wake up!" he ordered, kicking the kid in the leg for good measure. "You'll die if you sleep any more."

"Bollocks," came the weak but stubborn protest. "And I'll draw your cork if you kick me again."

Damian snorted. The lad didn't have the strength to roll over, but he was going to break Damian's nose? The duke had to admire the kid's spirit, but still, it was not enough to save the chap. An infection had set into the bullet wound, and the boy's breathing had changed to odd, raspy gasps.

"I'd like to see you try and draw my cork," goaded the duke, hoping to stir some life back into the weary chap.

But Quincy wasn't taking the bait. He merely grunted at the suggestion.

There was nothing more Damian could do for the kid. The gaol cell, with little food and water, no clean linens, and no surgical instruments, made for a very poor infirmary. Besides, Damian's medical talent was lackluster at best. After abandoning his castle, leaving the land steward in charge of the estate, he'd spent the last two years learning to sail, rig a mast, fire a cannon with deadly accuracy. He'd improved upon his fencing, his aim with a pistol, even his use of a knife. But he had no real use for the healing art. His purpose in life was to destroy: to destroy the piratical fiends who had murdered his brother.

Blast it! He should be out there right now, looking for the brigand swine, instead of playing nursemaid to a troubled buck. Curse the wretched storm that brought him here! But for the wild tempest that had thrashed his ship a few days ago, he would never have limped into port in desperate need of repairs. Repairs, of course, cost money, and since a good chunk of his coin had washed overboard during the squall, money was one thing he didn't have in abundance.

At first it seemed a trifle bind. In a safe aboard his ship was a series of credentials, all proclaiming him the duke that he was. He had only to saunter into the nearest bank, present the papers to a pudgy-faced banker, and acquire a loan for as much blunt as he wanted . . . if only the safe had been watertight. Damian had opened the iron door to find his credentials washed clean away, the ink smeared all over the raggedy parchments.

And so, adrift in New York harbor with a badly leaking ship and torn sails and scant supplies, he'd headed into port to *win* his wealth, leaving behind his lieutenant with the order to sell the damaged rig for whatever he could get and divide the money among the crew, should Damian not return within two days. Of course, he'd never expected *not* to return. His instructions to the lieutenant had been a mere formality.

But it mattered little now. He was stranded. Chained, penniless, and shipless, too. For by now his lieutenant had surely sold what was left of the vessel and divvied up the profit. Damian didn't even have a single coin. He'd been stripped clear of valuables before being shackled to the wall. Bloody hell.

Quincy coughed, a garbled, hacking sound that didn't bode well. "Why did you save me, Damian?"

Thoughts of Adam quickly flooded the duke's mind. At the sharp pain in his chest, he closed his eyes and fibbed, "I hate to see an American get the better of one of my own."

The kid raised an invisible glass. "Here, here."

Another round of hacking.

"Sit up, Quincy, you'll breathe better."

But the kid couldn't move, so Damian gathered the hay and mashed it together, cramming it under Quincy's head.

The coughing subsided, but it was a temporary respite, Damian knew. The chap wouldn't last much longer.

An owl hooted in the distance. A sick owl by the sound of its croaking cry.

Quincy's bleary gaze wandered over to the barred window. In a voice raw and faint, he wondered, "What time is it?"

"Near midnight, perhaps. Why?"

"Changing of the guards soon."

"So?"

"Never mind." Quincy looked away from the window. "So what brings a fellow sailor all the way to America?"

Damian had mentioned it before, his guise as a sailor. It offered him common ground with the kid, who claimed to be a tar aboard a merchant ship. Damian just couldn't tell Quincy the truth, that he was a duke, that he was captain of his own ship— former captain, he should say—for if rumor ever spread about his pirate-hunting mission, those dastardly pirates might up and disappear on him for good.

"I have a duty to see to my brother," said Damian instead. That much he was willing to admit.

A soft, choking laugh. "I have three brothers, all a bother, always interfering, claiming to do what's best for me."

The duke snorted. "Aye, I see how well you do on your own."

"That was a lark. Those bloody Americans accused me of cheating. Sore losers, I tell you, the lot of 'em.

All mortified to have lost their blunt to an English bloke."

"A seventeen-year-old English bloke," corrected Damian.

Quincy managed a proud but crooked smile. "That must have irked 'em a bit, too."

Damian, overwhelmed by a sudden urge to scold the impetuous chap, bit his tongue. Was he mad? Not too long ago he had lived the life of a heathen. And while eleven years Quincy's senior, he was hardly the appropriate figure to dictate on the value of responsibility. Besides, there was something inherent in his nature that went against the repugnant act of moralizing. Perhaps he could shake some sense into the chap instead.

"So this duty to your brother, what's it about?"

Damian shifted. His arse was sore. He was bloody tired, too. And Quincy's constant digging into his personal affairs was putting him in a more dour mood. "Why so many questions, kid?"

"Just curious." He shrugged. After another round of hacking, Quincy prodded, "Braving the Atlantic waves to fulfill a brotherly duty? That's some devotion."

A wave of grief smacked the duke. "I wasn't always so devoted."

"Neither was I," sighed Quincy. "I used to think I'd be better off without my meddlesome kin."

Damian swallowed the burst of bitter emotion that had welled in his breast, to ask, "And now?"

"I suppose I'm better off with 'em . . . but I'll never tell 'em so."

Damian quirked a brow.

"Tell you what," said Quincy. "When we get out of here, I'll help you see that duty to your brother to an end. I owe you that much."

When they got out? Damian had the sinking suspicion both he and Quincy would be left inside the rank dungeon cell to perish. That meant either the kid was a foolish optimist or the fever was making him incoherent. Damian wasn't sure which.

Moreover, the kind of help Damian needed wasn't something a chap still wet behind the ears could offer, even if they did manage to escape somehow. Stranded as he was, Damian had to sail home, commission another ship and crew, then hightail it back to America. Quincy wasn't the likely candidate to make any of that happen.

Just thinking about his plight had Damian's palms fisting. He had come so close to catching the miserable buccaneers. After years of fruitless searching, a tale had reached his ears of a marauding rogue, harassing English ships near the coast of New York. It was a frail lead, but one Damian was determined to follow. And he would have followed it, too, had it not been for the cursed storm . . . and Quincy.

"Thanks for the offer, kid, but I have to get home to England, and unless you have a ship, I doubt you can help me."

The thud was soft, but not so faint as to go unheard. Another thud followed, then another.

Damian scrunched his brow.

Keys jingled, and the prison door swung wide open

to reveal three titans filling the doorway. Hulking figures, every last one of them, with jet black hair and the same delft blue eyes Quincy bore.

" 'Bout bloody time," muttered Quincy.

Two of the titans entered the dungeon and knelt beside the kid. The third, and biggest of the lot, remained stationed under the doorway. A lookout, Damian supposed.

"Don't gripe," said the first titan. "It wasn't easy to find you in this maze of a city. We searched through brothels and gaming hells before finally coming to the gaols." Then, examining Quincy's arm: "Anything broken?"

"Only his pride," said the second.

"Sod off!" Quincy hissed. "Your owl cry still sounds like a parakeet, Eddie."

"Knock it off, all of you," from the third.

Definitely brothers. And not a single one of them paid Damian any heed.

Quincy was yanked to his feet, coughing. Stricken as he was, the guards hadn't bothered to shackle him to the wall. But before his brethren could drag him out of the prison cell, Quincy demanded: "Unlock his chains, James."

The third and most sinister titan deigned Damian a glance. "No."

"But James, he saved my life. We can't just leave him here."

"No."

"Damn it, James! I swore I would help him when I got out of here. You're not going to make a liar out of me, are you?"

"Oh, bloody hell." James tossed one sibling the keys. "Get him out, Will. Quick!"

Propping Quincy against his remaining kin, the one called Will hunched down to unlock Damian's chains.

The first key didn't fit, neither did the second. There were at least a dozen more on the ring, and the sound of distant movement in the courtyard, by a possible prison guard, was making everyone uneasy.

"Hurry up, Will!"

"I'm trying," Will shot back, inserting the third— and lucky—key.

The manacles sprang open.

Damian shot to his feet. Free but still stranded. One predicament was better than two, though.

The duke was about to express his gratitude when Quincy intervened, "He's coming with us, James."

"Are you ordering *me* around, little brother?"

"Come on, James, he's a sailor. And we need one more—"

"We don't need another sailor."

"Blister it, James, the man saved my life!" the kid croaked. "We can't just leave him stranded."

That gave the mulish brother pause—but not incentive. "No. Now let's go."

Quincy, hauled toward the door, reiterated all the way, "But James, we need another sailor."

"We don't need another bloody sailor! What we need is a navigator."

"I can navigate."

All four brothers paused to look Damian's way.

"You can?" said James, eyeing him closely.

"You can?" echoed Quincy, surprised.

"I can," Damian confirmed—somewhat. But he kept that part to himself. He had acquired many nautical skills over the course of his self-training. Navigation was one, only he wasn't proficient. He just didn't have a knack for calculations. Downright hated them, in fact, often trusting his own navigator to plot each course. But to get back home to England he'd bloody well dream of numbers and stars if he had to.

"Perfect," said Quincy. "Damian will be our new navigator."

James only growled. "We're not going to argue about this in here. Let's move!"

But Quincy took that as an affirmation, and grinned. "Welcome aboard, Damian."

Though he was not entirely convinced of his new appointment, Damian trailed after the brothers, stepping over the bodies of the three unconscious gaolers, and making his way through the foul-smelling passages.

Slowly, though, a prickle of hope spread through him. There was still enough time to fulfill his mission, he thought. It was only mid June. He could sail home and back before the winter gales hit the Atlantic, track the nameless rogue lurking along the American coast, and send him to a watery grave should he happen to be the murderous pirate Black Hawk.

That was the name the young cabin boy had uttered before he'd died. Black Hawk. It was a name Damian had dreamed about. It was a name that made the bile in his gut churn. The former "Duke of Rogues" would not rest until the day his brother's killers were dead. The piratical fiends would not ride the waves, a merry lot, while his kin lay rotting at the bottom of the sea.

Damian would see to it.

Out of the darkness and rank dungeon air, the duke took in a deep, lingering breath, relishing the cool breeze ruffling his hair.

Quickly the men skulked through the courtyard, along the shadowed walls, through the imposing iron gates, slightly ajar, and on to liberty.

Not three steps later, a bullet whizzed by Damian's ear, the blast so strident, he heard the bells of Westminster chiming in his head.

The men turned in time to see the hooded figure of a gaoler sink to his knees, clutching his bleeding hand, the pistol shot clean out of his grip and resting some yards away.

In unison, the bewildered men turned the other way, to see who had fired the bullet.

The vision rammed Damian in the gut.

She stood atop a boulder, the illustrious full moon illuminating the fine golden threads of her lengthy locks, lilting in the soft zephyr.

Her glistening eyes, piercing as a prowling cat's, met his, mesmerizing him. There was something dark and primal in those eyes, something familiar . . . something Damian recognized in himself.

She was adorned in all black, breeches and boots, tight leather vest. That vest! How he envied it. Strapped around plump and magnificent breasts. To taste such a flawless pair . . .

A hint of panic brewed inside him.

She was devastating. A true siren, with all her wiles, and he ached inside just looking at her.

It had been ages since he'd had the satisfaction of a woman's body. Nigh two years, in fact. While searching for the pirates, he had given up pleasure of all kind, lust and drink included. Pleasure only distracted the mind. But the stunning siren before him could foil even his hardened determination.

Damian closed his eyes, tamping the carnal yearnings into submission.

"Damnation, Belle, I ordered you to stay aboard ship!"

The blasted reproof brought Damian's attention back to the temptress. Slowly, she lowered the smoking pistol to her side, and in a voice just as smoky, shot back: "Good thing I didn't listen, James."

The man growled. "Let's get back to the ship before we're *all* rounded up."

His ears still ringing, Damian was sure he had misunderstood. The siren sailing home with them? Impossible.

But then Quincy said in his ear, "That's our sister, Mirabelle."

Sister? A sexy, curvaceous, golden-haired, keep-your-damn-hands-off-her sister?

Just his miserable luck.

Chapter 2

❝He's to be our new navigator?"

Mirabelle Hawkins stood atop the poop, staring at the formidable figure carting crates of supplies across the schooner's deck. Even in the moonlight, it was easy to see the muscular body moving with grace. A surprise really, that such a hefty man possessed such elegance of form.

With his forearms bare, the cuffs of his sleeves rolled up to his elbows, she could see the strength of his physique, the muscles flexing under the weight of each crate he carried. His long, dark hair was tied at the nape of his neck, stray strands whipping across his strong and rigid profile.

There was an aura of secrecy around him, a profound darkness under that brooding façade.

"He's to be *my* new navigator, Belle," James

interrupted her musing. Crouched over an open crate, he rummaged through the contents, checking to make sure all the supplies were there. "*You* are not a member of this crew."

She gnashed her teeth at the umpteenth reminder. Captain James Hawkins was adamant she would never serve aboard the *Bonny Meg*. Mirabelle was just as adamant that she would. And the two butted heads on the issue constantly.

"Why do you trust Damian more than me?" she demanded.

Damian stopped mid deck at the mention of his name. A shudder prickled through her. Hell's fire, but the man had a stunning pair of eyes.

"This has nothing to do with trust," said James, still groping through the paraphernalia, oblivious to the couple's exchange of heated looks.

Mirabelle shivered again and crossed her arms over her chest like a shield. She turned away, but Damian's intense stare still pierced her skin. "It has everything to do with trust," she contested, trying to dismiss the dazzling gaze of one dashing rogue sailor from her mind. "You think I'm incompetent."

"I think you're a woman." The lid thudded closed, and James stood to confront his sister. "You have no place aboard this ship."

They were a stubborn brood, her brothers. James, the eldest, more mulish than the rest. At the age of thirty-six, he was the tallest and wielded the greatest brute strength. And with those ebony locks and riveting blue eyes, he always maintained a daunting appearance. Just one scorching look was often enough to

put a disobedient tar back in his place. Not that Mirabelle heeded any of his attempts at intimidation. Certainly not. Her dream of being a seafarer was far too
precious. Even James's dark expressions could not dissuade her of her conviction.

Although she resented her brother's willfulness, she
at least understood it. James was worried a woman
aboard ship would be too disruptive. Rubbish, of
course, but that was his concern nonetheless. What
did not make any sense was the opposition from the
rest of her kin.

Her brother William, second eldest at thirty-four
and serving as lieutenant, was the most rational and
even-tempered of the lot. He could always see both
sides of a story, and had a knack for settling a conflict
before it got out of hand. But even he would not consider the idea of her remaining aboard ship.

And then there were her youngest siblings, Edmund
and Quincy. Babies really, at the ages of nineteen and
seventeen respectively. The duo were always at each
other's throats and didn't give a hoot for propriety or
order. But even *they*, reckless and impulsive fledg-
lings, were against her joining the crew.

Mirabelle took in a deep breath to soothe her rumbling temper. She was older than half of her brothers
at the age of twenty-one, more levelheaded for sure,
and still her tenacious brethren refused to let her serve
on board. All she wanted was a chance to prove herself. Just one measly opportunity to demonstrate her
sex did not make her incompetent or a menace to sta-
bility and order.

"I deserve to be here, James."

Her brother pushed the crate to the edge of the poop. "This goes to the galley," he ordered, then looked back at her. "How do you figure that, Belle?"

But she didn't answer him right away. Their spat postponed, Mirabelle studied the swaggering figure of an approaching tar with avid interest. Bloody big, she reflected. Almost as big as James.

Damian's booted steps were heavy, the footfalls resounding in her ears like rhythmic drumbeats, hypnotizing her. He came to a stop by the poop, his dark gaze settling on her, raking over her in a thorough assessment.

The fine hairs on her arms spiked.

What the devil was the matter with her? Knots in her belly? Goose bumps on her arms? Was she daft? So the bloke was staring at her; he wouldn't be the first. Mirabelle was used to such leering gazes. She was quite adept at ignoring them, too. So why couldn't she turn her head away from the man? And why was her heart starting to thump so fast?

Damian quietly collected the cargo and moved off.

"Well, Belle, why do you deserve to be here?"

"Hmm?" She looked up at James, a bit dazed. "Oh, right." With a quick shake of the head, she dismissed her bewilderment. "I've proven my loyalty, unlike Damian. That's why I deserve to be here."

There was something about the new navigator that made her uneasy. She didn't trust him, and she was going to find out more about him. If he was hiding something, perhaps then James would see *she* belonged here and not some strange scoundrel of a sailor.

"I'm not worried about Damian's loyalty," said James. "He thinks this a simple merchant ship, delivering cargo to England. He knows nothing that might put our lives at risk. Besides, we need a new navigator, and *you* can't navigate."

Her reverie shattered, she glared at her brother. "That doesn't mean I don't belong here."

"You *don't* belong here," he stressed in exasperation. "Look, Belle, Damian saved Quincy's life, which speaks something of his character. I'll learn more about him over the next few weeks, and if he navigates well and obeys orders, *then* I might ask him to join the crew."

Her hands went to her hips. "And Quincy? The boy is a disaster. You'd prefer him over me?"

"Quincy's young."

"And foolish."

"He'll learn."

"And I won't?"

"You've already disobeyed an order, Belle."

"But I *saved* one of you tonight."

"That doesn't justify your disobedience—again."

She snorted. "Stowing away doesn't count."

A dark brow lifted.

"Well, it doesn't," she insisted. "You never ordered me *not* to stow away."

He sighed at that. "Belle, you don't belong here."

"Yes, I do, and I'll prove it to you."

And she had the Atlantic crossing to do it. The voyage from England to America had been spent in seclusion, so she hadn't had a chance to demonstrate her nautical abilities. But the journey home would be different. She didn't have to hide in the galley anymore, fearing her brothers would turn the ship around and take her home too soon. She could now stroll along deck with everyone else, participate in all the chores and missions—well, some of them, anyway.

Needless to say, the Hawkins clan had not been pleased to find her on ship. She had foiled their main mission, for her brothers were not about to engage in their usual pursuits with *her* on board. After much haggling, it was agreed the *Bonny Meg* would stop in New York to obtain supplies and give the crew some leisure time before turning around to take her home. This was her one and only opportunity to prove to her blind brethren she deserved to be a member of the *Bonny Meg*'s crew.

"You know perfectly well I can't have you on board," said James. "You're a distraction to the crew, and the men consider you a bad omen."

"Bah!" She crossed her arms under her breasts. "Having a clumsy twit on board is unlucky. I'm no twit. I'm levelheaded, James. Father taught me everything he taught you."

"That was Father's mistake."

She took in a sharp breath, stung.

"Be sensible, Belle," he said softly. "You belong on shore. Why not get married and raise a family?"

"You're my family. I belong right here with you."

"I'm sorry, Belle, but I won't change my mind."

She would just have to see about that. The trip home would take a few weeks at least, enough time to convince her pigheaded brothers she'd make as good a pirate as any of them.

* * *

The *Bonny Meg* sliced through the black, velvety ocean.

Damian stood at the stern, hunched over the rail. He watched the bubbling waves, mesmerized.

A woman aboard ship? He had never heard of anything so daft. Who could think with a stunning siren strutting across deck? Not Damian, that was for sure. Warm blood rushed through his veins at the thought of Mirabelle. She was a bloody temptation. And she would destroy him if he wasn't careful. Just a short while ago she had said his name, and like an adolescent mooncalf he'd been completely bewitched. He had paused right in the middle of the deck—an obedient sailor heeding the siren's enchanting call.

Bloody idiot. Any more mishaps like that, and he was bound to find himself in the frothing water. If the brothers suspected he had any wicked intentions toward their sister, he'd be tossed overboard.

"Damian?"

She had a sultry voice. One that stirred the carnal heat in his belly. A sudden vision gripped him, an image of her lush and bare body writhing beneath him, as she cried out his name again and again in wanton desire.

Damian closed his eyes, banishing the erotic dream. "Yes, Belle?" Her name did her justice. She really was beautiful. Too beautiful.

"The captain wants to speak with you."

"About what?"

"Our course, I suspect."

He glimpsed at her sidelong. She had a dry

wit . . . and a devastating figure. Curse it, *why* was the woman here? It just didn't make any sense, the peculiar family union. To risk the welfare of one's own sister on the treacherous sea? The captain seemed the strict sort, certainly not the kind of man to allow any frivolity or a laxness of rules. So what the devil was she doing here?

Damian crammed the lustful yearnings deep down inside him. "How long have you been a member of the crew?"

She paused for a moment. "Not long. Why?"

"It's unusual to have a woman aboard ship."

"There's nothing wrong with my being here," she said, a tightness in her voice. "You're the intruder, remember?"

"I was asked to join the crew."

"For *one* voyage. Don't get too comfortable here."

He had ruffled her feathers. For some peculiar reason, he liked the thought of that. And he wasn't sure why. Feisty females had repulsed him in the past. He had always preferred an obedient woman, one to satisfy his carnal appetite. But the spark in Mirabelle was oddly fascinating. And that was treacherous. He could not let her stir his dormant demons of lust. He had a mission to complete.

To soothe her temper—and the heat in his belly—he deftly inquired, "What happened to the previous navigator?"

"Thomas?" She snorted. "Love drove him to shore."

"Love?"

She propped her hip against the rail and crossed

her arms under her splendid breasts. "So it would seem. Thomas had a ladybird in port, one he visited each time the ship moored. He hadn't seen her for a few months, though. Imagine his surprise when he came to call and she had a squalling infant in her arms."

A surprise indeed. Even more of a surprise was Mirabelle's candor. She behaved like a man, coolly chatting over delicacies like a mistress and a by-blow. Something a dainty maid would never do . . .

"Thomas decided to do the gentlemanly thing and marry the wench," she said.

There was enough emphasis on "gentlemanly" that Damian recognized the sarcasm. What, she didn't believe in love? That was odd for a woman. And speaking of odd . . .

"You speak your mind most freely," he murmured.

"Shouldn't I?"

He delved deep into her catlike eyes. "It's not something a proper miss would do."

Did she just shiver? He couldn't be sure. He was too enraptured by the shimmering strands of her honey blond hair lilting in the wind. Like streaks of moonbeams, he mused.

"And what do you know of a proper miss, Damian?"

Something glinted amid her breasts. A ring dangling from a thin gold chain. The bauble rested on the sleek curves of her folded arms. He reached out for her; the impulse to do so too great to ignore. He trailed a finger over her wrist. So soft. So warm. Was she a virgin? he wondered. She didn't act like one.

"I know enough to suspect an innocent maid would never speak of things lustful . . . which leads me to believe you might not be a very innocent maid."

In the bright night, he could see the goose bumps dot her arm, sense the fine hairs on her skin spike under his touch, envision her nipples hardening . . .

She brushed his hand away. "Who I am is none of your affair."

Well said.

Damian straightened, the hypnotic spell shattered. What the hell did he think he was doing, flirting like that? Had he taken complete leave of his senses?

"But *you* are my affair, Damian."

He bristled. "What do you mean?"

"Who are you?"

"The navigator." And he'd best remember that. He had not come this far in his quest for pirate blood to falter over a pretty face. And before she could grill him for more details about his identity, he moved off and said, "I'll go and speak with the captain."

Chapter 3

❦

The hammock rocked gently, Mirabelle nestled inside.

It was morning. A pale shaft of sunlight poked through the tiny window, brightening the captain's cabin.

James was already gone, his bed empty. She rolled her head to the side and decided to nap a minute more.

Her eldest brother had insisted she bunk with him ever since her discovery aboard ship. The man was too overprotective. True, there were forty crew members serving on the *Bonny Meg*, but four were her kin and the rest had sailed under the former captain, Drake Hawkins, her father. No one was going to do her any harm. She had known all the pirates for years . . . with the exception of Damian.

An image came to mind of the brazen sailor. What the devil had he meant by touching her like that? Making her skin tickle and her heart dance? And what about the way he had looked at her with those predatory eyes? Or the gruff way he had said her name, like a carnal growl? It had made her shiver. It *still* made her shiver, thinking about their brief interlude. Oh, why did *he* of all men have to be the new navigator? Couldn't James have plucked a sailor from port? Did her brother have to take the rogue chained next to Quincy in the gaol?

Mirabelle had never before felt the way she had the other night, so thrilled and anxious at the same time. Being close to Damian had had a disarming effect on her. One she didn't much like. She prided herself on her cool composure, and last night Damian had cracked her poise. Just a little bit, but still, it was enough to make her vexed. The cheeky bloke. Did he think to woo her with a mere touch or beguile her with a fluttering look? Never mind that he had come close to doing that very thing, the knave had no right to even try. She was the captain's sister. Didn't Damian care? Did he always tread such perilous waters?

Mirabelle hoped not. She didn't like the thought of such a reckless man guiding the ship . . . but she did like the thought of Damian in other ways.

Oh, of all the daft things to dream about! She wanted to be a pirate. She should stick to that seafaring ambition. Besides, Damian was just too mysterious for her liking. He deflected any questions about his identity. She didn't trust the man, remember?

So why was she *still* thinking about him? Mirabelle

didn't feel very collected this morning. She never got any sleep with James in the room. The man snored like a bull. Maybe that's why she was so befuddled. She could only hope.

After a few restful minutes, Mirabelle rolled out of the hammock and stretched, determined to forget all about her disagreeable encounter with Damian the other night.

She combed her fingers through her tousled hair and let out a gaping yawn. If only she could get some rest. Ever since she'd roomed with James, the maddening man had roused her from her slumber every night, and she had to wonder if he wasn't merely trying to deter her from her endeavors. Perhaps he thought to plague her with his incessant snoring until she couldn't take it anymore and, hysterical with exhaustion, demanded to be taken home.

"Well, he can rot," she whispered to herself. She'd nap when she could and suffer James's infernal snorts until doomsday if she had to. She would not be discouraged so easily.

Mirabelle shuffled over to a wooden chest. Lifting the lid, she snared a linen shirt.

The lid thumped closed. Slowly she fumbled with the laces of her black leather vest, sniffing the air attentively. Porridge? She scrunched her brow in disapproval. Breakfast was always the same.

She yawned again, and dropped her vest over the back of a chair. Neck sore, she massaged the muscles at the back of her head, realizing she still had on her necklace: a simple gold chain with a ring at the end. She removed the bauble.

A bowl of water had been left out on the table. She headed for it and set the necklace aside. She dipped her finger inside the basin. Cold. She shivered.

She scooped up a cloth saturating in the dish and wrung the excess liquid. With a sigh, she dipped her head back, relishing in the feel of clean water washing away the sweat and dirt from the previous day. She rubbed the cloth across her arms, her neck. She moved it over her belly in swirling motions, then stroked it across her breasts.

The door swung open.

Damian stood rooted to the spot. His lips parted in a soft gasp, his eyes darkened and narrowed on her. Eyes as blue as the high sea—a stormy sea.

The world seemed to fade away in that instant. Gone was the pitch and roll of the ship beneath her feet, the scent of freshly cooked fare, the creak of the deck boards. All those familiar sensations vanished. Only Damian's penetrating gaze was left, making her heart thump loud and fierce.

Mirabelle didn't shriek or holler, too enraptured by the intensity in Damian's eyes to move. He scorched her skin with one heated look, her flesh tingling, goose bumps prickling her arms, her chest. Her nipples, tight and pointy, jutted toward him.

Quickly she wrapped her arms over her breasts. She was trembling. From what, though? She wasn't cold. She felt quite the opposite, in fact. A fire sparked in her belly, the flames licked by the piercing stare of one dashing rogue sailor.

Men had looked at her before, she thought. Some had looked in admiration, others had gazed with obvious lewd intentions, but no one had ever made her feel so . . . alive. Every nerve inside her was humming, every bone rattling.

It was peculiar, the way her body responded to him. As if she had no control over her movements. As if *he* were in command of her limbs. And he was demanding she come to him, for her knees were quivering, and it took all her strength to remain entrenched right where she was.

Her mind still awhirl, she did have enough sense to pick up her shirt and drape it over her exposed front.

That seemed to snap Damian from his reverie.

He blinked. "I'm sorry," he murmured roughly, and stalked inside to grab the sextant.

He was out the door in an instant, the nautical instrument in hand, and she rushed after him to close the barrier.

Panic-stricken, she leaned against the door and let out a desperate groan. Oh, why hadn't she locked the door behind her brother as he'd warned her to?

Because you're not used to being aboard a ship, that's why.

True, she thought. At home, no one ever walked into her room—the girl's room—without knocking first. But she wasn't at home anymore. And she'd best get accustomed to her new surroundings, right quick at that.

Mirabelle thumped her head against the door. Even more distressing was the devouring look in Damian's eyes. She was in trouble. Big trouble. She was not supposed to cause any sort of disruption aboard ship. James was watching her, to see if she would drive the men to distraction. And Damian had definitely been distracted.

"Bloody hell."

She swiftly grappled with her shirt, tugging it over her head. If James even suspected she'd captivated the attention of one of his men, he'd never let her join the crew. A distracted sailor was a menace to the whole ship, especially if danger lurked. A distracted navigator was even more menacing, for a few miscalculated degrees and they'd end up in India instead of England.

Mirabelle left the cabin. Forget breakfast. She had to talk with Damian. She understood a man's nature. She'd overheard her brothers, on more than one occasion, recount tales of romps and would-be conquests. Men were always looking for a tryst, and if she corrected Damian's misconception now, she wouldn't have to worry about correcting it later.

But the thought of confronting Damian again provoked a flurry of fluttering sensations in her belly . . . and all because of that hot and spicy look in his eyes. That ravishing look, she realized, had stirred the jitters in her belly—and stirred them still.

Was this what passion felt like? Did it make you dizzy, even giddy? She had never had the chance to explore anything like it before, always too busy trying to impress her brethren with her nautical skill to bother with such distractions . . . And why the hell was she even thinking about it?

Mirabelle marched onward. She should not be so curious. The encounter with Damian had been an accident, pure and simple. A mortifying accident, granted, but an accident nonetheless. It would do her no good to dwell on it. And it certainly wouldn't do her any good to explore something so trivial as passion. For it was trivial, she was sure. Anything her brothers, especially the younger ones, adored was trivial. And Mirabelle hadn't come this far in pursuit of her dream to flounder over a petty quiver of the heart and a few flickering sensations in her belly—which could very well be due to hunger, she concluded.

Despite all her reasoning, though, she still didn't want to confront the new navigator. Luckily, a hoarse cry for a "bloody clodpole" stopped her in her tracks.

She opened the door to the cabin and peeked inside.

"What's the matter, Quincy?" she said, her words clipped.

"Well, good morning to you, too."

She stepped into the room and took in a deep breath, trying to calm her frazzled nerves. "Sorry, Quincy. My morning's gotten off to a wretched start."

"So has mine," he grumbled. "Eddie promised to bring me breakfast—a half hour ago. I'm starving!"

With a sigh, Mirabelle approached the bed. It was a good sign, Quincy's appetite. The boy was on the mend.

She sat down on the edge of the mattress and touched his brow. Still warm. She took the compress from the washbasin and placed it over his forehead.

"I'll go and find Edmund," she said.

"Don't bother, Belle. I can rail at the lout all the louder when he finally shows up."

"But I thought you were hungry?"

"I'd rather have Eddie's hide."

He was incorrigible, her brother. Rolling her eyes heavenward, she stood up to leave. "Fine, Quincy. Enjoy your ranting."

"Stay, Belle, and keep me company for a while."

"Bored?"

"Utterly."

She quirked a half smile and sat down again. "Serves you right for getting into that scrape."

"Don't harp, Belle. I've suffered plenty. Almost lost my head, and all. Isn't that enough?"

"I suppose it is," she grumbled. "Will you ever learn to behave?"

He snorted. "This coming from you? A woman who stowed away? A woman who disobeyed the captain's direct order to stay aboard ship?"

"It's not the same, Quincy. I had to do those things. I won't be left behind or treated differently just because I'm a woman."

"But being a woman *makes* you different, Belle. When are you going to realize that?"

"When you realize there's more to life than cards, brawls, and wenches."

"That long, eh?"

She gave him a wry look. "Besides, when I misbehave, I don't end up in a scuffle, fighting for my life."

"Point taken." He sighed. "I'm lucky Damian came around when he did."

Her tone softened a bit. "And if Damian hadn't come along?"

"I'd be dead, I guess."

The thought chilled her. Looking at Quincy, thinking about the young scoundrel not being around anymore, made her heart hurt, and for the first time, she felt a sense of gratitude toward Damian.

"You really think you'd be dead?" she wondered.

"Me against five Americans? Yah, I'm pretty sure."

"Five!"

He looked bewildered for a moment. "Did I say five? I meant two."

Mirabelle narrowed her gaze. "You told James the fight was with *two* men. He'll have your hide, Quincy, if he ever finds out you were daft enough to take on *five*!"

"And since I like my hide right where it is, promise me you won't tell him."

There was a pleading look in his wide blue eyes. He even batted his lashes to try and win her over. The scamp.

She wouldn't rat on him, though. James would skin him alive if he ever found out the truth. And what good would that do?

But she wouldn't give Quincy the reassurance he sought, either. Let the scalawag sweat a bit. Maybe next time he wouldn't be so eager to act the reckless fool.

Mirabelle leaned forward and pressed her lips to the ridge of her brother's nose. "I'll go and look for Edmund. I think you've waited long enough for your breakfast."

"First promise me, Belle, not to tell James."
She was up and heading for the door.
"Belle!?"
She was out the door, a smile on her face.

Damian looked through the sextant's eyepiece. The sun was somewhere in the heavens, but he didn't see a celestial orb reflecting in the mirror. All he saw were the two bountiful orbs of Mirabelle's breasts hovering above him.

He shuddered, a pang of lust gripping him. He had never seen such magnificent breasts before. The vision had lasted only a few precious seconds, but he had captured every detail in prefect clarity. The lone freckle dotting one globe. The way one swelling breast was slightly larger than the other.

Desire still twisting in his groin, the duke closed his eyes for a moment, taking in a deep and steady breath, dismissing the erotic vision.

How could a woman engage in the private matter of bathing and *not* lock the door on a ship full of men?

A woman not very chaste, he reckoned. One accustomed to men . . . so would her brothers really mind if he tangled with her, especially if she had been with other tars?

Damian stomped the thought asunder. He was *never* going to find out the truth to that query. He had to get home to England, and he wasn't about to endanger his mission to scratch an itch in his pants. He had survived two years without a woman. He could bloody well stay celibate for another few weeks . . . though he was beginning to suspect celibacy did more to distract a man than keep him focused. Two years of it had certainly taken a toll on Damian. One look at a woman's breasts and he was a mind-boggling fool.

Damian banished the thought of his unfulfilled lust and peered back into the sextant. This time he positioned the mirror until the sun overlaid the horizon. He then checked the angle on the scale and made a mental note of the figure.

He had to go back inside the captain's cabin to study the tables and charts, to obtain the chronometer, to plot a course back to England, but he wouldn't head back just yet. He would wait awhile longer, to make absolutely sure Mirabelle was gone from the room. He couldn't risk another sensual encounter with her. His resolve would snap.

"Something the matter?"

You, he thought. "Nothing's wrong, Belle."

"Good, because you have no right to be in a dander."

Her finger went to her well-endowed chest, attracting his attention. Even under the loose-fitting fabric, the full swell of her breasts was acutely evident.

Damian groaned quietly.

"You invaded *my* privacy, remember?" She poked her slender finger into her bosom. "I've had the miserable morning, not you."

Damian couldn't disagree more. He would bet his dukedom she wasn't suffering the same lustful urges he was struggling to tamp down.

"How dare you barge into the captain's cabin like that?"

"You should have locked the door," he accused, his tone biting.

"*You* should have knocked."

True, but he was still thinking like a captain, was wont to doing as he pleased, and the rules of an ordinary tar had yet to set in. And he was going to pay dearly for his misstep.

Damian looked away from her, his mind in turmoil, and growled, "I didn't know you were staying in the captain's cabin."

"Well, now you do. So keep your distance, Damian."

"I intend to."

"Good." A short pause, then: "And thank you."

"For *what*?"

"For saving Quincy's life."

He stared at her, taken aback. He couldn't remember the last time he had heard those words. And hearing them from Belle felt strangely good. It was pleasant, even, knowing he wasn't a complete failure.

Gruffly he bit back, "You're welcome."

She wrinkled her brow then. "Isn't that William's shirt?"

Damian glanced down at his apparel. "Aye. Your brother offered me the garbs, seeing as I was left penniless and all but naked on America's shore."

Was that color tinting her cheeks? And at the mention of him being naked? But before he could be sure, she turned to leave.

"Wait, Belle."

She looked back at him, her fiery gaze cutting up his soul. "What is it?"

He searched his brain for a reason to talk to her. That it was wholly senseless to keep her around did not cross his mind right then. He just didn't want the moment to end. There was something about Belle that aroused him. Both his body and his . . . well, he wasn't quite sure. His heart? Damian didn't think he had one anymore. Or if he did, it was as dark as cinder. Yet an emotion was buried deep within him. Too deep to be clear. But it clung to his breast with a fierce hold and he could not shake the sensation. It felt strangely warm. Even tranquil. And it had been a while since he'd felt something other than misery inside him. He wanted to hold on to the sentiment a bit longer.

His eye caught a speck on the horizon. "Is that a ship?"

She cast her golden gaze over the water. "Aye."

"I think it's sailing this way."

"So what?"

He studied her again, enthralled by the silky strands of her tawny blond hair shifting in the breeze. A stray lock whipped across her sun-kissed features and trapped between the soft curve of her coral pink lips.

Gripped by a yearning to wipe away the lock, his fingers twitched, preparing to move, but she brushed the wisp of hair behind her ear before he had a chance to do it. A good thing, too, for he wasn't overly fond of making a complete ass of himself.

Curling his restless fingers into his palms, he said, "Don't you ever worry about your safety out here?"

She shrugged. "No. Why?"

"What about a sea squall?"

"This is a sound ship." Her arms crossed under her breasts. "She can weather any storm."

"What about being lost at sea?"

She narrowed her amber eyes on him. "Do you plan on getting us lost, Damian?"

Indignant, he returned, "Of course not."

"Then I'm not worried."

He paused. "What about pirates?"

This time she snorted. "I'm not worried about pirates."

"Why not? That ship"—he nodded up ahead—"could very well be a pirate ship, tailing us."

"It's not," she said confidently. "Trust me."

Her smug assurance annoyed him. She was a bountiful prize for any pirate, who wouldn't hesitate to plunder her if at all given the chance. She could even be killed! Didn't she realize that?

"You should have more respect for the sea," he chided. "Instead you scoff at danger like your brother Quincy."

Her nostrils flared. "That ship"—she pointed to the horizon—"is just sailing by. It's *not* a pirate ship."

"It *could* be."

"Even so, we're armed, so I'm still not worried."

At her flippant response, he grabbed her by the wrist and squeezed.

Mirabelle's breath trapped in her throat at the sudden attack. "Are you crazy?" Her eyes darted to the crew, presumably to check if anyone had yet to notice their little entanglement.

"Break away," he bade.

She trembled in his embrace. He could feel it, the vibrations ripping through her. "If anyone catches us . . ."

"So fight," he demanded.

She looked at him as though he'd lost his mind. She made a noise of frustration and, wriggling, twisted her wrist this way and that, attempting to break free.

"Try harder, Belle."

Tight-lipped, she glowered at him, clawing at his clenched fingers, leaving glaring red marks all along his hand and forearm.

With a flick of the wrist, he jerked her closer to him, their noses bumping.

 Delving deep into the pools of her honey gold eyes, now flashing mad, he whispered roughly, "Remember, Belle, there is always someone bigger and stronger out there, just waiting for a chance to hurt you."

The salty musk of her hair swirled around him, and Damian suddenly realized just how close to her he really was, his eyes dropping to her full and rosy and damned kissable lips.

Sensing his poise was about to crack, he admonished, "Don't you ever make light of that again," and then let her go.

Mirabelle staggered back, massaging her wrist, her eyes burning orbs. She looked ready to hurl a slew of obscenities his way, but one look at the crew, casting her curious glances, and she seemed to reconsider.

In the end, she only warned, "Stay away from me."

I intend to, thought Damian, as he watched her

sultry figure stalk away. Being close to Mirabelle was a guarantee of hardship, physical and otherwise, for the woman sparked within him emotions he could not tame—or fathom.

Chapter 4

"**O**h, good. Someone to keep me company. I can't stand counting the wood knots in the ceiling anymore."

Damian stepped deeper into the cabin and closed the door. "Feeling better?"

"Aye," said Quincy. "I should be up and about soon."

"I'm glad to hear it. For a while there, I wasn't sure you'd make it."

"I'm tougher than I look," was his cool reply, but then his eyes lighted with anxiety and his voice took on a pleading pitch. "Oh, and if anyone asks, you saved me from *two* Americans, not five."

Damian quirked a brow.

"Just promise me you won't tell my brothers the truth."

With a shrug, Damian acquiesced.

The kid sighed, his demeanor blithe once more. "So tell me, how do you like life aboard the *Bonny Meg*?"

Collecting a nearby chair, Damian positioned it next to the bed and sat down. "It's . . . interesting."

"How?"

"The choice of crew."

"Belle, you mean?" Quincy chuckled. "She's a challenge, I know. The captain has trouble handling her himself."

Damian could commiserate. "So why did he bring her on board?"

"Bring her?" Quincy snorted. "That's not the way it happened. Belle stowed away."

Now *that* made sense. It had so often plagued Damian, the reason for her being on ship. A stowaway certainly explained everything. It meant the odd family union wasn't so odd after all—only Belle was odd.

"That must have been a surprise," said Damian, "finding her here."

"Was it ever! A fortnight into our journey, Eddie strolled into the galley—the lummox is always hungry—to ask Cook about dinner. And there she was, hunched over the piping cauldron, sampling the stew. Eddie couldn't believe his eyes. He lunged for her, but she got away, and he almost ended up *in* the bubbling cauldron. It was a lot of shouting and tearing around deck before we finally captured her. James was furious, we all were, but we were too far at sea to turn around and bring her home. We needed more supplies."

"And that's how you found yourself in New York?"

Quincy nodded. "We had to get rid of our plund—our cargo, load up some new supplies, and then head home."

"So you're taking Belle back to England?"

"Hell, yes! Why wouldn't we?"

Damian waved a dismissive hand. "Just the impression I got from her, that she was already a member of the crew."

"Belle wishes to be a member," grumbled Quincy. "That's the trouble."

Trouble indeed. Damian could still feel the heat twisting in his belly at the memory of his morning spar with Belle. To avoid her—and another sensual encounter—he had shut himself below deck, tending to navigational charts. But imagine having to endure voyage after voyage with Belle strutting around deck in her tight leather breeches, her arse swaying like the pendulum of a clock, mesmerizing all eyes. Nothing would ever get done.

"Why all the questions about my sister?" Quincy abruptly demanded.

Bemused, Damian glanced back at the kid. "No reason."

That got him a skeptical look. "You're to stay away from her, Damian."

He stood up. "I know."

"I mean it." Quincy eyed him intently. "I'm in your debt and all, but that doesn't mean you can do whatever you want with Belle."

Do whatever he wanted with Belle? Now there was a tempting thought.

"I don't plan on doing anything with her," Damian

insisted, more to convince himself than Quincy. He backed away. "I was only curious about her."

"She belongs on shore, Damian, married with a brood of children. Unless you want the job of hus—"

"I don't," he cut in, reaching for the doorknob. "I only want the job of navigator."

Quickly Damian escaped from the cabin, Quincy hollering after him, "Are you sure?"

Up on deck, Damian paused to inhale the briny sea air. *Him* a husband? Clearly, the kid's fever had yet to break. What a daft suggestion. It was no better than being tossed overboard, for the distraction of a wife would surely hamper his mission—especially if that wife happened to be a sultry siren. Besides, he could never take a wife. He was too much like his father. No woman would ever be safe with him.

The hammering overhead captured Damian's attention. He glanced up at the darkening sky, sucking in a sharp breath at the sight he beheld.

Mirabelle was perched on the mainsail yard, pounding away, her thighs straddling the wood beam, her legs crossed at the ankles.

Was the woman mad? Dangling up in the air like that? She had no business—

Wait. *He* had no business giving a damn. Let her brothers worry.

Damian headed aft, determined to find something other than Mirabelle to occupy his attention.

Passing the ratlines, though, he took no more than two steps before he turned on his heels and began to climb up the crisscrossing ropes.

* * *

Mirabelle took the nail from between her teeth and positioned it over the splint. She envisioned Damian's head and brought the mallet down with a resounding thwack.

Obnoxious devil. How dare he accuse her of being foolhardy? So she didn't fret over every potential peril. That did *not* make her reckless. Why, the ship could be swallowed up by a sea serpent at any moment. What good would it do her to panic over the possibility?

Another hard thwack.

It wouldn't do her any good, dreading unknown hazards. Damian knew it. He was just being an ass— like her brothers. Worse even, for he pestered her without benefit of kinship. But like her brethren, Damian had tried to frighten her into retreat. He had said it himself the other night; how "unusual" it was to have a woman aboard ship. He thought to disturb her with ghastly tales of sea misadventures. Unnerve her to the point where she demanded to go home— where she belonged.

Bah! What was it with the crew of the *Bonny Meg*? All seemed to think she lacked a healthy dose of feminine hysteria.

Mirabelle hammered away for a while, fixing some minor damage amassed during the last spring storm they had weathered.

She paused in her repairs, looking out to sea, trying to quiet her troubled spirit.

The glow of the setting sun warmed her skin. She

inhaled the fresh tang of salty sea air, listened to the ballooning sails stretch under the pressure of the surging winds.

She loved being on board, feeling the breeze whipping through her hair. Even staring at the rhythmic swell of the water gave her pleasure. It soothed her soul.

Resuming repairs, Mirabelle glanced down and spotted a lone figure scaling the ratlines with obvious prowess.

A sudden giddy unease enveloped her. "What are you doing here, Damian?"

A head popped up to glare at her. "What are *you* doing here?"

"Fixing the yard."

Damian straddled the wood beam opposite her. "You shouldn't be up here. It isn't safe."

She snorted. Life on a pirate ship was never safe. Always being hunted and all. It was the very reason her brothers had set sail for the Americas. Plundering near the English coast had become a hazard. Ever since that incident with an English passenger vessel two years ago, too many scout ships prowled the waters in search of the *Bonny Meg*. It being time for a change of venue, her brothers had crossed the Atlantic waves to find it. Of course, Damian wasn't privy to any of that.

"I told you to stay away from me, Damian."

"And I told you to be careful." Then tersely he said, "It seems neither of us listens to the other."

She huffed. "I'm not in any danger." Though perhaps that wasn't entirely true. Hell's fire, but the man had such stunning eyes. She was woozy just looking at him. "My father taught me how to sail—and hammer a nail."

The autocratic brute was quiet for a moment. "Was this your father's ship?"

She glanced down at the yard, pounding away. "Aye. He was captain for almost twenty years."

"So who is Meg?"

Mirabelle paused, a welter of emotions swimming in her breast. "My mother, Megan. She died in childbirth to Quincy."

Mirabelle wished she had known the woman better. She was often told how much she resembled her mother, with her golden hair and eyes, while her brothers distinctly mirrored their father. It was why she liked being aboard the *Bonny Meg*. She felt close to her mother here. And her father. As though both parents were watching over her, hugging her in their arms.

She took another nail from the satchel tied at her waist, and positioned it over the splint. "So you see, Damian"—bang!—"I belong here."

"Not *way* up here."

"I'll have you know, Father was a wonderful teacher." Bang! Bang! "He had faith in me."

Memories squeezed at her heart. Memories of her father. It had been a year since the death of Drake Hawkins. The worst year of her life, for with all her brothers at sea, she had been left home alone for the first time in her life. The silence had been agonizing.

The ache in her lonely heart consuming. But out here she was close to her brothers—and her parents. Out here she belonged to a crew, a family. She didn't need anyone else. She certainly didn't need a husband and children, as James had suggested. Such a family would only bring her grief . . . as it had her mother so many years ago.

Oh, the Hawkins clan had been happy for a time, blissfully so. And then tragedy had struck, a great upheaval that had devastated many lives, her mother's most of all. It'd been more than twenty years since the awful event, but still Mirabelle feared the kind of heartache that had plagued her mother. She would much prefer the life of a seafarer. And there was nothing in the world that could make her give up her dream. Not a stubborn troop of brothers or a pigheaded navigator.

"You should appreciate that more, Damian, the lessons of a father. Mine made sure to teach me everything about sailing." While the ship was moored, of course. Drake had never taken her out to sea. This was her first voyage, in fact. "Didn't your father teach you how to be a tar?"

"My father wasn't a sailor . . . and he never taught me anything of value."

She looked into his azure blue eyes, so gloomy for an instant. She recognized that doleful expression, having often felt the same way herself. But the intensity in Damian's gaze was unique. A depth of sorrow even she couldn't fathom.

Suddenly curious, she decided it was time to learn

more about the mysterious navigator and put her suspicions to rest. "If not a sailor, who was your father?"

Damian appeared to dislike the question. A pulse ticked in his neck. "He was no one special."

Well, that wasn't very informative. "Yes, but *who* was he—"

"Enough of this, Belle," he said roughly. "Get down."

Her flicker of curiosity smothered, she returned his poignant glare with a tart, "I will not."

"Get down or I'll haul you down myself."

He wouldn't dare, the blackguard! "I have to fix the ship, Damian. Captain's order."

"I'll fix it."

"It's my ship. *I'll* fix it."

A black brow cocked in disbelief.

"Well, it is—sort of. It belongs to my brothers and I, so I have as much right to be here as any of them."

"So why did you stow away?"

She took in a sharp breath. The conniving bounder! "You had no right to pry like that, Damian."

"*You* have no right to be here."

She snorted and whacked the nail head hard. "My brothers are just being stubborn."

"More like wise."

Affronted, she demanded, "And what does that mean?"

"You shouldn't be on the ship, Belle—at all."

Oh, men were such a tenacious brood! "That's not your choice to make, Damian."

He glowered at her. "Get off the yard, Belle."

"Why?"

"Because you have neither the strength nor the proper balance to be up here."

"I'm hammering a piece of wood, not towing the ship." She glared at the iron nail and imagined Damian's head. Thwack! "How much strength do you think I need?" Thwack! Thwack! "And my balance is perfectly fine."

Of course, the ship chose that very moment to dip and roll, tipping her sideways.

Damian reached for her, her muscles aching under the pressure of his grip.

He yanked her forward.

She gasped at the feel of his nose bumping hers. Dark eyes, burning hot, scorched her soul. He was so close. The heady scent of him swarmed her senses, making her heart tick hard and fast. She could almost taste him. She almost wanted to . . .

"Get down, Belle. Now!"

It was a cold command. Cutting and to the point. She didn't argue. She could see it in his gaze, the tenacious resolve. If she so much as parted her lips for a breath, he'd take it as a sign of willfulness and toss her over his shoulder.

And what would James think with Damian dragging her down the ratlines? That she was stirring up trouble, that's what. It was always *her* fault.

Snapped from her reverie, she gnashed her teeth and resisted the urge to clock Damian over the head with her mallet.

After a quick scan of the deck below, to ensure no

one was watching, Mirabelle swung her leg over the yard and began to climb down the ratlines, Damian in tow.

She hit the deck.

Offering Damian one last scowl, she flounced off, fuming.

Chapter 5

The sounds coming from the belly of the ship had Damian bristling.

He had come below in search of canvas, ordered by the captain to replace one of the badly worn jibs, but the noises stemming from the bowel of the ship, akin to groans, had him rooted to the spot.

Mirabelle.

He would recognize that smoky voice anywhere. And that she was making the most sensuous racket he had ever heard in his life had his body simmering with rage, for *he* was not the one making her sing like a wanton.

The abrupt compulsion to tear off limbs overwhelmed him. With nary a thought for the impropriety of barging in on a most intimate act, Damian stormed into the storage nook—and smiled.

It wasn't much of a smile. A quirk of the lips, really. He rarely expressed the sentiment of amusement. He didn't have much in life to be happy about. But this . . .

Damian cocked his head to the side to better view Belle's plump behind wedged firmly between two wood posts.

She was stuck.

And she groaned with each failed attempt to get *un*stuck. The lofty posts, it seemed, were quite determined to keep her ensnared. Damian didn't blame them. He would love to have Belle in a similar position—in his bed.

Dismissing the wistful fantasy, he was content to observe her wiggle for a while. How did she find herself in such a precarious position? Eyeing those voluptuous curves, though, was it really a wonder she got trapped?

The ship dipped forward.

Damian heard something roll across the floor.

Mirabelle cooed. "Oh, there you are—"

Her cooing quickly turned to shrieking.

Damian noticed the rat scurry by and disappear through a crack in the planks.

But the trinket continued to tumble toward Damian.

He lifted his boot and stepped on the bauble. Arching forward, he picked up the shiny ornament.

A ring.

He eyed the jewelry carefully. It was a large ring. Too large for a woman's finger. Crafted from gold, the emblem in the center depicted a winged hourglass.

Time flying away.

And so it was. He could stare at Belle's delectable arse all day long. Nothing would ever get done.

Enough of the frivolous pleasure, he told himself. He was on a mission to avenge his brother. And while he wasn't the least bit looking forward to the task at hand, for it would bring him even more unease, he couldn't very well leave the woman squished between two posts like that.

Stifling a groan, Damian slipped the ring over his finger. Without a word to Belle, he came up behind her and spread his legs apart.

She gasped. "Damian!"

He hooked his arms around her belly, the twitch in his groin painful. Bloody hell, it was hard to be slumped against her in a most intimate way. Such a perfect position to *take* her hard.

He tugged.

Out popped Belle—and they both crashed to the floor.

"Get off me, Damian!"

Rather obtuse of her to say such a thing, considering *she* was sitting on top of him, every delicious curve rubbing against him, taunting his shackled arousal.

"You mean 'let go,' don't you, Belle?"

She scrambled to her feet as soon as he opened his arms. "I told you to stay away from me."

"Aye, you did." Damian was more slow to stand, the stiffening in his groin uncomfortable. "So should I stick you back between the posts and holler for one of your brothers to come instead?"

She made a wry face.

"I didn't think so." He dusted off his trousers. "Well, Belle, don't I get a thank you for my effort?"

"Effort? Was it really so grueling? I'm sure you found the whole thing rather amusing."

Don't forget arousing.

He slipped the ring off his finger and held it in the air. "Looking for something?"

Belle eyed the bauble, then snatched it from his grip.

"You're welcome," he drawled, and headed for one of the crates. He had to look away from her. She only stirred in him unquenchable lust . . . confused his senses . . . made him restless. It was pure torment being so close to her.

Lifting the lid, he searched for the canvas.

Mirabelle slipped the ring on a chain. "It broke."

He paused to glance at her. "It seems fine to me."

"Not the ring, the chain." She sighed. "I can't wear it anymore."

He went back to work, rummaging. "It looks familiar."

She stopped fiddling with the clasp to stare at him. "What does?"

"The ring."

"How?"

Damian closed the lid. No canvas. "I don't know. I've seen it before, I think."

"Where?"

She sounded rather desperate. Or was it panicked? "Like I said, Belle, I don't remember."

Her amber eyes drifted to the floorboards. "It was a gift from my father for my twentieth year."

He went to the next crate to grope. "Does it have any meaning?"

"No."

Well, that was uttered posthaste. Damian stuck his head out of the crate to stare at her. "You don't know its meaning?"

"It has sentimental meaning."

"So your father gave you a ring without bothering to understand its message?"

Those amber eyes, alight with fire, pinned back on him. "I would think the message was rather clear."

"Aye, time getting away. But why give *you* such a ring?"

She shrugged.

"So you have no idea? Rather odd if you ask me."

"Well, no one's asking you," she snapped. "And there's nothing odd about my father."

She blushed when she made the assertion. Now *that* was definitely odd.

"Something you're not telling me, Belle?"

"Never mind." She huffed and headed for the door.

He grabbed her by the arm. He wasn't sure why. He should let her go. He had work to do and she only distracted him. But he held her steadfast.

"Don't worry about your peculiar family," he murmured. "Mine's not normal either."

She made a moue and broke free of his hold, verily stomping out.

Mirabelle wrinkled her nose at the pungent scent. It was making her a bit queasy. She was entombed below deck, ordered to disinfect the causeways with vinegar and salt. After a brief repose, she went back on her hands and knees and scrubbed away, but in the shiny, wet wood planks, she imagined the rugged features of one aggravating navigator, a seductive glow in his deep blue eyes, and her whole body started to hum.

Mirabelle sloshed more vinegar over the floor, scouring across the haunting face. She was a bloody half-wit, letting Damian affect her so. She had so much work to do. Precious time should not be wasted on idle daydreaming.

And why the devil was she thinking about *him* of all men? The arrogant blackguard who ordered her about like a tyrant? He only upset her at every turn. Unnerved her, too, with all that huffing and glowering . . . and grabbing.

The queasiness in her belly grew worse. She closed her eyes and tried to ignore the sultry sensation of his hard-muscled thighs pressed against her buttocks as he'd yanked her from the wood posts. But it did no good. She shuddered in remembrance. Her body wasn't willing to forget the tingles of excitement that had washed through her when he'd strapped his large body behind hers. The power surging through him had been palpable. It'd scorched her flesh, whipped her insides into a frenzy. Something had stirred deep within her womb. A pulsing need she had never felt before.

Mirabelle opened her eyes and blinked a few times. She really had to stop her woolgathering. She had been washing the same spot for the last five minutes. At this rate, she would never get done.

Moving to a new area, she set to work on polishing the floor. But try as she might, she simply could not dismiss the thought of Damian from her mind. Worse, prickles of pleasure dotted her skin, as though the man were still touching her, staring at her . . .

Mirabelle glanced over her shoulder and stifled a gasp.

Damian stood at the far end of the gallery, thick arms crossed over his strapping chest, hip cocked and resting against the wall. He was watching her, intent in his smoldering gaze. Intent to do what, though?

She shivered under the lazy caress of his burning blue eyes. He moved from the wall and started toward her, a slow saunter that made the nerves in her body dance a jig.

It was hopeless, evading the man. On a ship like the *Bonny Meg* there wasn't much room for privacy. She had to accept that. She had to get used to the new navigator and bring her capricious emotions under control. Otherwise, the journey home was going to be a thorny pain in the—

"I remember now, Belle."

Damian came to crouch beside her, dark indigo eyes peering at her from under a thick fringe of sooty lashes.

She shivered under his seductive stare and dropped her scrub brush into the bucket of vinegar, perching on her heels. "Remember what?"

"Where I saw the winged hourglass before."

The jitters in her belly intensified. "Where?"

It was a damn bother, always sinking into the pools of his sea blue eyes. She needed her wits about her—especially now. The ring was tucked away in James's cabin, but it still might prove a danger.

Her father had worn the bauble for much of his pirate career, so if he'd ever raided a merchant vessel that Damian had sailed, the navigator might just remember the ring—and the formidable captain who had sported it.

"I saw it in a book," he said smoothly.

Mirabelle let out a soft sigh, her heart thumping at a steadier pace. Odd, she thought. The winged hourglass was a pirate symbol, often part of the pirate flag. It was warning to a ship being preyed upon that time was running out: the vessel was doomed. What on earth would it be doing in a book?

She made a face. "What book?"

"*Robinson Crusoe,* I think. I remember a picture in the book, an engraving of a winged hourglass on a pirate flag."

The fine hairs on her arms spiked. "I've never read the book."

"It's been so long since I've read it, too." Something flickered in the dark pools of his eyes. Something raw and emotional. "I had to steal the book from my father's library."

She snorted. "Your father had a library? What was he, a gent?"

He seemed taken aback. "No, I mean, he had a few books."

"So why did you have to steal it?"

He looked off for a moment, peering into the empty gallery. "I wasn't allowed to go near the books."

"Why?"

"It doesn't matter." He glanced back at her, his reverie shattered.

What had just happened to the man? That poignant expression, so full of grief?

"Why do you have a pirate ring, Belle?"

Oh, why couldn't she grab hold of her wits when he looked at her like that?

"My father got the ring in the Caribbean from a friend." From a pirate friend, but she managed to keep that part clandestine. And the rest was entirely true. She was just too befuddled by that damn predatory stare of his to conjure up a fib.

"Your father sailed the Caribbean?"

She nodded. "A long time ago. He liked the picture in the ring. It reminded him of coming home, of not letting too much time pass away at sea."

Damian touched her lips. She bristled at the soft caress, her heart throbbing like a wild winter storm.

He brushed away the lock of hair trapped between her lips. Had that been stuck in her mouth the whole time? She hadn't even noticed.

"You should be careful, Belle." The low rumble of his voice made her all hot and sweaty. "A ring like that is nothing but trouble."

Damian lifted off his haunches and sauntered away.

Funny, but Mirabelle suspected it was not the ring that was the trouble.

Chapter 6

Dinner was over. Mirabelle found herself in the mess, surrounded by her brothers. Even Quincy was present, ensconced in a chair, a blanket wrapped tight around his shoulders.

Slumped in her seat, she twirled a lock of hair around her finger. "So what's this all about?"

James had summoned the family to a meeting, but had yet to reveal what the meeting was about. He stood at the head of the dining table, burly arms folded across his wide chest, legs braced apart in an imperious stance.

She wasn't impressed by his daunting posture, though. She had seen it far too often to feel intimidated. Her other brothers appeared equally unmoved, especially Edmund, who found the grease stain on his palm more interesting. Only William reflected the captain's grave countenance.

"We have a problem," said James.

With a sigh of impatience, Edmund wondered, "What problem?"

"Our new navigator is infatuated with Belle."

Mirabelle's jaw dropped.

A chorus of protests and stunned exclamations erupted promptly.

Moving away from the wall, his grimy palm no longer appealing, Edmund cried, "You're not serious, James?"

"This is all a mistake," Quincy asserted.

"Really, James," from William, "what brought on this accusation?"

The captain's fist came down, making the dirty dishes on the table dance. "Quiet! All of you. I want to hear from Belle."

All eyes went to Mirabelle.

Stunned, she countered, "It's not true!"

James gripped the edge of the dining table and leaned forward. "Then tell me why the two of you were perched on the mainsail yard a while ago?"

Blast it! So James *had* seen her with Damian. She was definitely going to have to clout that lout of a navigator over the head with her mallet. Look at all the trouble he had caused!

In a perfectly smooth voice, she fibbed, "Damian was helping me with repairs."

James cast her a dubious look. "And this morning?"

"What about this morning?"

"You were seen with Damian—in his embrace."

Another round of boisterous objections.

"The man is dead," vowed Edmund, fist slamming into his palm.

Mirabelle rolled her eyes. It was the plight of all women, she supposed, to have overprotective, and often hypocritical, guardians of her virtue always buzzing about. Really, what a farce. True, she was their sister, but so what? The women her brothers dallied with were all someone else's sister in the end, and if one was never allowed to touch another man's sister, then what would her brothers do with all their spare time? But she couldn't mention that discrepancy to any of them or the four would be scratching their heads in confusion.

"Damian is *not* chasing after Belle," Quincy affirmed once more with a confidence Mirabelle found puzzling. She wasn't sure why her youngest kin kept dismissing the notion so entirely. It certainly wasn't *im*possible that Damian found her attractive.

Bloody hell. She was doing it again. Being too curious. She should be rallying behind her youngest brother, not thinking up ways to dispute his claim.

"Well?" James pressed her when she still didn't answer.

"There was no embrace," she refuted at last. "Damian simply"—she grappled with her brain for a reasonable excuse, and finally blurted out—"caught me."

A frown wrinkled the captain's brow. "Caught you?"

"I lost my balance." She shrugged. "A wave hit and Damian took me by the wrist to stop my fall. I would hardly call it an embrace."

He didn't believe her. She could tell by that poignant look in his eyes. Trouble was she wasn't clumsy, and James knew it. She never lost her balance—unless, of course, accosted by a big oaf some fifty feet in the air. But that was a moot point. What mattered was her reputation for a sturdy grip and foothold. The notion that she should lose her poise on deck during clear sailing was more than a little suspect.

But what else could she say? Certainly not the exasperating truth, that the new navigator also happened to believe she didn't belong here. Why, that fact might even endear Damian to her kin, and then the whole lot of them could band together and squash all her hopes and dreams. Mirabelle wasn't about to let that happen.

"Belle," said James, voice low, glare steadfast, "Are you sure Damian isn't bothering you?"

"*Yes*." If she admitted the opposite, James might assume she was enticing the navigator in some way, hence why he was pestering her. And that would give her brother ideal grounds to banish her from the ship forever.

With a smug air, Quincy smiled. "I told you he wasn't after Belle."

Edmund stalked up to him, demanding, "And how did you know that?"

Quincy shrugged. "Because Damian told me so."

It was Mirabelle's turn to explode. "*What?*"

William came forward next. "You spoke with Damian about this already?"

"So he *is* infatuated with Belle?" From James.

"No, no." Quincy gestured with his hand. "Nothing like that."

The captain, too, moved toward the youngest Hawkins, until all three men had circled his chair. "Quincy, if you spoke with Damian, you must have assumed something was wrong."

"Well, yes, but I overreacted." Glancing at each of his hovering brothers, Quincy resumed his narrative. "You see, Damian had a lot of questions about Belle and I suspected he was smitten with her. It wasn't true, though. He was just curious to know why a woman was aboard ship. He wants nothing to do with Belle, he assured me. He doesn't find her the least bit interesting."

The men in the room all puffed a sigh of relief, but Mirabelle felt as though she'd been smacked in the face.

"And you're sure about this?" said James.

"Aye." Quincy nodded. "Damian bolted when I suggested he either do right by Belle and marry her or leave her be."

It was a sturdy punch to her gut, his words. Quincy had tried to *marry* her off? She didn't know what was worse, that he would do such an unseemly thing or that the boorish navigator didn't want her.

"Now, Belle," said William, the first to notice her crimson complexion. "Quincy didn't mean to upset you."

The fledgling of the family finally glanced her way, his expression contrite, his tone placating. "I didn't, Belle, really. I was just looking out for you."

"That's the very reason you shouldn't be here," grumbled Edmund, his temper mellow. "You're a distraction to the crew, Belle."

"And while you haven't charmed Damian," James went on to point out, "you might very well charm another sailor." He sighed at that point. "I just can't have you on board, Belle. You're too damn beautiful for your own good."

She was on her feet and marching toward the door, the humiliation suffocating. So Damian didn't want anything to do with her? Not that she craved his attention. Certainly not. But still, all those fiery looks were nothing more than expressions of curiosity? He thought her *odd*? What a fool she was!

"Belle!" Quincy wailed, as she thundered past him.

But William rested his hand on Quincy's shoulder, stopping the entreaty.

The brothers let her go.

Tears pooling, Mirabelle let them gather. She didn't even wipe them away when they dripped down her flushed cheeks.

Too beautiful, was she? What rot! But if her infuriating brethren believed it so, she could fix that. In a few minutes she would be as ordinary and unattractive as any poor and weathered tar aboard ship.

Bursting into the captain's cabin, she lit the oil lamp suspended on the wall and set to work. First she headed for the table, tossing aside the papers and nautical charts. Nothing. Her wet gaze then lit on the wooden chest at the foot of James's bed. She tore through the clutter of clothing, looking for the knife she knew her brother kept hidden somewhere in his cabin.

The knife was a gift to James from their father. It had a decorative ivory handle and a long, glossy, five-inch blade—a sharp blade.

The lid crashed closed. Still nothing. The bed was next. Crouching on her knees, she groped under the prickly straw mattress.

Aha!

Fingers circling the sheath, she yanked the knife free. For a moment she cradled the weapon, tracing her finger along the intricate carving. The scene depicted wild animals in the jungle. It was a priceless souvenir, the knife. One her father had obtained while stationed in India, long before he ever became a pirate.

Slowly, she pulled the blade from its sheath. The metal glinted in the fiery light and she blinked at the glare.

Mirabelle walked over to the captain's shaving mirror, peering into the murky glass. Shadows masked her face, but there was still enough light to go about her task.

Too charming, was she? Not anymore.

Grabbing a clump of her long and treasured hair, she lifted the knife to her scalp and cut.

The knife, wrenched from her grip, went flying through the air, piercing the opposite wall.

Clutching a small cluster of hair in her palm, Mirabelle whirled around to confront the hulking figure towering above her.

She was thunderstruck, met by a tangle of dark curls swirling across a strapping chest. She had never seen Damian like this before, his shirt wide open, his lengthy, raven black locks fanning free. He was too ruggedly handsome for words, leaving her belly in knots at the sight of him.

"What are you doing here?" she demanded, flustered.

"I've come to study the sea charts. What the hell do you think *you're* doing?"

"Get out, Damian." She averted her stormy eyes. "This doesn't concern you."

Turning quickly, she went over to the other side of the room and jerked the embedded blade from the wall. She didn't want Damian to see any more of her tears—or the blush that had adorned her cheeks at the sight of him so scantily attired.

His rough voice faded to a husky whisper. "What's wrong, Belle?"

She faced him again, confident her flushed cheeks had lost some color. But one look at his muscled form, and a spark flared deep in her belly. She wondered, unabashed, what it would feel like to rake her fingers through the matted curls on his chest . . . or to have those lush and arrogant lips pressed hard over hers.

And then she remembered the bounder didn't want her, that he didn't find her the least bit interesting, and she promptly pushed her absurd yearnings aside.

"It seems I'm too beautiful," she said, her remark smothered in sarcasm, for she didn't feel the least bit pretty at the moment, her eyes all puffy and swollen from tears, pieces of her hair hacked away. And knowing Damian didn't think very much of her, either, made her feel even worse. It appeared only her brothers thought her a temptation, but since they were her brothers, their opinions didn't count. All doting brothers thought their sisters comely and a target for seduction.

It didn't bode well for her dream, she realized, that her kin believed her too attractive to remain aboard ship. No one else considered her fair, but her blind brethren continued to insist she was a menace to the crew with her "charming" good looks. If she didn't change their minds about the matter soon, she just might find herself dropped back on England's shore— for good.

"I have to do away with my beauty, you know?" She walked over to the mirror again, knife in hand. "Tars aboard the *Bonny Meg* must be ugly. Captain's order."

She lifted the blade to her scalp once more.

Robust fingers latched onto her wrist.

"You'll do no such thing," Damian admonished, the low timbre of his voice prickling her spine.

She gazed up at him. Piece by piece he took her apart with those heavenly blue eyes. It was as if he could see right inside her heart.

She didn't care about his mysterious past right then. Her absurd yearning was back. The yearning to be wanted—even if by him. She was just so tired of being tossed away all the time. Of being told there was something wrong with her. There was a desperate need inside her for acceptance, a need to belong.

But she would never belong in Damian's arms, she

told herself. It was too great a risk. A risk of the heart. One she wasn't willing to take. Besides, the oaf didn't want her, remember?

She twisted her wrist free of his grip. "Get out, Damian."

His sensuous sapphire eyes flared. "Give me the knife."

Taking a few steps back, she tried to ignore the jitters in her belly. "I will not."

His hand came out. "The knife."

"Forget it." She clasped the blade's handle even harder. "I have to do this. Don't pretend like you give a damn."

He took a daunting step forward. "And what does that mean?"

The butterflies wreaked havoc on her insides. "I know you don't care about what happens to me. You just want me off this ship and rotting on land with some oaf of a husband and a brood of children."

A dark brow cocked. "What the devil gave you that idea?" Another step forward.

Mirabelle bumped into the wall—trapped. "Quincy told me about your little chat." The tears and humiliation welled in her throat once more. "But you're wrong, you know? I do belong here."

There was a thoughtful look in his smoldering blue eyes. "I don't care whether you marry an ogre or have a dozen squalling brats, but you do *not* belong here. It isn't safe."

He was towering above her now, and her heart was pounding away like a blacksmith on an anvil.

"It isn't safe for my brothers, either," she said, breathless. "I'm no different from any of them."

"The hell you're not!"

The man was so close, she couldn't help but peek at the wide expanse of muscle and the dark tufts of hair that made up his strapping chest. Nor could she ignore the swell of his tight and chiseled pectoral muscles or the nubs of his nipples puckering in the crisp night air.

Mirabelle squirmed in her spot, a moist heat invading her belly . . . her loins. The daft desire to press her lips over one of those jutting nipples skipped through her mind, the salacious image sending her heart thumping loud and fierce.

Blast it! What the devil was the matter with her? Where had such bold passions come from? She had never felt this way before, so enamored, so eager for more. It was gripping and frightening at the same time, the emotions inside her. All sorts of mystifying sentiments swirled in her gut. She couldn't make any sense of the feelings bombarding her. And the confusion only grew worse . . .

Damian traced his thumb along the line of her brow in a slow and sensual caress. "You're so different, Belle," he murmured.

Lost in the zeal of his fiery stare, she flinched at his tender touch. It scorched her skin, the warmth of his finger stroking her brow.

Breath trapped in her throat as he trailed his thumb softly over the ridge of her nose, making her shiver and her heart throb.

"So very different," he said again in a husky drawl, eyes dark and penetrating. There was awe in his voice. She heard it clearly. He looked for answers in the way that he touched her. Answers to one imperative query: why was she so different?

She sensed he did not mean her sex alone. It was much more than that that baffled him, though she wasn't quite sure what it was. Perhaps if she could get her thoughts to string together in one coherent line, she might be able to figure it out, but alas, she was blissfully distracted by the thrilling touch of one dashing rogue sailor, and could not think straight to save her soul.

Damian's fingers trailed roughly down her arm, her skin tingling, and when he took the knife from her hand, she didn't protest. She let the handle slip free.

The blade point hit the wall behind her.

She couldn't move. Figuratively, of course. It would be so simple to duck out from under Damian's embrace and dash out the door, but her feet wouldn't budge. She didn't want them to budge. She was content to explore the feelings inside her just a tad longer. She was going to regret it later, she was sure, but right then, she didn't care, too engrossed by what was happening to bring the erotic moment to an end.

Damian pressed the pad of his thumb over her mouth.

She took in a sharp breath. It felt so good to be touched by him. Too good, perhaps. She didn't understand why. But she was sure it was the most arousing sentiment she would ever experience in her life. And she wanted to make it even more stimulating . . .

Mirabelle let her lips close tight over his thumb.

He bristled. The tension in him hummed through every pore of his body; she could feel it.

She flicked her tongue over the pad of his finger in a wet and lanky stroke.

Kiss me, Damian.

She looked deep into his eyes, dark as a watery sea at midnight. Tremors rolled along his limbs. He was tempted to take her and fighting it. Soon, though, his lips parted . . .

Mirabelle thought her heart would stop.

"Oh, Belle," he whispered in a wretched groan, his lips brushing hers in soft whisks. "You're going to destroy me."

A hot mouth pressed hard over hers.

Blood roared in her ears, her heart pumped furiously. Hell's fire, but the man tasted good. His mouth was burning and wild, his days-old stubble scraping back and forth along her cheeks and chin, adding to the frenzy of sensations already whipping around inside her.

She didn't think a kiss could feel this way. So good. So liberating. So intoxicating. She had never been kissed before. Well, there had been a few stolen kisses in her adolescent years, but nothing compared to what Damian was making her feel.

She took in the heady scent of him. So masculine. So virile. His hands were all over her, roaming and caressing, stirring the heat in her belly.

What a thrill! She gripped his robust neck, her fingers weaving through his thick mane, twisting around the ebony strands. Her other hand went to his chest, resting over a hard pectoral that jumped in response to her brazen touch.

He groaned into her mouth. Skin, so hot, scorched her palm. The vibration of his heart thundered against her hand, and she sensed the tremors spread along her wrist, her forearm . . .

A whip of heat lashed her skin, as his hand slipped boldly under her shirt, his fingers stroking the ridges of her spine in slow and tantalizing movements, making her shudder.

Muscles taut and thrumming, she inhaled a sharp breath when his palm slipped over her waist and cupped her breast.

At her gasp, his tongue dove into her mouth, brandishing, evoking a deep-rooted moan from her throat. Powerful fingers massaged and rubbed her swollen breast, his thumb swirling round and round over her tight and jutting nipple, so sensitive to his touch.

She was sweating, her skin prickling with little goose bumps of desire. *This has to stop!* a voice cried inside her head. *It's madness!*

But she didn't want it to stop. She wanted to tell the annoying little voice to hush, but then it shouted, *You're getting too close to him!*

Now *that* was a frightening thought.

Panicked, Mirabelle pushed the navigator away.

Damian was breathing hard. The sultry flame in his deep blue eyes impaled her and would likely haunt her for some time to come.

She had to get out of the cabin. She had to get away from Damian.

Mirabelle bolted, her body trembling, and dashed down the corridor. A hopeless wreck, she chastised herself over and over again for allowing the kiss to occur—for enjoying it so immensely.

What if James or another tar had stumbled into the cabin? How could she have risked her very dream of becoming a seafarer—her heart, even—for one measly peck on the lips?

Oh, who was she kidding? A peck on the lips? Measly? The kiss had been anything but. No wonder her brothers adored this sort of thing. Passion was nothing to scoff at, she'd just realized.

Mirabelle burst out onto the deck, a gust of warm wind greeting her.

A spring to her step, she headed aft, beneath the ropes and ratlines. She passed a few of the loyal tars, shuffling about, preparing the ship for the evening voyage under the boatswain's command. At the helm, the quartermaster nodded to her in greeting, his hands locked on the steerage, as he navigated the vessel through calm waters.

She paused at the stern and closed her eyes, trying to quiet her rumbling heartbeat, to ease the blood rushing through her veins. She was a mess. She was on fire. For the first time in her life she had lost control of her senses . . . and all because of Damian.

He had kissed her? Quincy had vowed Damian wanted nothing to do with her. Evidently her youngest sibling was a terrible truth getter. Bloody hell. If her brothers ever found out, her goal of being a pirate would be smashed to bits. She couldn't let that happen. She had come too far in her pursuit of seafaring to sabotage her own efforts by indulging in a kiss—a torrid and soul-wringing kiss, but still just a kiss.

Mirabelle opened her eyes, mesmerized by the frothing waves caressing the hull. Mirrored in the dark sea, starry twinkles winked up at her. It was so peaceful, she reflected, so unlike the storm raging in her breast.

Chapter 7

The gentle pitch and roll of the rig did nothing to soothe Damian's troubled spirit.

His body gripped in agony, he imagined all sorts of hideous things, trying to banish the erotic memory of Belle's plump breast cradled in his palm, the taste of her sea-doused flesh, the fiery warmth of her mouth.

Nothing helped, though. The ache in his groin remained. Repulsive thoughts turned sensual once more. Carnal and wicked acts skipped though his mind. Belle's legs splayed in one instance, as he devotedly tended to the folds of her feminine flesh with his roving tongue. Suckling her breasts was another favorite fantasy, and he closed his eyes at the enticing vision of her silky smooth areolas shoved in his hungry mouth.

Damian clenched his teeth at the stiffening in his

groin. Bloody stupid of him to have kissed her. Now all he could do was think and dream about her.

Tense and disgruntled, he rolled out of the hammock, unable to get any rest. Weaving through the columns of snoring tars, he headed topside, his path lit by soft shades of violet and sapphire creeping down the hatchway.

The breaking light of dawn greeted him on deck. Not that he paid the rising sun any heed. He was too roiled up to notice much of anything. Only the demon of lust inside him, chained and ranting for freedom, gripped Damian's attention. How he hungered for Belle. How his body ached for the touch of her . . . and more.

He remembered the pressure of her fingers sensually stroking his bare chest, cradling the flexing muscles . . . and his heart. He wanted something from her. Something more than physical gratification. He could feel it inside him, rumbling quietly alongside his raging lust. He couldn't imagine what it was, though. Nor could he fathom the intensity of his desire for Belle. Such a powerful yearning to be with a woman had never before overwhelmed him.

Marching aft, Damian paused at the stern and let his eyes fall on the birthing sun.

It had to be the years of celibacy warping his mind. It was the only reasonable conclusion for his wild sexual cravings.

Yet all this hankering for Belle was going to drive him mad. Even now, struggling against the twisting pain in his groin, he imagined her bent over the rail, her bare arse thrust against his throbbing rod. He could hear her moaning as he pushed hard into her, feel the muscles of her warm and wet passage clench around him in spasms of ecstasy.

Damian groaned and gripped the rail. It was insufferable: trapped on a blasted ship, with no means of assuaging the savage lust inside him. How was he going to endure the next few weeks?

"Have you forgiven us, Belle?"

Forgive her hard-hearted brethren after all the miserable things they'd said to her the other night? Not in this lifetime.

She offered the mediator of the family a cutting glance. "No, Will, I haven't."

She went back to scrubbing the deck, her brother's long-winded sigh tickling her ear.

"Come on, Belle, we're sorry. What more can we do?"

He went to stroke his knuckle across her cheek, but she jerked her face away. A mollifying gesture wouldn't suffice. If he wanted clemency there was only one thing in the world he could offer her: a chance to prove herself a worthy seafarer. But she wouldn't waste her breath making the suggestion. She already knew what the mulish man would say.

Scouring the deck boards, she returned stiffly, "There's nothing you can do to make it up to me, so just leave me alone."

William took her by the wrist and pulled her to her feet. In a huff, she dropped her scrub brush and glared at him.

"Do you know what I want, Will? To wash the

deck boards in peace. And if you tell me I can't even do that because I'm a woman, I'll toss you overboard myself."

With resentment—and more—bubbling inside her, cleaning the ship was one way to rid herself of the burden of fervent emotions. If nothing else, the hard work would tire her out, for she hadn't nabbed a wink of sleep since Damian had kissed her.

That kiss, so hot and sensual. Memory of it had her belly in a whirl. Tingles of heat washed over her as thoughts of Damian invaded her mind. She had to keep her distance from the man. He aroused in her feelings of intense desire . . . and something more. For a brief and terrifying moment, he had stirred something strange within her. A deeply buried emotion that made Mirabelle panic. She would *not* give her heart to a man. She would not give a man power over her. Emotions of love and devotion could be a source of great comfort and joy . . . but also misery. And Mirabelle had no intention of being miserable.

A troubling thought hit her. What if James asked Damian to join the crew? And if she stayed as well? How would she perform her duties under the torrid looks of the navigator? The man already had a mystifying hold on her she couldn't shake. He had ordered her not to cut her hair, for instance, and for some daft reason, when she'd returned to her brother's cabin the other night, she had put away the knife and simply tied a kerchief around her hair to conceal the missing part she'd hacked away. It was disturbing, her compliance, and she still couldn't understand why she had done it.

Her meditation unsettling, Mirabelle reached for her scrub brush, anxious to get busy again—and forget all about Damian. But a hand on her wrist stopped her from her task.

She glanced back up at William to find him smiling. The galling man was actually grinning at her.

"*What* is so funny?" she demanded sharply.

"I remember when you came along, Belle. The first girl of the family, you were quite a novelty. Even James took an avid interest in you, and we all know how indifferent he feels toward children."

"Will, I don't want to hear any family stories right now."

He put his finger to her lips to hush her. "Just listen to me for a moment. I remember one particular instance, when James was about sixteen. He was determined to teach you how to fish and perched you on his shoulders, heading for the nearest trout stream."

She quirked a dubious brow. "But I couldn't have been more than one year old."

"More like one and a half," he said, eyes cheery. "I tagged along that day. When we reached the stream, James set you down to help me with my fishing line, and *you* suddenly sprouted the legs of a race horse. A hopping ball of fluff caught your eye and you were off." Will chuckled. "You should have seen the look on James's face when he turned around to find you missing. Utterly dumbstruck. But surprise turned to horror soon enough. We both feared you'd toddled over to the stream and fallen in. James was ready to dive into the water in search of you, but then we heard a squeal of delight. We found you a little ways off, crouching by a boulder. There you'd cornered a rabbit, pointing your finger at the little critter, desperately trying to gurgle something past your lips.

"You were safe. James fell to his knees in relief. You know, I don't think he's ever gotten over the scare of nearly losing you. I think that's why he maintains such a strict watch over you to this day."

Her black mood somewhat fading, she asked in a low voice, "Why did you never tell me this before?"

He shrugged. "Truthfully, I'd forgotten all about the episode until just now. It wasn't my worst moment, after all."

"I appreciate your love and concern."

"Now Belle." He smiled in response to her dry tone. "I didn't mean it like that. You know I love you, but the incident weighs more heavily on James's heart. *He* was the one responsible for you. If anything dreadful had happened to you, *he* would have to live with the guilt for the rest of his life."

Her arms went under her breasts. "Are you trying to appease me with this childhood tale?"

"I'm trying to make you understand *why* James is so set against you being a pirate."

"You're *all* set against my being a pirate," she corrected, the tension back in her voice.

William set his hands on his hips. "Well, you're special, Belle."

"Special? As in peculiar?"

"No," he was quick to refute. "We just don't want to lose you to the sea. You're our only sister."

She snorted. "So I have to wallow on land—alone—because you think I'm special?"

"Ugh!" His hands went to his hair. "I swear, Belle, out of all of us, you were the only one born with pirate's blood already coursing through your veins."

She flushed at the reminder. From a tender age, too young to understand even the basic laws of nature, she would take a toy, bury it in the ground, and then dig it up a week later to see if it had turned to gold. Her endeavors never proved triumphant, but her resolve was unwavering, and week after week she'd inter some little knickknack.

One day, curious to know what had happened to all her belongings, her father had inquired about the missing paraphernalia. Patiently, she'd explained she was turning her toys into gold so the family would want for nothing in the future. Drake Hawkins had been touched, if not a little tickled, by her confession. But the toy burying would have to come to an end, he'd explained, for none of the items she'd masked with dirt would ever turn into gold.

And so she'd unearthed her belongings, vowing if she couldn't make gold, she'd find it. It wasn't long before the yard of their home had no level ground. But with her kin always tumbling into one hole or another, her excavation days had come to a swifter end than her alchemy ones.

"You were all so determined to see my innocent treasure hunting come to an end," she griped.

"Innocent? I nearly broke my ankle—twice— falling into one of your many pits."

"So I have an adventurous spirit." She shrugged. "All the more reason to let me join the crew."

His eyes lifted heavenward. "Belle, haven't you listened to a word I've said?"

"I've heard plenty—of rubbish. First, I can't become a pirate because I'm a distraction to the crew, then I'm an unlucky omen, and now I'm *special*. Which is it, Will?"

"All of those reasons, I suppose. We're just too afraid of losing you."

Her finger poked into his broad chest. "And I'm afraid of losing all of you. But nobody seems to care about my feelings, do they?"

"We care, Belle—a lot. That's why no one wants to see you get hurt."

She snorted. "A few days ago, Quincy nearly lost his life. *He* got hurt. Why aren't you hauling him home to England? Why just me?"

"Belle!"

Back on her hands and knees, she resumed polishing the deck. "Forget it, Will. I'm still angry and I still want to become a pirate. You haven't changed my mind about either."

She heard the disgruntled sigh and footsteps receding.

After a few minutes of vigorous deck scrubbing, she rocked back on her heels and stared at the puddle of water, letting out a noisy exhale.

She *would* change her brothers' minds, she vowed. She was determined to do away with their doubts and fears. Her future happiness depended on it.

Later that night, alone in the galley and peeling potatoes, Mirabelle glanced up to find James filling the doorway.

His expression inscrutable, she didn't care to decipher what he was thinking. Instead she resumed her task, knowing it would annoy her brutish brother. James hated to be ignored.

"Still not talking to me, Belle?"

She didn't say anything; that seemed answer enough.

Heavy footsteps approached, but Mirabelle kept her eyes on the potato.

James hooked his ankle around the leg of her chair and spun it about until she was facing him.

She cried in surprise, her potato popping clean out of her grip and tumbling onto the floor. As the ship dipped, it rolled away.

Mirabelle glared at her brother. He swiped a nearby chair and swiveled it around, straddling the seat, his burly arms perched on the chair top.

"You have some gumption, Belle, being so miffed. And after all the trouble you've caused me by stowing away."

All the trouble *she* caused! What tripe! If James wasn't such a dogged dictator, he wouldn't have any trouble—not from her anyway.

"So you want to sit here all night, Belle, frowning at me? Fine . . . But you're going to miss the star shower."

Her eyes brightened. Forget the potatoes—and her temper. Eagerly, she jumped from her seat.

But a robust hand grabbed her by the wrist and yanked her back down into the chair.

Spending the evening gazing at a star shower was preferable to staring at her surly brother, so she broke her silence to demand: "What do you want, James?"

"A truce."

"What kind of a truce?"

"Well, what will it take for you and me to stop bickering?"

"That's easy." She crossed her arms under her breasts. "Give me a chance to prove myself a worthy seafarer."

He let out a disgruntled sigh. "Not this again."

"If you want a truce, James, then give me a chance. I deserve one. You took Quincy on board without even testing him first. I'm at least willing to show you what I can do."

His delft blue eyes brimming with misery, he grumbled, "You're determined to put me through hell, aren't you?"

"You're putting yourself through hell." Her voice softened then, as she reached over to place a reassuring hand on his forearm. "I'm not a little girl anymore. I won't fall into a fishing stream—or the Atlantic, for that matter—and drown."

James's look of misery turned murderous. "Will and his yapping."

"Forget about Will," she said. "And don't worry about me, either. I can take care of myself. Let me show you."

That stubborn blaze in his eyes dwindled to a mellow kindle. He took in a few loud breaths, likely in protest, before relenting, "All right, Belle, you can prove yourself."

She squeezed his forearm in excitement. "Really?"

"Aye," he said gruffly, "but you'll be treated just like the rest of the crew."

She jumped up and kissed his brow. "Thank you, James. You won't be sorry, I promise."

"I mean it, Belle, no special treatment."

Another kiss on the brow. "I know."

And before he could stress *again* how hard life would be for her as an ordinary tar, she ran from the galley and up onto the deck, determined not to miss another moment of the star shower.

The evening was late, the moon high in the heavens. Her heart was light. Lighter than it had been in a long time. She wanted to hoot with laughter, but she contained her joy. Instead she celebrated by feasting her eyes on the glittering specks of light shooting across the night sky.

She was in awe. She always was whenever she had the privilege of witnessing one of nature's finest performances. And how appropriate to have a star shower on the night James finally surrendered his stance, giving her the opportunity to prove herself a capable seafarer. It was as if fate itself was congratulating her on her success.

Mirabelle clasped her hands together under her chin and reveled in the unearthly display, so brilliant. Out here, on the clear and crisp ocean, the falling stars seemed brighter, more magical than on land. Another great reason to be a sailor.

A soft breeze drifted through the ship, teasing her long hair. It was an enchanting moment. Life stood still for just a second, and her heart captured every detail in perfect clarity to cherish for years to come.

Staring at the plummeting stars, Mirabelle suddenly found herself wondering if Damian would enjoy the vision. Would he appreciate the dazzling sight as much as she did?

Without thinking, she abandoned the spectacle in the heavens and scanned the deck, searching for Damian. Her eyes rested on his tall, wiry frame, leaning against the starboard rail. Despite the hovering darkness, she recognized his figure instantly, having become so well acquainted with it the other night. And although it was too dim to see his face, she could *feel* him looking at her.

A warmth spread through her. Titillating . . . but also comforting.

Mirabelle returned her gaze to the glimmering lights in the sky. She finally had her chance to become a seafarer, and it was more imperative than ever that she prove herself an admirable tar. Nothing could jeopardize her chance for victory . . . nothing save one very sexy and mysterious navigator.

She definitely had to keep her distance from Damian. She sensed he was the only man in the world who could thwart her dream of sailing now.

Chapter 8

⁓ ◦◯◦ ⁓

The sailors erupted in a chorus of hoarse guf-
faws.

Damian had been dragged into the fray of things by
a well-recovered Quincy, forced to partake in the revelry with a mug of ale in his hands. He hadn't touched
the spirit, though. Little by little, when the chap
wasn't looking, he dumped more and more of his ale
into Quincy's mug.

Assembled on deck, most of the crew had gathered
in celebration. There was no particular cause for celebration, Damian had discovered. The men simply
enjoyed toasting to freedom. Or perhaps it was broth-
erhood? In any event, the jokes and ale poured forth,
the men besotted and loving it.

The captain was conspicuously absent, as was
Mirabelle. Damian looked up ahead to find James

conversing with the helmsman, but Belle was nowhere in sight. He had watched her earlier in the night, gazing at the plummeting stars with obvious awe and appreciation. She was more breathtaking than any twinkling light, though. More fascinating, for sure, and he had found himself captivated by her earnest expression of joy rather than by any falling star . . .

"And then," said Brice, the quartermaster, gesticulating with his fingers, "Johnny over here eyes a plump redhead by the bar."

Young Johnny blushed and muttered, "Shut your mouth, Brice."

But Brice wasn't about to do that, not when he had so many eager ears his way. "Johnny gathers up his valor and swaggers over to the redhead, but she's too busy chortlin' with another wench." Brice puffs out his chest in imitation. "Johnny taps the redhead on the shoulder and utters some lovin' words . . ."

Johnny tackled Brice to the deck at that point, but a wheezing Brice managed to rasp, ". . . and then the redhead, lookin' all confused, asks, 'Which one o' us are ye talkin' to, mate? Me or my friend here?'"

Another burst of boisterous laughter. Damian commiserated with the poor cross-eyed Johnny, who turned a bright crimson red just then. But Johnny was a relatively fresh member of the band of merchants, a brother to one of the older men, according to Quincy, and the chap needed to be properly initiated—in other words, ribbed until thoroughly mortified.

Damian glanced around the circle of merry tars. All brothers, really. Some bound by blood, others by friendship. Whatever their relation, their tight comradeship was evident, and he was gripped by a sudden pang of loss at the sight of them.

Clutching his mug of ale, Damian resisted the impulse to down what was left of the frothy liquid in one greedy gulp. The carousing around him reminded him of his own empty existence—of the loss of his brother. Suddenly he wanted to immerse himself in the familiarity of depravity, like one of the heckling sailors around him. He was tired of enduring his miserable existence in stark sobriety.

But despite that pressing urge, he would not give in to temptation. He had a duty to carry out. And as difficult as it might be to withstand his oppressive loneliness, Damian would not surrender to his old dissolute ways until his obligation to Adam was satisfied. If he took so much as one sip of ale, he knew he wouldn't be able to refrain from another and another still. Before long, he'd end up foxed and incompetent, just like his former worthless self, and his duty to Adam would be forever unfulfilled.

He couldn't do that to his kin. The one small, untainted part of Damian that had loved his brother, that still loved his brother, gave him just enough strength to face each and every wretched day. He would see his vow of vengeance to an end. He was adamant.

But he could not sit and listen to the brotherly banter any longer. It was like a knife to the heart. Quietly, he excused himself. The laughter still rife, only Quincy took particular notice of his withdrawal, quirking a curious brow.

Damian made his way down the hatchway, his

heart thundering. Memories of his old degenerate ways came back to haunt him. He could still recall the nights of illicit decadence, the obscenity of three women at a time, drowning in liquid fire—brandy was always his particular favorite. He'd lose a small fortune at the turn of a card and not give a bloody whit. Aye, he could remember. Remember the lonely despair whenever he sobered up. It was a gaping chasm he could never fill. He had dumped lust and drink and coin down that hole in an attempt to fill it. An endless stream of debauchery into a bottomless pit.

But the true infinity of his misery didn't strike him until after Adam's death. Once his brother was gone, Damian had realized the only semblance of peace, of companionship, he had ever felt in this pitiful world was when he was with his kin. But with Adam now dead, so, too, was the chance of ever finding that peace again.

A crushing weight on his chest, Damian was oblivious to his surroundings, conscious only of the pain slicing through him. So when a warm and soothing feminine body crashed into him, he wrapped his arms tight around it, desperate to banish the solitude suffocating him.

Without thinking, he pressed his mouth hard over Belle's, stifling her protest, drinking in the sweetness of companionship . . . of life. She tasted so bloody good. Like hope, if hope had a taste. But he didn't give a damn about technicalities right then. He cared only about the warmth sweeping through him, smothering him, taking away the darkness that had lived so long inside him.

Damian pushed her up against the wall, the yearning to never let her go blanketing him. At some point in the kiss, Mirabelle had stopped struggling and returned his embrace with the strength of an Atlantic winter gale, squeezing his neck and hooking her leg around his calf. The desire to consume her intensified the more she offered herself to him, and he began to fear letting her go, losing the connection that had been forged between them.

He had been alone for so long. Alone in hell. And Mirabelle's company was like balmy rain to his burned and tattered spirit. She washed away the misery of so many desolate years. It was intense—and frightening—at the same time.

"Damian?"

The intruding voice jostled Damian from his spiraling thoughts. He parted from Belle, slammed against the opposite wall in his haste, all the while devouring her with a raw and undeniable hunger in his eyes.

She was breathless, like him. Stunned, like him. And if his imagination wasn't deceiving him, gripped with unquenched desire, like him.

Damian tore his gaze away from her and looked down the hall to find Quincy approaching.

"Damian, are you all right?" The kid glanced between him and Mirabelle, a puzzled expression resting on his brow. "Why did you leave the deck so suddenly? Is something wrong?"

"No," said Damian, curtly. That was all the breath he could muster to make a reply.

And before Quincy caught on to what had just happened between him and Mirabelle, Damian marched down the corridor, abandoning the siblings.

His soul was in turmoil, twisting in every conceivable way. The desire to return to Belle and carry her off to an isolated cabin for a thorough bedding engrossed him. And an equally overwhelming desire to stay the hell away from her consumed him.

Shit, was he really so weak? Could he truly have disgraced his brother over the stirrings of his cock? Over the pathetic cries of one lonely voice inside him? Another second more and Quincy would have witnessed the embrace. Then what? Was he to swim back home to England once the furious brothers had tossed him overboard?

Guilt and self-loathing quickly replaced what little comfort he had found in Belle's arms.

Damian clenched his fists. He *would* stay away from her, he vowed. He had not come this far in his quest for pirate blood to fail over a kiss.

Chapter 9

❦

Damian slammed against the wall, then toppled to the floor. He tried to stand, but the ship lurched beneath him, tossing him back to the ground as a child would a rag doll. Deafening cracks of thunder exploded overhead. The rain beat down in sleets.

"Bloody hell," he muttered.

There had been tepid weather the last week or so. A few days of northwesterly winds, a few days of idle drifting. Nothing to predict the monstrous gale that had hit the vessel not a quarter of an hour ago.

Ensconced below deck, tending to minor repairs, Damian had felt the pitch and wallowing of the floorboards beneath him. At first, buried in the hold, he'd assumed the tempestuous movements nothing more than the result of being immersed so deep below sea level. Apparently that was not the case.

Not entirely sure how he managed to get up *and* remain standing, Damian forced his wavering self through the stairwell, staggered down the corridor, then stumbled up another set of steps that led to the main deck.

He stepped into the deluge, at the mercy of the lashing waves. A gust of wind blasted him, whipping piercing spray into his face and body, nearly knocking him back down the opening whence he'd come.

The smoky sky, congested with sinister, billowing clouds, banished the afternoon sun. But there was still enough visibility to outline the silhouettes busily taking in the fore and mizzen sails. It was the mainsail that was stuck, however, and if it wasn't reefed soon, it would shred under the overwhelming pressure of the storm, bringing the mast down with it.

Braving the opposing winds, Damian made his way over to the distorted figures.

His heart tightened.

Faint shadows, illuminated under the sizzle of lightning, revealed the most incredible sight.

What the devil was *she* doing out here?

Struggling with the brail, Mirabelle tried to bring the thrashing rope under control. Just then, a mammoth wave surged and crashed onto the deck. It was a few heart-stopping seconds before the tumultuous waters receded and Damian could breathe once more at the sight of her still standing on deck.

He was going to wring her neck if they survived this ordeal. She had no business being out in such a devastating storm. She had no business being on the blasted ship in the first place!

Making his way over to Mirabelle, Damian smothered her in his embrace. It felt so good to touch her again, to envelop her in his arms. He hadn't come near the woman in more than a week, and the fact that he had nearly lost her just a moment ago made his euphoria all the more potent.

Grabbing the stubborn brail and winding it around his palm and wrist, Damian yanked it tautly, the rope thrumming with strain in the tempest's frenzy.

Belle shouted over her shoulder, "I have to cut the tangled rigging loose!"

"Are you mad?"

She'd be washed overboard the moment she released the rope. And just to prove his point, another comber sloshed over the deck, its stinging numbness taking away his breath—and almost taking away Belle.

The rope dug into his hands, red welts appearing in the wake of the burning friction. His muscles hardened around Mirabelle, keeping her locked between his arms, while the retreating waters poured back into the turbulent ocean.

"Don't argue!" she shouted. "You're strong enough to pull the canvas down. When I let go, you'll have the brunt of the weight. Hang on!"

The woman was daft. He noticed her swipe a dagger from her boot and wedge it firmly between her teeth. Like hell he'd let her go! Let another sailor risk his neck to cut the tangled rigging. She wasn't going anywhere. And she realized that soon enough, squirming in his arms when he refused to release her.

Another wave slammed onto the deck, fiercer than

the last. The body pressed hard against him was gone, his arms empty. Damian's heart stopped beating.

"*Mirabelle!*"

The added pressure on the rope, leaving him struggling to control it, had his frantic eyes sweeping the deck up ahead, and his heart pumping blood once again.

He was definitely going to throttle the woman when this was over. She had slipped out from under his embrace in the confusion of the pummeling waves, and was now gradually making her way over to the mainmast, gripping the brail for support. Though visibility was scarce, he watched her shadowy figure every step of the way, and unbeknownst to him, it was a long while before he took another gulp of air.

Mirabelle choked back the rain and coiled her arms around the mainmast. What the hell did Damian think he was doing, trying to hold her back like that? He hadn't said a word to her in more than a week, had barely glanced her way, and *now,* when all their lives were at risk, his despotic tendencies returned? The temperamental bounder. If he wasn't kissing her, he was berating her. If he wasn't ignoring her, he was crushing her in his embrace. And always at the most importune times!

Removing the knife from her mouth, Mirabelle began to saw at the interwoven lines. The heavy bonds refused to give way, though, so she intensified her efforts. But with her fingers numb from the frigid waters, her progress was slow.

Curse the wretched storm! The squall had come

from nowhere, giving no more than a moment's notice of its imminent arrival. There was so little time to pull in the sails, and virtually no time to batten down the ship.

Mirabelle couldn't even spare a glance to see if the crew were still holding on to the brails. She prayed that they were. The *Bonny Meg* had been through worse storms than this, but she'd had her sails furled at the time and weathered the turmoil.

The mast groaned and splintered. If they survived Poseidon's current wrath, it wouldn't be by much.

Her teeth clenched in defiance of the storm, Mirabelle sliced through the bonds at last. The canvas came skidding down, the crew grappling to tie it flat against the boom.

Another slash of lightning sliced through the angry heavens, and Mirabelle caught sight of the jibs still flying. It was never-ending, the pitfalls to this voyage. They'd already done battle with one tempest on their way to New York, and were now fighting their second. The mainmast had nearly collapsed, and now the jibs were threatening to tatter to pieces. She had to lower them. Inflated by the surging winds, the ballooned sails could mean the difference between the ship staying in one piece and being ripped apart.

Had she already cursed the storm? Well, she cursed it again.

Lodging the knife between her teeth, she slung her arm over her brow and pushed her way over to the bowsprit. Hoisting her knee up onto the rail, she crawled along the extended spar.

The grueling minutes it took for her to reef the

sails seemed to stretch on forever. When at last she brought the jibs down, she inched her way backward along the spar . . . but she didn't get very far.

Mirabelle gawked in awe of the black wall of water racing toward her. There was no time to think or even fear. Instinct took over and she draped her arms around the bowsprit, holding it tight. But it was futile, she knew. She would never withstand such a monstrous comber.

Like shards of glass lacerating her skin, the surge pummeled her. It was so cold, so biting, she couldn't breathe. She spit out the knife. Water clogged her mouth. She couldn't even scream.

The sudden pressure around her midriff was crushing. A robust arm pulled her through the water and hoisted her over the rail.

She went crashing to the deck. Dazed, she couldn't move for a few moments, and then slowly she tilted her head to the side and caught a glimpse of Damian's pained expression. He'd slammed his head against the ground when they'd toppled over.

Still gripping her in a mighty hold, he glared at her—with relief or fury, she couldn't tell—before his eyelashes fluttered closed.

Chapter 10

⁓◌◠◌◡

Damian sensed a moist cloth bathing his chest, the soothing movements allaying his scorched skin and evoking a heavy sigh from him.

Fingertips, tepid and damp, gently pried apart his parched lips, allowing icy drops to seep into his mouth and trickle down his dry throat. Swallowing, he grimaced at the shooting pain.

Once one body part grew conscious of its torment, all body parts rang out with the same anguished cry. Muscles ached unmercifully. A throbbing at the back of his head pounded with mounting intensity.

What had happened? Where was he?

Darkness clouded his mind. He tried to remember . . . a roar of thunder clapped in his ears. The wallowing ship lurched beneath his feet.

A storm.

There had been a storm.

Damian opened his eyes. A pale mist still shifting through his vision, he adjusted his gaze to the dimly lit cabin and scanned his surroundings, only to blink in bewilderment at the sight of Mirabelle seated on the edge of the bed.

The bed? He glanced around the room once more. He recognized the space. It was the same infirmary where Quincy had recovered. The same bed, even. The only thing different was Belle's tender bedside nursing. She hovered above him, dousing his fevered flesh—his naked flesh.

Damian was suddenly all too mindful of his undressed state, his body rigid with the realization that there wasn't much obstruction between him and Belle, only a thin blanket covering his lower region.

The twinge in his head ebbed away, replaced by a more critical ache in his loins.

She was oblivious to the fact that he was studying her. With each graceful stroke, she mapped the contours of his abdomen, her eyes traveling in the same direction, at the same leisurely tempo of her roving hand. But Damian felt the caress of her amber eyes more than the fondle of the wet cloth. And despite the agony tearing through every fiber of his being, he wouldn't have twitched and disturbed her salacious rubdown to save his soul.

With the cool compress, Mirabelle gingerly traced a path from his navel to his neck, her meditative eyes absorbing every part of his body. Up and up went her golden gaze, until their eyes locked.

Damian had never seen such scarlet color rush into a woman's cheeks so quickly.

His voice rumbled, his throat raw with pain, "Were you enjoying yourself?"

Mirabelle cleared her throat and chucked the cloth into a bowl of water, spray splashing onto the floor. "Drink some water."

She was stunning when mortified, blooming rose pigment accentuating the soft lines of her regal features. He could spend an eternity admiring her.

But Belle had another idea. When he still didn't move, she shattered his reverie by bracing one hand beneath his neck and picking up a glass with the other. She pressed the rim to his lips and he greedily drank.

Setting the glass back on the table, she wondered, "How do you feel?"

"Awful," he admitted gruffly. "What happened?"

"Don't you remember?" She eyed him closely. "We sailed through a squall two days ago. You hit your head during the storm and have been asleep ever since."

The heavy mist enshrouding his thoughts slowly began to lift. More images came to mind: images of shadows taking in the sails, strikes of lightning . . . and a woman perched on a spar, about to be swept away by an enormous swell of water.

"I remember," he said roughly, passion and fury now intermingled in his heated glare. "How could you be so daft, crawling out onto the spar like that?

She stood up, hands hooking around her hips. "I *had* to lower the jibs or the ship would have torn to pieces."

"You were almost killed."

She snorted in rebuttal.

"Damn it, Belle, you can't be that foolish again!"

"Foolish?" Her amber eyes flared. "If the ship went down, I *would* have been killed. So how was I being foolish by trying to keep the rig afloat?"

He gritted his teeth. "Someone else should have taken in the jibs."

"I did what had to be done," she said. "I'm not the half-wit you and my brothers seem to think I am."

Her outburst at an end, she proceeded to the table and vented the rest of her temper on a folded sheet of linen, tearing it into long strips.

Watching her massacre the linen reminded him of the cloth already coiled around his head, and he demanded, "How did I strike my head?" Damian had captained his own ship for the last two years. He was not a fresh sailor, prone to slipping and skidding and knocking himself senseless whenever the waves grew rough.

Mirabelle heaved a deep sigh and paused. "Saving my *foolish* hide, that's how you hit your head."

More memories flooded forth: Mirabelle in his arms as he'd yanked her from the death grip of a monstrous comber. He had collided with the deck boards in the wake of the violent upheaval, like a boulder plunged off a cliff, smashing against the rocks below.

Damian winced in discomfort, reliving the entire scene again in his mind. No wonder he had such a pounding headache.

"Are you hungry, Damian?"

For you, he thought, then shoved the carnal impulse aside. He was already in agony, and didn't need the added burden of lust to cause him even greater torment.

"I'm not hungry," he said, voice hoarse and strained. "How's the ship?"

She went back to shredding the linen. "The mainsail was badly damaged, but it's being repaired now. We should be under way in a few days."

Silence.

All he could think about was her spicy touch and the arousal he was still struggling to tamp down. The quiet that had settled between them only ignited his imagination, giving him the opportunity to study her without distraction and envision all sorts of decadent things, like her tearing those strips of linen without a stitch of clothing on.

He pictured the naked swell of her arse, the smooth and creamy skin pressed against the eager palms of his hands as he caressed her bare bottom.

He closed his eyes and groaned softly.

What the devil was the woman doing in here anyway? Damian had a hard time believing the captain would send his own sister to nurse an injured man who was not her kin. A naked man at that!

The provocative thought struck him soundly. Had Belle been the one to undress him? Had she stroked and fondled him in more intimate ways while he was asleep? Better yet, had she enjoyed it?

Bloody hell, she was driving him mad.

"What are you doing in here?" he suddenly snapped.

Belle dropped the linen back on the table and glared at him. "Making bandages. What does it look like?"

He delved deep into the honey gold pools of her eyes, fringed with long, flaxen lashes. "You weren't making bandages a few minutes ago."

A blush adorned her cheeks. "I was *trying* to bring down your fever. Your skin is on fire, you know?"

Thanks to you, Belle, he wanted to growl aloud. Did the woman think him so daft with the chills that he couldn't recognize the desire in her eyes?

Blast her! She was going to destroy his resolve, hack it to pieces like that unfortunate scrap of linen.

He couldn't bear to have her as his bedside nurse, rubbing his fevered flesh each day, making his groin throb and his heart pound and his fingers ache to hold her. It was even more insufferable knowing her attraction to him wasn't just in his head anymore, that she really did feel something for him in return.

"You shouldn't be here, Belle."

"Fine." She stalked over to the door. "Quincy can see to the rest of your needs."

Flustered, she left the cabin, and Damian was both glad and sorry to see her go.

She was a temptress all right. Heaven to look upon and hell to resist. At least he was laid up in bed and couldn't go about seducing her—if he was daft enough to even try. That was one small consolation. His only hope was that *she* stayed away from him. If fate had even a measure of pity for him, he wouldn't see Belle again until the ship docked in England.

Damian could wish.

"Bloody stink hole."

Crammed in the narrow corner of the bow, with a bucket of tar in one hand and strips of old canvas in the other, Mirabelle patched up the tiny leaks that had sprung during the ocean voyage.

She had volunteered to do the disgusting job in the hopes of proving to her skeptical brethren she was a capable seafarer, that she was just as hardened as any of them. Even the churlish captain would have to concede that point after she flawlessly demonstrated her nautical skills . . . or so she tried to convince herself. Deep down, though, she knew the real reason she had asked James for the most vile task aboard ship. To keep her mind—and hands—off Damian.

Mirabelle let out a heavy sigh, the memory of Damian's exquisite muscles beneath her fingertips still sizzling in her mind. She hadn't meant to get *that* close to him. Truthfully, she hadn't. Her intention had been to check on him. Nothing more. After two days, he had yet to regain consciousness, and she'd started to suspect he might never wake up. That Quincy was designated nursemaid didn't help soothe her unease. Her young scamp of a brother was the most irresponsible of the lot, and she was convinced he wouldn't make a proper aide.

Skittish and inconsolable, Mirabelle *had* to see

Damian for herself—even though she was expressly
forbidden to do so. James had issued the order soon
after Damian was injured. It had never occurred to
her why she wasn't allowed in the infirmary. The
order seemed rather unreasonable, but she had followed instructions without protest, not wanting to
come off as a disobedient tar . . . until the paranoia
had gripped her. What if Quincy forgot to check on
Damian's head wound and the man bled to death?
Or what if her brother didn't give Damian enough
water and he died of thirst?

The constant fretting was making her restless and
she'd decided to put her frazzled nerves at ease. Just
one quick peek at Damian was supposed to quiet her
jitters.

It did anything but. After sneaking into the infirmary, she had discovered Damian was fine, all
right—and naked as a Greek god. No wonder James
had threatened to chain her to her bedside if she ventured anywhere near the navigator while he was recovering.

But the deed was done. Damian looked in good
order—incredibly, Quincy was more attentive to his
needs than she'd thought he would be—and she
should have walked away at that point. But something had compelled her to stay.

Damian's bare chest.

She blushed. She was stuck in a dark corner of the
ship, alone, and still she blushed. Well, it wasn't her
fault the man had such a virile physique. She was
drawn to his muscular curves, as she'd been drawn to
them on the night he'd first kissed her. And she'd as-

sured herself a quick touch, to appease her carnal impulse, wouldn't do any harm.

But one touch had informed her Damian wasn't doing as well as he appeared. On that point, at least, Mirabelle could console herself with the knowledge that if she hadn't ventured into the cabin, Damian might have perished from his fever. The thought helped quiet her raging guilt over the pleasure she had felt staring at—and touching—Damian's magnificent form.

Mirabelle sighed again. Her back twisted with pain, she stood up to stretch. It wasn't doing her any good, all the difficult and repulsive labor. Damian was still wedged firmly in her thoughts.

Feeling a little light-headed from the tar fumes, she decided to head topside for a break. She found Quincy on deck, arms folded over his chest, staring up at the sky with apparent fascination.

"What are you looking at?"

Quincy flashed her a quick and devilish smile. "Eddie's tending to the last yard."

Mirabelle looked up to find her brother Edmund perched on the mainsail yard, pounding away at the extra supports. His legs straddled the beam, and with a mallet in one hand, he reached for the nails tucked between his teeth with the other.

"Are you expecting him to do something amusing?" she asked in confusion.

"Yup. Come crashing down on his head."

She made a noise of disgust. "You have a twisted sense of humor, Quincy."

He laughed at that. "It runs in the family."

"*I* wouldn't find Eddie tumbling down the ratlines very funny."

He offered her an odd look. "No, you wouldn't, would you? I suppose you take after Mother."

She pursed her lips. "What does that mean?"

"Only that Mother was solemn, that she rarely laughed, or so I heard from our brothers."

"Well, that might have had something to do with the fact that she didn't lead a very happy life while Father was away."

He shrugged. "Perhaps."

Mirabelle turned away from her brother, and cast her eyes over the somber gray waves and the congested midday sky, billowing with clouds. She caught sight of a ship on the horizon, drifting aimlessly like the *Bonny Meg*. The squall must have disoriented a whole slew of vessels, she thought.

After a short pause, she asked quietly, "How's Damian?"

"Fine. He's awake now."

Her heart thumped a bit faster. "That's good." She waited to hear if Quincy would mention anything about her being in the cabin. She wasn't sure if Damian had confessed her presence there. After all, she had left in a huff, miffed that he had all but ordered her out of the cabin. Though she still wasn't sure why. Why she was miffed, that was. She should be grateful that at least one of them had enough sense to realize she shouldn't have been in there. Anyway, she never got the chance to ask Damian *not* to reveal her visit.

"Yah, I'm glad he's doing better, too," said Quincy.

"I just changed his bandages a little while ago. He grumbled the whole time, though."

Solace came over her when Quincy didn't say anything about her spat with Damian. The man must not have mentioned it to her brother. But then bafflement replaced her relief, and she furrowed her brow. "Why was Damian upset when you changed his bandages?"

"I think I tore too many strips of linen. His head's as big as a bull's." Then, mystified: "I could've sworn I made just enough strips for one dressing."

Mirabelle didn't say anything. Bloody stupid of her to have mucked up the cabin space like that, shredding all that linen. But she'd needed *some*thing to tear to pieces after Damian had called her a fool.

It was still a sore point for her, being castigated for doing what any other sailor would have done. But being a woman, she wasn't suppose to do things like help save the ship from sinking.

Men and their ridiculous reasoning!

An elbow to the ribs brought her out of her pensiveness.

"Eddie's on his way down," said Quincy, "with all his tools in tow. I wonder if he'll come fumbling headfirst?"

"Please don't sound so hopeful."

The siblings watched as Edmund made the steady descent, Quincy grinning in anticipation of a fall, Mirabelle apprehensive of one.

When Edmund safely set foot on deck, she sighed in relief.

Quincy, on the other hand, clicked his tongue in disappointment. "He didn't even swallow a nail!"

She rolled her eyes heavenward. When would her two youngest siblings give up the constant sparing? James and William got along just fine. Why couldn't these two be friends?

It was only in times of danger that Edmund and Quincy banded together in complete accord. But did the ship have to be under constant attack for the brothers to get along? Mirabelle hoped not. She trusted it was their tender age making them so quarrelsome and nothing more. In a year or two, when each matured, the back-and-forth bantering should come to a stop. If she had to endure their pugnacious tendencies for the rest of her life, she might seriously reconsider her dream of being a seafarer.

Edmund soon approached them, holding his finger and glaring at it intently.

"What's wrong?" she asked.

"I have a splinter."

"Let me tend to it," Quincy offered.

Edmund cradled his hand against his chest. "Not on your life."

Quincy snickered. " 'Fraid, are you?"

"I'll tend to the splinter." She stepped between the two warring titans, then nudged Quincy in the arm. "Go and fetch me a needle."

When he didn't budge, she gave him a shove. "Go!"

With a sigh, Quincy headed off to find a needle, and Mirabelle turned her attention to her remaining kin. She examined his finger, doing a little poking and prodding to asses the minor abrasion, Edmund hissing and wincing the entire time.

A short while later, Quincy returned with the needle, and a whole new round of poking and prodding began, with Edmund jerking his hand away and griping over the unnecessary pain.

It was a few combative minutes before the splinter was finally retrieved.

"I've got it," she said.

Peering over his sister's shoulder, Quincy examined the tiny sliver of wood, then focused his gaze on his brother. "*That* little thing had you hopping in anguish?"

Edmund, having lifted his finger to his lips to suck on the drops of blood, mumbled, "Would you like me to give you a splinter up your—"

"Enough." Mirabelle cut them each a disapproving glance. "What is wrong with the two of you? Always puffing out your chests and squawking like roosters. There are more important things to worry over." Such as the welter of emotions swirling around in her gut whenever she thought of Damian. Like the fear of losing him to his injury, gratitude for saving her life, and the desire to put her hands back on his fevered flesh . . . maybe even press her lips to his chest for a decadent taste.

Mirabelle sucked in a sharp breath. "Oh, forget it. I don't care anymore. Just kill each other and get it over with. At least then we can have some peace aboard ship."

She stalked away, her brothers staring curiously after her.

"What's the matter with her?" wondered Quincy.

"I don't know," said Edmund, his attention back

on his finger. "Maybe she's having her monthly courses."

Quincy looked back at his brother. "I'm going to knock your teeth out for putting that thought in my head."

Chapter 11

❦

Damian battled the turbulent waves, the chill of the water sapping his strength. He cried out Adam's name, but wind and spray whipped across his face, snuffing his voice.

Soon he would slip beneath the waves and sink to the bottom of the sea. Soon his struggle would be over.

But a hand suddenly broke through the thrashing water. A hand of hope. It clasped his wrist and yanked him back to the surface.

Damian opened his eyes to find Mirabelle hovering above him, ensconced in a rickety little boat, urging him to climb aboard. The sight of her made his heart hurt, but in a way he had never felt before. Not with pain, but with . . . joy.

At her behest, Damian attempted to pull himself

up into the boat, but something snagged his ankles. He glanced down to see the grim face of his brother, distorted by the violent waves. Adam tugged and tugged, pleading with Damian to join him on the seabed. Damian looked back at Belle, who was shouting for him to ignore his brother, to climb up into the boat.

But Damian could not.

He couldn't leave his brother alone in the dark ocean. He deserved to share in Adam's fate. His brother had set sail for home in the hope of saving Damian from his monstrous self. Had Adam remained in Italy, he would still be alive. He would be settled in England, blissfully wed, with a child perhaps.

But Adam was gone. Murdered at the hands of pirates. And all because Damian couldn't take care of himself.

The least Damian could do was join his brother on the ocean floor. It was where he rightfully belonged. Besides, he could never be happy with Belle. He was a scoundrel, just like his father, and he would only hurt her in time.

With one last look into Belle's lovely eyes, Damian let go of her hand and drifted away into the cold darkness.

Mirabelle poked her fingers into her ears. Hell's fire, but she could *still* hear the blasted snoring!

Gnashing her teeth, she glared at her lump of a brother, stuffed under the bedcovers, blissfully sleeping away.

She wished James to purgatory right then.

Her eyes closed, she steadied her ragged breathing, quelling the urge to smack her kin over the head with her boot. She turned her thoughts to less maddening matters, going over her chores for the following day, but wherever her mind wandered, it always seemed to return to one constant spot—Damian. The meddlesome navigator who bothered in her affairs . . . and who risked his life to save her.

Why?

Why would he do such a thing? He had known her a fortnight. Why save her at detriment to himself? He wasn't her kin. They weren't even friends.

So what were they then?

The question haunted her. And that damn snoring didn't give her a moment's peace to think.

Gracefully, Mirabelle rolled out of the hammock and treaded softly toward the door. She scooped up her boots on the way out of the captain's cabin and paused in the corridor to slip on the leather pair.

She needed some fresh air and headed down the gallery, but the muffled noises coming from Damian's room gave her pause—and had her pressing her ear to the door.

Prudence eventually gave way to curiosity, and she stepped into the cabin.

Damian was asleep in bed. Still nude, still ruggedly handsome . . . still tempting to touch.

You shouldn't be in here, Belle.

True, she thought. But she had to check on Damian. Just a quick peek to make sure he was all right.

But in the dimly lit room, the shadows emphasized the contortion of pain on his face, and she realized he wasn't sleeping very soundly. The incoherent rambling wasn't comforting to hear, either.

Worry sprouted in her breast.

Mirabelle walked over to the bed and gripped Damian by the arms. "Wake up, Damian."

"No," he resisted, fighting her off. "Let me go. Let me die in peace."

"Like hell I will!" She gave him a firm shake. "If you think you're going to die and leave *me* to suffer the guilt of it, think again. Now open your bloody eyes!"

He did.

Damian blinked once, twice, the mist of drowsiness dispelled. "I'm not in the ocean?"

"No," she assured him with a sigh. "You're safe aboard the *Bonny Meg*."

His gaze narrowed. "What are you doing in here?"

"I heard noises." Moving away from the bedside, she allowed the lamplight to fall on his bronzed and rough features, casting him in a fiery glow. Tempting indeed. She hooked her hands behind her back to resist touching him. An idle caress might ease the restless twitch in her fingers, but only for a short time. One caress would eventually inspire another and another. It was a risky path to tread: one she wasn't willing to take. "I came to see if you were all right."

Damian reached for his temples. As soon as he fingered the thick head dressing, though, he scowled. With a flick of the wrist, he whipped the bandages off his head and tossed them to the floor.

She reached down to pick up the discarded cloths.

"I know it's a nuisance, but you really should wear the bandages a while longer."

But the moment she stepped toward him, he visibly tensed. "Don't touch me."

She froze and raised a questioning brow.

"I mean, I'm fine." His words were clipped. "I don't want the bandages."

The strips of linen landed on the table. "You're a grumpy patient, you know? More so than Quincy."

"Quincy didn't have a pounding headache to be grumpy about." He sighed and rubbed his temples. "By and by, why would *you* suffer guilt if I were to die?"

She shrugged. "You did save my life. If you die, I guess it would be my fault in some way."

"Well, *if* I die, don't feel guilty, Belle. It was my choice to pull you from the wave."

"About that . . ." She crossed her arms over her chest. "Why did you save my life?"

He seemed deep in thought, troubled even. Not that she dwelled on it for very long. Hell, no. She heard the sharp intake of breath, observed the wide expanse of his magnificent chest heave, and all other thoughts went overboard.

It was disgusting, really, how easily her mind wandered when confronted with a patch of bare skin. But Damian was different from any other man she had ever seen. He was not a brother or a familiar sailor. He was new and interesting and virile and . . .

"I guess I didn't want to lose another innocent soul to the sea," he rasped.

She blinked. "What?"

He cleared his throat. "I lost someone to the sea once. I didn't want it to happen again."

"Oh." She didn't press him further. She could tell by the tightness in his voice it was a sensitive point for him. It was also one of the few things he'd offered to tell her about his past, so she wouldn't badger him with questions—yet. Maybe later, when he was feeling better. After all, her curiosity was too keen to simply let the matter rest. "Well, whyever you did it, thanks." She headed for the door. "I'll let you get some rest now."

"Wait."

"What is it?"

"Stay, Belle. Talk to me."

Really, she shouldn't. She had come to make sure he was all right. He was fine now. There was no reason for her to stay . . . except that she wanted to.

"It's not right for me to be here, Damian. Those were your words."

"I know, but . . ."

"In need of a bedtime story?"

"Something like that."

Oh, what the hell. Mirabelle straddled a nearby chair. "I can't sleep, either."

"Why?"

"James snores." She gesticulated with her fingers. "It's like a trumpet blast to the ear all night."

"I wonder if I snore?"

"You probably do. All men snore."

Damian tucked a strapping arm beneath his head and cocked a brow. "Is that so?"

Hell's fire, the man was sexy, lounging in bed like a

fabled titan, his dark hair unruly, his jaw dusted with the shadow of a beard. And that broad chest! Big and built of muscle and covered in a mat of sable curls. And what about those lips? So lush. So well suited against the backdrop of his sharp, chiseled features. So tasty to look at . . .

Mirabelle pulled her wayward thoughts together and focused on the question at hand. She really had to stop ogling the navigator like that.

She counted off on her fingers. "My father snored, James snores, Quincy likes to talk in his sleep—which is just as bad. I've never heard a peep out of Eddie or Will, though. That's three men out of five who snore, so chances are, you snore too."

"I see."

"I think you men do it to irritate the women in your lives."

He shrugged. "It's possible."

"All I know, my brothers take great joy in pestering me."

"Did they always pester you?"

"Always?" She thought back. "No. They doted on me as a child, but the attention wasn't quite so aggravating back then."

"What was your life like as a child?"

She hesitated. "My life?"

"You mentioned before your father was a sailor."

She nodded warily. "He was a merchant sailor for a few years before he wed and retired from the sea to become a cabinetmaker . . . and then he joined the Royal Navy."

"Why? A cabinetmaker earns more, doesn't he?"

How much to tell him? Mirabelle wasn't sure. Secrecy was imperative during the voyage home. Damian could not be trusted with the crew's identity yet. But there was no harm in telling him a little about herself, surely.

She took in a deep breath, the dark memories coming to fore. "Father didn't want to be in the navy, but he didn't have a choice in the matter."

His brow furrowed. "What do you mean?"

"They just took him off the street one night."

The bitterness in her voice was clear. It had happened so long ago, before she was even born, yet the story of her parents' suffering still made her seethe with anger.

"They?" said Damian. "A press gang?"

She nodded. It was the year 1788. The Royal Navy was desperate for sailors. Few enlisted voluntarily—likely due to the dismal pay and horrid treatment aboard vessels—so press gangs were hired to "collect" young and healthy men and bring them aboard. Drake Hawkins had been one of those unfortunate men.

"Father never had a chance to say good-bye to the family. He was attacked coming home from work one night. Hauled into the nearest port, he was thrashed into submission. The next few years aboard the *Neptune* were pure hell for him."

"And your mother?"

Mirabelle shrugged. "She didn't fare much better. Alone with two small boys and little money, she had to take on a lot of work. Milkmaid. Apple seller. Scavenger. She was up at four every morning, and always went to bed well after dark, but still, the few pennies she earned didn't help much. Sometimes James and William went to bed hungry. Sometime the cold winter winds broke through the rotting roof. And she missed my father the entire time."

It was that very grief Mirabelle wanted to avoid. She would not give her heart to a man as her mother had done, and then risk that heart being broken. The years Mother had spent apart from Father had darkened her spirit. She had loved him so much, and when he had disappeared, the pain of it had overwhelmed her, nearly shattered her. She never did recover from the separation, from the years of toil and wretched loneliness. Even after Father's return, she was not the same woman anymore. She had changed irrevocably. Joy and laughter did not come easy to her anymore. Mirabelle didn't want that kind of a life. She didn't want to be so attached to a man that his every breath determined her very happiness. She didn't want to give a man that kind of power over her: the power to destroy her.

In a low timbre, Damian wondered, "How long was your father gone?"

"About twelve years." Mirabelle wrapped her arms around the back of the chair and rested her chin on the rail. "Father tried to appeal to the Admiralty about his impressment, but his plea went unheard. He was stuck aboard the *Neptune*. The commander never let him off the ship . . . well, sometimes Father was allowed to go on land, but only in really dreadful places, where no one would think of deserting."

"I guess that explains the age difference between you and your older brothers."

She nodded. "Mother never remarried. She was convinced Father was still alive and would come home one day."

And her mother's conviction hadn't been in vain. After more than a decade at sea, visiting countless foreign and inhospitable lands, the battleship *Neptune* had crossed paths with the pirate ship *Jezebel*. After a triumphant battle, more than a hundred pirates had boarded the navy vessel, taking the crew hostage. While ransacking the ship for supplies, the pirate captain, Dawson, had invited any weary sailor to come and join his band. Her father had been the first to volunteer.

Never mind that Drake Hawkins was committing treason. He had lost the love for his king long ago. Being forced to abandon a family had a way of hardening a man's heart. But Drake had forever vowed the king his enemy on the day he'd been whipped for opposing the commander's brutal treatment of the crew. Twelve lashes with the rod, salt rubbed into the bleeding and blistering wounds. Drake had not a smidgen of loyalty left for the crown after that.

Her father would spend another year aboard the pirate ship *Jezebel*, touring the Caribbean. His carpentry skills proved invaluable in repairing the frigate. In time, Drake even befriended the pirate captain. It was that friendship that eventually led to her father's release from servitude. Captain Dawson even gave her father a parting gift: a ring with a winged hourglass emblem.

"My father came home one day. He just appeared in the doorway, having escaped from the navy. Mother wept for days. The family was reunited and I came along a year later."

There was a thoughtful look in Damian's smoldering gaze. "So life was good once more."

Mirabelle glanced away for a moment, tickles of delight scampering along her spine. The man really had eyes too beautiful for words. And it frightened her, what he could do to her with just one scorching look. She had to be more like her brothers. The Hawkins boys were renowned for their interludes— and for keeping their hearts locked up tight. She had to be the same way. She could not let her fascination for Damian go beyond desire.

"Life?" She maintained her vigil of the floorboards. "It was fine for a while. Father took to the sea again, but as captain of his own ship."

"How did he afford the vessel?"

She blinked. "Oh, he, ah, got an inheritance. A wealthy aunt died." She had to omit the part about Drake's tour as a pirate, and how it ensured him a fair share of the booty. Once back in England, he could afford to captain his own vessel—and he chose to captain a pirate one. "Father didn't travel too much as captain. He was home with us a lot."

"But then?"

"Mother died in childbirth." Her lips quivered slightly. "A governess came to take care of us then."

"*You* had a governess?"

She met his wide gaze, her brief sadness forgotten. "Why do you sound so surprised?"

"I just can't imagine you in a schoolroom, taking orders."

She snorted. "I wasn't very good at it. Taking orders, I mean. But I did like school."

"What did you study?"

"Everything."

"Latin? Philosophy?"

"Geography and mathematics." She sighed. "But what I really wanted to do was sail."

"I would never have guessed."

Her lips twisted at his sarcasm. "Don't start that again, Damian. I really do belong here, whatever you or my brothers might think. Father taught me everything about seafaring." After letting out a frustrated huff, she resumed, "It isn't fair, really. James and William have served abroad the *Bonny Meg* since she first set sail. And then, two years ago, Eddie and Quincy joined the crew, both restless on land and needing some *adventure*, as they'd put it."

"And you were left alone in England," he concluded with a knowing look.

"At first, I didn't mind being at home. Honest. I had Father to keep me company."

"So he retired as captain?"

"He had to." Her voice softened a bit and she looked down at the floor again. "He wasn't feeling well, always plagued by headaches, sometimes bleeding from the mouth, and he was growing feeble. Father didn't want to appear weak in front of the crew, so he gave the ship to James and came home. We were together for almost a year before he died." She gave another heartfelt sigh. "It was a good year. Father even took me to London."

A black brow cocked. "And what did you think of the city?"

"Loud. Dirty. But it had its admirable features. Riding in Hyde Park, for one. Or betting at Ascot's. I liked Vauxhall Gardens, too."

"Good Lord, you got around that season. In your leather breeches and all?"

"No." She snorted. "Father made me wear a dress. More than one, actually. He had a seamstress come to do a proper fitting, made sure I had the latest in fashion."

A soft whistle. "That must have cost him a penny or two."

"Father could afford it. As captain of his own ship, he'd profited from his many ventures."

"So what did you think of Londoners?"

"Stuffy, the lot of 'em . . . well, except for Henry."

Damian's deep voice rumbled in the small cabin space, and she could feel the rumble echo in her breast like a storm. "Henry?"

She shivered at the sudden coolness in his voice. "Aye, Henry's a real spitfire."

"Is that so?" he drawled.

Brooding. Snarling. What the devil was the matter with the man?

Mirabelle decided to ignore his churlish temperament and went on with her story. "Henry and I met in a tree."

His brow furrowed. "A tree?"

She smiled in fond remembrance. "Henry was in flight, desperate to get away from a certain admirer."

"Sounds like a bloody clodpole to me," he grumbled.

Mirabelle bristled in defense of her comrade. "She's not a clodpole. She's just a little eccentric."

"*She?*"

"Aye. Henrietta Ashby." She wrinkled her forehead. "Did I not mention that?"

"No," he said in a low but more tepid voice. "You didn't."

Mirabelle was confounded by the sudden improvement in his mood, but didn't dwell on it too much. Thoughts of Henry filled her mind, and she grinned. "You see, Henry didn't want to meet a certain dandy her mother had picked out for her, so she clambered over the balcony ledge to escape."

"Why didn't she just use the stairs?"

"Her mother was stationed at the foot of the stairs to 'escort' her to the sitting room. Henry had to go over the balcony and down the tree. She didn't have any other choice."

It was still clear in Mirabelle's mind, that first encounter. A crisp autumn morning. A light fog churning. "I was walking through the West End alone. Father wasn't feeling well, and so stayed behind at the hotel to rest. All of a sudden, I heard an odd groaning sound coming from one of the fancy houses. I was curious and peeked over the iron fence, into the courtyard."

"And there was Henry."

"Trapped in a tree." She smiled. "I felt sorry for

her, so I quietly opened the gate and tiptoed through the yard."

"I'm sure Henry was happy to see you."

"*Very* happy." *Oh, bless you!* Henry had cried. She had chattered on in appreciation for a full five minutes. "I scaled the tree and set Henry's foot loose. Together we headed down. But Henry slipped. She knocked me clear out of the tree. We both landed in a pile of leaves. Dazed, it took us a few minutes to gather our wits, and then we burst out laughing."

"Instant solidarity."

"Exactly."

Damian shook his head in wonder. "Why do you call her Henry? It's so masculine."

"She was christened Henry—unofficially, of course."

"By who?"

"Baron Ashby, that's who. You see, the baron was desperate for a son and heir, and when his wife produced a *fifth* daughter, the baron simply decided to name the girl Henry. Lady Ashby made sure the church scribe recorded the name Henrietta, though."

"The poor girl."

She chuckled. "Don't feel too sorry for Henry. She's quite fond of the name. It's a term of endearment, really." Reserved for family members and intimate acquaintances alike, so when Henry had informed Mirabelle she could call her by her nickname, Mirabelle had been mawkishly pleased. She had never had a close friend before, being a pirate's daughter and all. Not that Henry was privy to her true identity. Certainly not.

She sighed in longing. "I haven't seen Henry in almost a year."

"Why?"

Mirabelle shrugged. "Father was very ill and I had to take care of him. Once he died, I was determined to be a sailor." She gripped the chair back tighter. "I still write to Henry, but I don't know when I'll get the chance to see her again."

It was a gloomy thought, being friendless and alone. She had already lost her parents and Henry. She might lose her place aboard the *Bonny Meg*, too . . .

She quelled the sorrow gurgling in her throat and looked back up at Damian. "That wasn't a very cheerful bedtime story, I'm afraid."

"But it was an interesting one."

She quirked a half smile and stood up. "Then you owe me a story, Damian."

"What?"

"Next time James bothers me with his snoring, it'll be your turn to tell a tale. Your life's, preferably." She headed for the door. "Good night, Damian."

With a smoky look in his eyes, he said softly, "Good night, Belle."

Chapter 12

"That does it. I'm going to kill him!"

Damian popped open his eyes to find a tempestuous siren strutting across the cabin, her long golden hair billowing with each sharp step, her arms tucked snuggly under a pair of heavy breasts.

After last night's visit, Damian had given up hope that Mirabelle would stay away from him for the remainder of the voyage. And while he couldn't stop her from invading his room, he was determined to stop her swaggering. Watching her parading around in a brilliant display of temper, all her best features showcased, was making his groin ache.

"Dare I ask whom you're going to murder?" he rasped, throat still sore.

"The captain, of course."

"Snoring again, is he?"

"Like a bear!" She stopped pacing and gripped the roots of her hair. "I haven't slept in days. I'm going mad!"

"Couldn't you talk to your brother? Ask him to—"

"What? Cut out his tongue? Plug his nose with canvas?"

"I was going to suggest move you to another cabin."

She snorted and resumed pacing. "He'd never do that. He *wants* to annoy me, to make my life miserable so I beg him to take me home. This way, it's *my* choice to leave, and I can't blame *him* for it." She let out a growl. "Brothers. All a bother. Why couldn't I have had four sisters instead?"

"The fates love to torment us."

Her heated gaze skipped over him, burning him, before returning to the floor. "Do you have any brothers, Damian?"

An unexpected twinge in his heart. "One."

"And is he an obnoxious lout?"

"No, Adam is without fault. My exact opposite."

She paused in her ramble, honey gold eyes connecting with his. "What do you mean? You're stubborn, granted. Overbearing at times, too. But you have a few redeeming qualities."

After that scalding review, it was a wonder she believed him to have any good qualities at all, and in a dry voice, he wondered, "And what would you consider to be my redeeming qualities?"

"You're a good sailor."

"That's a skill, not a quality."

"You have courage, then."

"Meaning?"

"You saved Quincy's life . . . and mine."

"Aye, I did." He gave a wry, hoarse chuckle. "But there was a time in my life when I would have done neither. When I would have watched you and your brother die—in amusement."

"I don't believe you."

"Oh, believe me, Belle."

A blond brow tilted. "So what prompted you to change?"

He could tell by the tone of her voice she still didn't believe him, that she didn't think him capable of such cruel apathy. But she didn't know him very well, did she?

"My brother prompted the change in me," he said.

"How?"

"He died."

"Oh," she said softly. "He died at sea, didn't he? The lost soul you mentioned the other night?"

Damian nodded. "So don't mistake the guilt I feel for courage. Guilt makes one do balmy things, like risk one's neck for the welfare of others." Though that wasn't entirely true, not in her case anyway. With Belle, his emotions ran deep, beyond guilt, and into a realm unfamiliar to him—even frightening.

"Why do you feel guilty?" she asked.

"Because Adam was sailing home to save me when the ship sank."

"Save you?" She dragged a chair over to the bed and sat down. "From what?"

"From myself." He tucked an arm under his pillow to better prop up his head. "You see, I wasn't always such a 'good sailor.' In fact, I wasn't good at much of anything. Anything useful, that is. I had a tendency to be something of a rogue."

She snorted. "All men are rogues to some extent. Just look at my brothers. When not at sea they're getting into drunken brawls and chasing after skirts. I'm sure you're no different from any of them."

"Your brothers take pleasure in somewhat tame pursuits."

She snorted again. Only this time, she didn't elaborate.

His brows pinned together. "Their pursuits are not so tame?"

"Let's just say my brothers enjoy one pursuit I would not consider tame."

"Such as?"

"Never mind that. We were talking about you." Her arms hugged the back of the chair, her chin resting on the rail. "Why do you consider yourself to be more of a rogue than any other man?"

Because any other man was not dubbed the "Duke of Rogues." Though he kept that thought to himself. "I had an infamous reputation among . . . my kind." He was about to say "the *ton*" but caught himself in time.

"Infamy can be a burden, true." She sighed like a woman well acquainted with notoriety. Before he could question her about it, though, she added, "But just because you're infamous for something doesn't mean you're guilty of it."

"I happened to be guilty of my infamy."

"All right, Damian," she said in the same skeptical tone. "What were you renowned for?"

"Where to begin?"

His sarcasm must have triggered an idea in her head, for her expression grew thoughtful. "Well, why not at the beginning? I told you about my childhood. Now tell me about yours."

Fair enough, he supposed. Though he really abhorred thinking about those days gone by.

"I don't know what to say," he admitted honestly. "It wasn't much of a childhood."

"Full of hard work, was it?"

Work? Damian had never worked a day in his life. No. That wasn't entirely true. Damian the duke had never worked a day in his life. Damian the sailor had worked his *entire* life. Or so Belle had to believe. Damian couldn't confess his true identity to her, to anyone else for that matter. He trusted no one with his secret. If word ever spread that the Duke of Wembury was hunting the pirates who had killed his brother, those pirates might catch wind of it and disappear on him. Then how would he honor his vow of vengeance?

"Hard work, yes," he fibbed. "But there was something more."

"Like what?"

An overwhelming darkness he didn't care to dwell upon. "It was a very unhappy childhood . . . thanks to my father."

"What did he do?"

She was adamant in her curiosity, wasn't she? And

Damian wasn't sure why he was confessing his life to her—or why he found it so easy to do.

"My parents had an arranged marriage, you see." He thought back to those awful early years. "I was the firstborn, so Father took an avid interest in my upbringing. He'd decided to make me into his image, and no one was to interfere with his plan, not even Mother."

"What do you mean?"

"I wasn't allowed to speak with my mother growing up."

Her golden eyes widened. "At all?"

He shrugged. "I spoke to her at times, when in the company of others, but I was never allowed to be alone with her. Father made sure to keep us apart."

"But why?"

"Because a mother's influence would soften a boy, he thought. Make him into a hen-hearted ninny. And I was destined to be a devil, just like my father."

The memories suddenly welled in his breast, pounding on his chest. He took in a ragged breath to quell the turmoil gushing around inside him, but it did no good. The demon of pain was released.

Damian couldn't believe it could still hurt after all these years, the separation from his mother. He had cried for her as a babe. And each time he'd wailed, he remembered being chained in the dark and dank castle dungeon as a punishment. Mother had once tried to sneak down into the dungeon to comfort him, but Father had caught her traipsing in the stairwell and beat her senseless. It didn't take long for Damian to learn that crying only brought about more pain. And so he'd stifled his woe, buried it deep within him.

"Mother eventually accepted that I was lost to her," he went on to explain, steadying his voice. "Then four years after I was born, Adam came along. Father didn't care about the second born, handed him right over to my mother without a qualm."

An image flashed through Damian's mind. An image from long ago. It was hazy, but still clear enough for him to make out the nursery, all decked out in pale ivory sheers and blankets of lavender and powder blue. He had wandered into the west wing of the castle by mistake—a wing he was forbidden to enter. And he'd found himself on the threshold of the baby's room.

It had looked like a faerie world to Damian. Infant furniture and toys were scattered across the floor. Flowing lace adorned the windows, bright rugs bedecked the floor. His bedchamber didn't look anything like that. It was frighteningly somber in comparison, with bloodred curtains and hideous gargoyles perched on either end of the mammoth hearth. He remembered thinking about the striking difference between the two worlds. And he remembered hating his brother for getting the better of the two, for Adam had not only the more peaceful room, but Mother as well. She had been perched in a rocking chair that day, murmuring softly, trying to soothe a fidgety Adam in her arms. The afternoon sun was coming in through the windows, casting a warm and fiery glow over the couple.

But what Damian remembered most was the look

in his mother's eyes when she had glanced up to find him standing in the doorway. Utter fright. If Father had discovered him there, it would be the dungeon for Damian and perhaps something worse for Mother, like the loss of Adam.

Her panicked expression had told him clearly she didn't want him to be there. And that had hurt him more than anything else.

Damian cleared his throat, cramming the bubble of emotion back down into his gut. "Mother doted on Adam. And she made sure to keep him far away from Father."

Belle's voice was gentle, soothing. "And from you?"

He nodded. "She was afraid of what Father would do to her if she allowed us brothers to be together."

"But?"

"But Adam was too curious about me to listen to either of his parents." Damian actually cracked a slight grin in fond memory—one of the few he had. "I had found Adam one night, tiptoeing through the corridor, looking for his mysterious older brother. He was four years old at the time and stout as a warrior. But I didn't want anything to do with him then, and tossed him out of my room. Adam came back night after night. And each night I knocked him flat on his arse. But one night he appeared holding two boiled apples rolled in brown sugar."

Mirabelle laughed, a soft, husky rumble that struck a chord of arousal in him. "So Adam won you over?"

"Right then and there. Adam and I visited each another in secret for years. But that all changed soon enough."

"What happened?"

"I grew older. Old enough to start learning some of Father's favorite pastimes, like drinking and gambling."

"And whoring?"

He raised a brow.

She shrugged. "I have four brothers. Do you really think I don't know what they do with their spare time?"

She likely had experience in that area herself, he mused, then quickly slew the salacious thought.

"I spent days away from home by the time I was twelve," he said, and since Belle wasn't such a naïve miss, added, "living in and out of gaming hells and whorehouses."

"At *twelve*?"

He nodded. "Father wanted to make sure I didn't develop a will of my own and thwart his plan of making me into his image. The older I got, the less likely I was to do as he bade, so he made sure to teach me young."

"Is that why you had to steal your father's books?"

"Aye. Father believed reading would lead to ideas. And ideas might change my immoral way of thinking. He was so adamant, he even destroyed *Robinson Crusoe* when he caught me reading it one night, tossed it right into the fire." *And then tossed me into the dungeon.* But Damian kept that part to himself. "Father was determined to make me into a wastrel."

"And he succeeded?"

"I'm afraid so. By my thirteenth year, I was thoroughly enjoying my depravity."

The hurt of being alone had flittered away by that time. Adam had filled that empty void for a while, but the debauchery Damian had grown accustomed to had hardened his heart to the point where even Adam could not wriggle his way into Damian's affections— or so he had believed. Of course, Damian's heart hadn't hardened enough, or the pain of losing Adam wouldn't have affected him so profoundly.

Belle's voice intruded on his pensive thoughts. "So you became just like your father?"

"Through and through. I even surpassed him in escapades and scandals alike."

"What happened to your father?"

"He died during my twentieth year—of overindulgence."

"And you didn't stop *your* overindulgence once he and his influence were gone?"

"Stop? I was a foxed, disoriented, rowdy bounder. I couldn't have saved myself even if I had wanted to . . . but Adam could. He always came to visit me, to pull me out of my lairs of decadence. But as soon as he was gone, I went back to my old immoral ways." He paused, the ache in his chest growing more intense, making it hard to breathe. "Ever loyal, Adam was on his way back home to England to haul me from my drudgery yet again. The fool. He should have stayed in Italy. He should have given up on me like everyone else. Then he and Tess would still be alive."

"Tess?"

Damian took in a ragged breath, the twinge in his heart suffocating. "Adam and Tess were on their wedding tour. If only they had stayed in Italy, neither one of them would have drowned at sea. It's all my fault."

"No, Damian, it's not," Belle said in a tender voice, rising from her chair and coming to crouch by the bedside. "You couldn't have known the ship would sink."

"I should have died instead of Adam."

"Don't say that, Damian."

"I should be the one lying at the bottom of the sea, just like Mother said."

She captured his face, taking him by surprise. The kiss was hot and hard, smothering the pain inside him, pounding it into oblivion until only a burning desire to be with Belle remained.

He grabbed the back of her head, wove his fingers through her thick golden mane to keep her from pulling away from him. Not that she intended to, if her zeal was any indication. The woman moved her lips over his with a hunger that rivaled his own. And that was a feat indeed.

She tasted divine. Like all the sweetness in life he had been denied for so many years. She was beautiful and spirited and she made him feel hopeful. Like he could be happy in life—with her.

Damian dragged her onto the bed, wrapping his arms tight around her, crushing her to him. Her weight overtop of him was heavenly, but he wanted to feel and taste all of her. To move deep within her until they were one.

Already naked beneath the thin bedsheet, he could sense every part of her body rubbing up against him, scorching his skin. He wanted to know her even better, though. Every intimate part of her. Her bountiful breasts, the nook of her neck, the dip of her belly button, the smooth groove behind her knee . . . the warmth between her thighs.

With a desperate groan, Damian rolled her onto her back, his lips still devouring hers. He grappled with the buttons of her trousers, then slipped his quivering hand between her legs, cupping the warm and dewy flesh.

She gasped, then moaned against his mouth, arching her hips forward to meet his deliberate caress.

His wanton siren.

She goaded him with her urgent movements. And he appeased her lustful cravings by slipping a finger into her wet passage, stroking her on the inside, stirring up another primal moan from the pit of her throat.

Ah, his beautiful Belle. She called to him, enchanted him, soothed his troubled heart . . . and she made his blood run hot.

But the erotic moment shattered at the sound of a voice seeping in through the fissures of the planked walls. It called for Belle, and Belle heeded the call.

She scrambled to her feet in alarm, a soft cry escaping her lips. "It's James," she whispered breathlessly. She was shaking so hard, she couldn't do up the buttons of her breeches right away. "He'll kill us both if he finds us together."

Damian swallowed a few gulps of air. He was still thrumming with lust, his cock hard and ready for Belle.

"Get out," he said roughly.

"I *will*," she shot back in a low voice, her lips swollen and red and ever so tempting. "Just as soon as James wanders by. The bloody codpole. He could sleep through cannonfire, but *now* he decides to wake up and come looking for me?"

"And don't come back, Belle."

She tossed him a flustered and confounded look. "What?"

But Damian had meant what he said. He could *not* keep his hands off Belle to save his life—or his soul. He realized that now. Even the memory of his brother was not strong enough to draw Damian away from Belle's enchanting grip. He had to keep his distance from the woman or he would not survive the journey intact.

"If you come back in here," he warned between uneven breaths. "I'm going to finish what we started—to hell with both our lives."

Chapter 13

To hell with both their lives?

That didn't sound very appealing. But the thought of finishing what she'd started with Damian the other night did.

Mirabelle was still tingling all over with pleasure, her skin overly sensitive to touch. She had bathed in the morning with a cool, wet cloth, for instance, and had imagined Damian's hands roving over her the entire time. It had left her weak and breathless, that brief rubdown. Not to mention aroused. And curious. Curious to know more. To feel more. Last night's interlude had been far too short. Though she'd been unprepared to abandon herself to Damian completely, a few more moments with the navigator would have been immensely gratifying, she was sure. Intense feelings of bliss had slowly developed inside her. A need so profound, it made her heart flutter just thinking about it. But her need had been left unfulfilled. Interrupted by an interfering older brother.

Mirabelle grimaced in remembrance. Roused from his sleep to find her gone from the cabin, James had assumed something was amiss, and had scoured the ship looking for her. He'd found her—eventually—topside and breathless. She had escaped Damian's room undetected, and had made her way up onto the deck, where she'd admitted to James having a spell of insomnia and nothing more. Ordered back to bed, she'd complied, but she didn't get a wink of sleep the entire night. And for once, her wakefulness had nothing to do with James's snoring. For once, it had all been Damian's fault.

After letting out a gaping yawn, Mirabelle stretched her arms high over her head. Perched in the crow's nest, she was assigned the first watch of the night and already she was feeling restless.

She shifted in her cramped spot, her bottom numb, then returned her attention to the setting sun and the horizon, dreamy thoughts of Damian filling her mind once more.

She could still remember the haunting look in Damian's eyes, the bitter pain in his voice. Last night, she had yearned to banish the hurt tormenting him . . . but now she just yearned for him. Yearned for him to do all sorts of things to her. Like touch her in intimate places.

She shivered in fond memory of his fingers gliding inside her, stroking and stroking, whipping her insides into a frenzy. What a delightful, no, delicious way to spend one's time. No wonder her brothers found this sort of amusement so engaging. Mirabelle was beginning to understand more and more their eagerness to dock after a long voyage at sea. One could get merrily accustomed to such wonderful feelings. All she had to do was keep her heart at bay, and then she, too, could explore these arousing emotions without consequence.

She yawned again. So many sentiments struggled inside her: unquenched passions, a curiosity to appease her inflamed yearnings. So much to think about and work out and so few hours in the day to get any of her chores done, never mind any soul searching. And so many aggravating brothers to battle and so little sleep and . . .

Mirabelle's lashes fluttered closed. She needed just a minute to rest her eyes. Just a quick repose to settle her errant thoughts.

She took in a deep breath and sighed . . . and then a sound smack across the boot roused her from her rest.

James glared at her. "What the hell do you think you're doing?"

"I just closed my eyes for a second," she murmured. "No need to get in a huff."

"A *second*!" He grabbed her by the ankles and yanked her roughly forward. "Get down, Belle. Now!"

"But why?" And then she noticed the night sky—black as pitch. "Oh no."

"Oh no indeed. You're damn lucky Quincy noticed

that ship heading in our direction. If we hadn't changed course in time, we might very well be at the bottom of sea. Now get down!"

Crimson color filled her cheeks. How could she have been so careless? The dangers that lurked at sea were boundless. All their lives were at constant risk. She knew that. The watcher's post was vital . . . and she had fallen asleep at it.

The shame that welled in her breast made it hard to breathe. She followed her brother down the ratlines, as ordered. As soon as her boots hit the ground, James hooked his fingers around her arm and hauled her across the deck like a naughty schoolgirl—in front of the entire crew.

"Into the nest, Quincy," James barked, then ushered her down the hatch. "To my cabin, Belle."

She treaded the corridor in the same brisk strides of her brother, but the shame simmering inside her soon gave way to rage.

Inside the cabin, James closed the door—slammed it was more accurate—and blasted, "How could you fall asleep, Belle?!"

"It was an accident." And then with more venom: "How could you drag me across the deck like that in front of the whole crew? I'm not a child. Now the men will never trust me."

"They have reason not to trust you."

"Damn it, James, I said it was an accident! A mistake. The *first* one I made this trip."

"Your *mistake* nearly claimed all our lives."

She gulped in a ragged breath, quelling the tears

into submission. "You've ruined everything, James. The crew now thinks me an irresponsible little girl. They will never come to respect me."

"It's your own fault, Belle."

"But *you* didn't have to humiliate me in front of them. You did it on purpose. Damn you!"

James grasped her wrist before she could clout him. She gasped when she realized what she had done—or almost done. She had never hit her brother before or even tried. But he had never humiliated her in such a way, either.

James leaned in close, still holding her wrist, and admonished, "Whatever embarrassment you've suffered, you've brought it upon yourself. If you can't handle the responsibilities aboard this ship, then you don't belong here."

"I *do* belong here. I made one mistake. I was tired and—"

"No excuses, Belle," he cut in sharply. "You're restricted to quarters for the rest of the night. I'll decide your punishment in the morning."

He left the cabin then.

Alone, Mirabelle fought against the sorrow and rage and disgrace all clashing inside her. She wanted to scream. She sent her boot into the door instead. Over and over and over again.

Tears soaked her soul. Darkness swamped her. All her hope for a future aboard the *Bonny Meg* seemed to be slipping away from her and she could do naught to grab hold of it.

How could James have done this to her? Disgraced her in front of the crew? Her own brother!

She wanted to disappear under the deck boards and never come out again. What was she going to do now? How was she going to repair the damage James had done? It was important to maintain a comradeship with her fellow tars. Otherwise, each voyage would be filled with misgiving about her seafaring abilities. The men might even refuse to sail with her on board, fearing her incompetent, and then James would have to kick her off the ship.

It was a horrifying thought, being stranded on land, cut off from all that she loved. And it hurt like hell knowing her own brother might have helped to make it happen.

Mirabelle slumped against the door and dug her palms into her eyes. She gulped back a sob and slumped to the floor in despair.

Hours later, tucked away in her hammock, she still battled the same turbulent emotions.

One mistake. Granted, it had been a serious one, but she could count on and on the number of times her brothers had made mistakes just as grave.

James was so quick to forget Quincy's transgression. Not a fortnight ago the boy had landed himself in the gaol, and all her kin had risked their lives to set him free. But Quincy was a man, and as such, prone to stupidity. He was expected to make mistakes. No big deal. Hence scolding him for foolish behavior was a waste of time. But *she* was a woman. *She* had to be perfect. One misstep, and to hell with all that she had done right. It was only the error that mattered.

Mirabelle tried to steady her uneven breaths, to smother the tears, but the grief spilled forth nonetheless. James might have devastated her dream of being a seafarer. Thanks to him, the crew, already wary of her presence aboard ship, would now be downright alarmed to have such a "bad omen" strutting about. She might lose everything . . . but it was the betrayal of her brother that hurt the most.

Mirabelle couldn't lie still. The turmoil inside her was suffocating. She rolled out of her hammock with ease, careful not to disturb James.

Once in the corridor, she sprinted. Barefoot, her steps were quiet. She didn't even think about where she was going. It was instinct, really.

She burst into the dimly lit cabin, tears streaking her cheeks.

Damian stood against the wall, his hands at his temples. Evidently he couldn't sleep, either. Due to the pain in his head or another nightmare, she couldn't tell. Nor did she think to ask, for the sight of him knocked the wits from her head and the breath from her lungs.

He was in the buff, every glorious male part of him exposed to her wandering eyes. Hell's fire, the man was big. Big and beautiful and strong. And it was his strength she needed right then.

He looked at her, eyes turbulent and confused. Such dreamy eyes, full of passion . . . and pain. She saw her own pain reflected in the deep blue pools.

Before he could utter a protest, she closed the door—and the gap between them.

Hooking her arms tight around his neck, she pressed her lips hard over his. She hungered for the touch and taste of him. For the solace she felt when in his embrace. She didn't want him to push her away, to reject her. She wanted him to banish the torment inside her, to make her feel good again.

Blessedly, Damian wasn't opposed to the task. He groaned into her mouth. His robust arms went around her back, cradling her, squeezing the agony from her veins.

It was a swift surrender on his part. A good thing, too, for she wasn't in the mood for a fight. All she wanted was to touch him and kiss him—and to have him do the same to her.

He bussed her cheek, drinking in her tears. "What's wrong, Belle?" he murmured, a husky sound that made her shiver right down to her toes.

"It doesn't matter."

Stubble tickled her skin as he kissed her other cheek, over and over, taking in every teardrop. "Are you all right?"

"I will be," she said, breathless, and closed her eyes. "Just put your hands on me."

He let out another soft and aching groan at her command. She felt the tremor along his neck, but didn't think too much about the effect her words had on him, for he did as she bade just then, letting his powerful fingers roam all over her backside. He cupped her bottom and thrust her higher against him, his mouth crushing hers in a steamy kiss.

Don't let me go, she thought. *Don't ever let go.*

He pushed her up against the wall, his long black hair dipping forward like a curtain framing his face. He looked so much more handsome, so much more rugged and dangerous without his locks tied back.

Dark indigo blue eyes scorched her soul, as deft fingers went to work on the laces of her shirt. He tugged and tugged, widening the collar, then slipped the garment over her head in one fluid movement.

He pressed her back against the wall. She shivered. The chill of the wood planks against her bare back contrasted sharply with the heat of Damian's skin on her front.

His skin.

What a glorious sensation to feel his naked flesh, moist with sweat, meshed against her own fevered flesh. And it was even more glorious to feel his hands caress the mounds of her breasts. She inhaled a quick breath at the intimate touch. His large palm cupped one swollen breast, then the other, massaging, sending shudders of pure bliss dancing along her woozy limbs.

"Oh, Belle," he moaned. His lips went to her cheek, to the crook of her neck. "You taste so good."

Prickles of delight dotted her skin at his whispered words.

Damian kissed the center dip at the base of her throat, then dropped to his knees. His hands went to her backside, rubbing in slow and tantalizing movements. His mouth, hot and moist, licked the space between her breasts, making her quiver with desire.

Mirabelle wove her fingers through his dark and unkempt hair, gripping him close to her skin, not wanting to let him go. He licked and he kissed, whipping her insides to a frenzy. When his hungry mouth found one jutting nipple, and he parted his lips to take in the puckering bud, she all but collapsed onto the floor beside him. Nothing had ever felt so good. The pleasure was shooting through her every pore. Every nerve felt alive and was ringing out for the same wanton attention.

The emotions bubbling inside her were strong enough to make her weep. With pleasure, she assumed. What a mawkish sentiment! But the sob welled in her throat nonetheless. She kept it from escaping, though. She let out a half croak, half moan instead.

Damian flicked his tongue over her nipple, then laved the sensitive area with a languorous caress. He sucked at her breast for a while, cradling the swollen mound in his palm, draining the strength from her limbs.

She dug her fingers tighter into his mane, wrapped one arm around his neck and shoulder to hold him even closer. He could take all her strength, she thought. She just didn't want him to stop.

But he broke away from her breast at last, leaving the wet skin to wrinkle in the nippy night air. She gave a soft whimper of protest, but he quickly tended to her other, neglected breast, and, appeased, Mirabelle found the tight, pleasurable knot winding in her belly once more.

Her breasts felt raw and ravished from his salacious ministrations. Yet she wanted more. She yearned for his lips and his hands on other parts of her, too.

He must have yearned for the same, for he let her breast slip between his teeth just then, making her shiver, before he turned his ravenous attention to her belly.

Hot lips pressed against the taut skin of her

abdomen, branding her in the most wicked way. Her entire body was trembling. But at least she had the cool and sturdy wall behind her for support, or she surely would have found herself sprawled across the cabin floor.

When Damian's fingers moved to unfasten the buttons of her trousers, she dragged in a deep breath and held it for a moment.

Slowly he undid one button at a time, kissing each newly exposed patch of skin.

She finally had to breathe, and let out a noisy exhale, her next breath just as deep and ragged.

Damian peeled back the folds of the trousers. "I want you so much, Belle," he whispered hoarsely, warm bursts of air tickling and rousing the fine hairs on her skin.

"Then take me." It was a quiet request. She wondered if Damian had even heard her, for she hadn't the strength to utter the plea in a louder voice. But the groan that soon followed told her plain enough he had heard her clearly—and was keen to do that very thing.

A good thing, too, for she didn't think she could take much more of his slow and deliberate seduction.

Damian pushed the trousers off her hips, slipping them down her thighs, her calves, and finally discarding the garment altogether.

His hands went between her thighs, burning her skin. He parted her legs, made her take a step in both directions.

"Lift your leg," he bade, voice rough and turbulent, the strain in it evident.

Without a thought, she did as he commanded. Damian hooked her leg over his shoulder, raising it high. The flesh tingling between her legs was exposed to him—and he took eager advantage of that.

His fingers parting the curls at her junction, Damian lowered his head.

She stiffened in shock at his hot, slick tongue lapping the sensitive area. Her hands hit the wall behind her to support herself. She let out a deep and guttural groan, as surprise gave way to intense, soul-wringing pleasure.

He kissed the dewy folds of flesh, softly, almost reverently, then flicked the tip of his tongue over a most delicate spot, causing that sob she'd been holding back to bubble forth.

"Oh, Damian," she gasped.

His lips moved over her flesh in deft and fluid strokes, stirring a welter of emotions in her belly, causing her entire body to shake in unrestrained longing.

He broke away from the kiss.

No," she whimpered. "Don't you dare stop now."

"I have no intention of stopping," was his gruff retort.

He was back on his feet. She met his stormy blue eyes, so dark and smoldering that she shivered at the intensity reflected in the deep pools.

In one easy swoop, he scooped her up into his arms and carried her over to the bed.

The power surging through his muscles made her almost giddy. She wanted him so badly, it hurt. Ached deep inside her belly.

He placed her on the bed. Her legs parted in instinct, allowing him space to settle on top of her, and it was then she noticed the turgid flesh, throbbing and swollen red with blood.

Giddiness was swiftly replaced with panic. As much as she loved his lips and his hands on her, she didn't think she'd like *that* part of him inside her.

Damian slipped a finger into her wet passage first. "You're too tight," he breathed. "Relax, Belle."

Easy for him to say. *He* wouldn't be feeling the pain in a moment's time.

But the finger inside her, thrusting in and out, had the most disarming effect on her, easing the tightness in her muscles and joints, evoking first a heavy sigh, then a low, whimpering moan from her.

When he slipped another finger inside to join the first, the pleasure intensified, and she thought: *This isn't so bad.*

"That's it, Belle," he coaxed, voice rough. "Let me give you more pleasure."

She looked into his eyes then, so dark and passionate and soulful. The fear and panic ebbed away.

"Yes, Damian, show me more."

The tip of his shaft pierced her slick passage. She arched her hips forward, her neck back. He slipped inside her all the way.

Mirabelle stiffened. *Okay, this is bad,* she thought.

Damian's eyes widened. "You've never done this before, have you?"

She swooshed her head back and forth in denial, the discomfort slicing through her making it too hard to speak.

"Why didn't you tell me?" he growled.

Before she could think to answer, his fingers were between her legs, softly stroking the sensitive bud of nerves at her apex. He was still embedded inside her, but he didn't stir, and the more he stroked, the more the tension withered from her limbs.

"Oh, Belle," he whispered against her neck, kissing her cheek, "you should have told me."

But had she confessed she was a virgin, he might have turned her away. And Mirabelle didn't think she could have handled a rejection from him after everything she'd already been through.

"Forget about it, Damian," she said, the pain inside her dissolving. "Just finish it."

He cocked a sable brow. "Finish it?" A wicked gleam sparkled in his burning indigo eyes. "I don't think so."

Fingers still rubbing between her legs, Damian bent down to kiss her neck, her shoulders, planting his lips on every bare patch of skin he could reach.

Mirabelle closed her eyes, taking in the newfound comfort of his tender kisses and caresses, but when he stirred inside her, all thoughts of tenderness went out the cabin window.

He withdrew slightly, then dipped back into her. Slow at first, he eased himself from her sheath, then pushed back inside.

Mirabelle felt like cooing, a whole new sensation brewing deep between her thighs. Her hands went to Damian's back, gripping his shoulders. He thrust into her over and over again, adjusting his tempo, each thrust deeper, quicker than the last.

She moaned in ecstasy.

Damian offered her a seductive look. "Do you still want me to 'just finish it'?"

"No," she breathed weakly. "You can take all the . . ."

She was going to say, "all the time you need," for she didn't want the glorious feelings inside her to come to a stop, but she was too preoccupied with *feeling* those feelings to finish her thought.

Damian chuckled softly by her ear. "As you wish, Belle."

He pumped harder into her. Steady plunges, each more thrilling than the last. The swift and piercing strokes whipped her insides into a whirling fit.

Mirabelle clamped her arms around his neck, holding him close. His skin was hot and wet. There was so much of him to explore, she thought, but the tight and thrumming need within her ranted for satisfaction. There would be time to explore later, she assured herself. Now was the time for other, more primal things.

Blood pounding through her veins, she gasped for breath. His body rocked against hers in urgent strokes, the undulations swift and rhythmic, the knot at her junction tightening and tightening . . . and then a burst of satisfaction wracked her limbs. A quake of pure pleasure rushed through her, releasing all the tension stored in her flexing muscles.

She buried her face in Damian's shoulder and cried out in gratification. He thrust hard into her, then withdrew, giving a guttural cry of his own, as a warm and sticky fluid spread out along her belly.

As the climactic moment passed, her heartbeat dwindled to a more steady pace. "Why did you do that?" she asked weakly.

Damian sighed, still on top of her, their limbs intertwined. "So I wouldn't get you with child."

"Oh," was all she said.

Mirabelle cherished the brief repose, so soothing after such a soul-wringing experience.

Breathing more evenly, Damian locked his arms around her and rolled onto his back, perching her across the great expanse of his chest.

They both rested for a time. Neither said a word to the other. Mirabelle only stroked the rough curls of his chest hair with her fingertips, getting better acquainted with his physique without the distraction of unsatisfied lust obstructing her enjoyment.

She liked being with Damian. She liked that he had been the first one to show her the true meaning of passion. If she ever got to serve aboard the *Bonny Meg*, there would be no more opportunities to experience such pleasure. It would have been a mighty shame if she had gone her whole life without ever knowing desire. And despite the risk she had taken to be with Damian, she realized then, it had been worth it.

"Are you sated?" she whispered in his ear.

He moved his head to the side to meet her gaze. "Belle?"

"I want to feel all of you." She snuggled against him and licked his neck. "You won't deny me this, Damian."

He buried his face in her mussed hair, the low

timbre of his voice almost aching in response. "I could never deny you anything, Belle."

Such heartfelt words. She definitely liked the sound of them. "I'm glad to hear that."

Propping her weight on an elbow, she let her eyes— and hands—roam over him in a thorough assessment, taking in the hard contours of his chest muscles, the robust swell of his arm, the flat ridge of his abdomen, the flesh between his legs . . .

"That's enough, Belle." He gripped her wrist. "Or you won't be leaving this cabin until dawn."

"I suppose you're right." She sighed. "I should be going before James comes looking for me again."

But first she dipped her head down and took his nipple in her mouth as she had longed to do since the night he'd first kissed her.

Damian inhaled sharply, gripped her hair, and she moved her lips . . . her teeth . . . her tongue over the hardened nub for a while more.

When he started to moan, she smiled and stopped. She didn't want to get him too aroused. She would never get out of the cabin otherwise.

Crawling overtop of him, she treaded toward her discarded clothes and slipped back into them.

As soon as she turned around, she found Damian standing above her. He kissed her. A hard, quick kiss. Then he stroked his knuckle across her cheek in mesmerizing tenderness.

"Little witch," he murmured.

He was scolding her for the wanton way she'd sucked his nipple, and she purred, "You didn't like that?"

He grunted as though to say, *Of course, I did. That's the problem.*

"You never did tell me why you came in here, Belle."

But she didn't want to tell him her sorrow. She didn't want to taint the experience they had just shared with a somber tale. "I just wanted to be with you."

He lifted a brow in disbelief, but didn't press the issue further. "We can't do this again," he said, a rueful note to his voice. "We'll both lose our heads if anyone catches us."

"I know."

But it was a lie. Deep down, they both knew neither would be able to stay away from the other—not now, anyway.

Chapter 14

❦❦❦

"Wake up, Belle."

Mirabelle groaned and rubbed her eyes, burning from lack of sleep. She looked up to find James hovering above her and murmured, "What time is it?"

"Time for your punishment."

Her punishment. Right. How could she forget? On second thought, after the wonderful night she had shared with Damian, it was easy to understand how the repugnant thought of a reprimand could be forgotten.

Tingles of warmth spread through her just from thinking about the navigator. He was the one man on the ship to whom she could go and not be cast aside. Odd, considering their tumultuous past.

"All right." Mirabelle sighed, still drowsy. "What will it be?"

"You're to spend the rest of the day stitching all the torn canvas that was damaged during the storm."

"What?"

His burly arms crossed over his chest. "Do you have a problem with that?"

"I most certainly do." She rolled out of the hammock and grimaced a bit at the stiffness in her nether region. But she quickly recovered to demand, "What kind of a half-wit punishment is that?"

James flushed. "What did you expect? A flogging?"

"I expect something more appropriate." She jabbed her finger into his chest. "Any other sailor would get the brig for the day. Why not me?"

"Because . . ."

"Because I'm your sister, right?" When he didn't say anything in rebuttal, she made a noise of frustration. "Damn it, James, I deserve a chance to redeem myself in front of the crew. If you give me the lackluster task of sewing canvas, the men will resent me. I'll be considered the captain's pet."

"Deal with it, Belle."

Her black mood was back. "I *want* the same punishment as any other tar."

A dark brow lifted. "You want to be locked in the brig?"

"If I deserve it, then yes. I need the respect of the men, James."

It was his turn to grumble in frustration. "I'll have a bloody mutiny on my ship thanks to you, Belle."

She snorted. "Don't be absurd."

"The men don't *like* having you here."

"The men will get used to me, James. More so if you treat me like an ordinary tar."

"But you're not an ordinary tar, damn it! Can't you see that? *I* can't treat you like one of the men. You're my sister and I'll never consider you a sailor. I can't change how I feel."

"You mean you won't change how you feel. You don't want to give me a chance, admit it."

He walked away from her then, moved to the cabin window at the far side of the room. "You're my weakness, Belle. I'll never be at peace so long as you ride the waves. I'll always be looking out for you, worrying about you. The ship, the men, the missions will all suffer so long as you're on board. And it will always be that way."

Blast the man! Did he have to sound so sincere? Mirabelle was beginning to feel what little was left of her hope crumble before her.

"You want to stay in the brig?" James confronted her again. "Fine. You can spend the rest of the day there. And maybe then you can think about what I said."

In two brisk strides, he reached her. "Come on, Belle." He cupped her elbow. Out in the corridor, James handed her over to a passing Quincy. "Lock her in the brig, Quincy."

The boy's eyes rounded in obvious disbelief. "Are you craz—"

"You heard me," James cut in sharply. "She goes to the brig. Now!"

The captain then stalked away. Mirabelle was left alone in the gallery with a baffled Quincy, her heart ready to shatter.

"What the hell is going on?" Quincy demanded.

"Just do as the captain ordered," she said quietly.

Flustered, Quincy raked his fingers through his ebony mane. "I can't believe I'm doing this." He then took her by the wrist and escorted her to the brig, a small nook of the ship partitioned by iron bars.

"Belle, what's going on?"

Mirabelle stepped inside the cell. "It's my punishment for falling asleep during the watch."

"But to lock *you* away?"

"It's just for the rest of the day, Quincy. I'll live."

But she wasn't so sure of that. Like James, Quincy was confounded by the notion of *her* being imprisoned. The captain had been right. No one thought of her as an ordinary tar. No one could look past her sex or her kinship. And that meant her chance of becoming a seafarer might just have fizzled away in front of her.

If she couldn't sail the *Bonny Meg*, what would she do for the rest of her days?

Later that night, Damian prowled the infirmary. His headaches plagued him less and less. He felt strong enough to return to his regular duties, but the captain had ordered him to rest for a few more days. Damian didn't think he could last that long, though, cooped up in the cabin with nothing but erotic thoughts of Mirabelle to keep him engaged.

He slumped against the wall and raked his fingers

through his hair. "Oh, Belle," he groaned, and closed his eyes, sweet thoughts of last night spiraling through his mind.

How he'd missed being with a woman. After such a lengthy sexual lapse, it had been a thrill to inhale the heady musk of feminine skin, to caress a smooth and plump breast, to hear the cry of wanton satisfaction.

No. That wasn't entirely true. It was not the years of celibacy that had made last night so wonderful—it was Belle. She and she alone invigorated his spirit. It was the touch of *her* creamy flesh, the scent of *her* sweaty skin, the sound of *her* husky voice that had made the experience so memorable. No other woman would have incited similar feelings, he was sure. Only Belle stirred the deepest and darkest parts of his soul. And that was frightening.

It was also bewildering to realize she had been a virgin. His sassy siren, so provocative in her tight leather breeches, *had* been an innocent maid, after all. And she had gifted him with her first time.

Primal gratification coursed through him. He had been the only man to ever touch her. He liked the thought of that. Somehow it made her his. He liked the thought of that even more.

The soft squeak of iron hinges captured Damian's attention. He glanced up, his heart pounding with awakened vigor. "What are you doing in here?"

Mirabelle slipped into the room and closed the door quietly behind her. "Looking for you."

Her woebegone expression, her golden eyes so doleful, had him entreating, "What's wrong?"

"Everything," she said weakly, her lips trembling.

"I don't know what I'm going to do. All day today
I was locked . . ."

He moved away from the wall and folded her in
his arms, his fingers twisting in her long and flowing
hair. "Tell me."

She embraced his waist. "Kiss me."

"Is that your solution to every trouble?"

"For now."

He grunted in defeat. Her lips so rosy and tempting parted before him, and he dipped his head to
capture her mouth in a ravenous kiss.

Damian's spirit came to life, thrummed with re-
newed energy at the sweet taste of her. It had been a
day since their coupling. One whole day. Yet the
randy enthusiasm storming his breast would augur it
had been a year.

He hankered for Belle with startling intensity.
His lust overshadowed any threat of discovery, as he
quickly went to work on the laces of her shirt. He
even tore at the fabric in his haste to divest her of
the obtrusive garment.

Her breeches were next, stripped in a rush. Neither
one of them had any intention of a deliberate coupling. It was apparent in their anxious groping, their
hasty breathing. And to move the encounter along,
Damian tore off his own trousers.

Naked, their bodies flush and grinding, the couple
practically stumbled toward the bed and collapsed.

Belle was clutching him so hard, he had to ease her
arms off his neck. On his knees, Damian swiveled
her around until her rump was pressed against his
throbbing erection.

"What are you doing?" she said breathlessly.

"Trust me," he murmured into her ear, then sucked at the nape of her neck, his palm caressing a swollen breast in slow, methodic ministrations, soothing her skittishness. When she let out a deep and primitive moan, he braced his hands on her shapely hips and gave her a push forward. "Bend over."

She didn't protest. Her hands came forward, gripping the mattress for support, as she thrust her smooth arse into the air.

What a heavenly sight! Damian positioned himself between her splayed legs. "Are you ready for me, Belle?" And to make sure that she was, he slipped a finger amid the dewy folds of her feminine flesh.

She was hot and wet, and he groaned in ecstasy. Removing his finger, he pushed into her in one swift stroke.

Mirabelle moaned again and dropped her head down, her long hair spilling over her shoulders.

Damian maintained a firm hold of her hips as he thrust into her. Quick and steady plunges. He rocked her with a burning desire that consumed all his senses.

It was better than he had dreamed, taking Mirabelle from behind. The euphoria was palpable as it invaded his blood and rushed through his veins. Such energy, such potent life.

He struggled to control his orgasm, clenched his muscles to keep from spilling into her. It was too soon. She needed more time. He wanted her to experience the ecstasy of their coupling, to cry out in fulfillment.

And she was definitely feeling it. He sensed her climax approach. Each moan grew louder. She was so wet inside. Before the spasms erupted, though, he withdrew from her warm sheath.

"Damian!"

He was breathing hard, had barely enough control to keep his own climax in check, so he didn't respond to her outrage in words. Instead he hoisted her back on her knees and turned her about.

Her breathing ragged, she was a wanton sight. Lips flush, breasts swollen with blood, eyes sensually slanted in unquenched desire.

He quickly drew her into his lap until she straddled his thighs. "I want to see your face while I make love to you." Guiding her hips, he brought her down on him.

Mirabelle groaned and grabbed his shoulders. She bowed her head forward. Their brows touched. Their eyes met, reflecting such passionate need.

"That's it, Belle," he encouraged, voice rough and strained, as she took control, moving over him in haste. "Ride me as fast and as hard as you'd like."

She kissed him then. A deep and soulful kiss that made his heart hurt. How he adored her. She brought him peace and passion and made him feel so alive. He could stay in this moment with her forever, he thought. It was true bliss. True rapture.

Mirabelle's climax was quick to come. Her muscles shuddered around him in spastic pulses, blanketing him in warmth and satisfaction. Soon he sensed his own climax about to spill forth and he lifted her off him, spilling his seed with a great growl of gratification.

He had never cared about such delicacies before, thinking only of his own pleasure and fulfillment, but with Belle, he wouldn't risk her becoming enceinte with no husband and four brutish brothers to confront.

When it was over, she draped her arms around his neck and buried her face in his shoulder.

Damian cradled her in his lap, gently stroking the ridges of her spine, wet with sweat. Closing his eyes, he just held her, touched her, committed her to memory.

Breathing more mellow, he eased Belle back onto the bed. He kissed her brow and brushed the wet and straggling strands of her hair behind her ear.

"Now will you tell me what happened?"

She didn't say anything for a while. Then, softly, "I don't think James will ever let me be a sailor."

"He told you so?"

"He always tells me so." She made a moue, then sighed. "But this time was different . . . this time I believe him."

He stroked her flowing golden hair in tender regard. "Why do you believe him now?"

"He made a rather convincing point today. And I had a lot of time to think about it while locked away in the brig."

Damian's hand stopped mid stroke. "The brig?"

"Aye, I spent the day in there. Quincy let me out a while ago, but I had to wait till James was asleep before I could come to you."

He liked the thought of her coming to him in need. It evoked his most primitive instinct to protect her. But he did not like the thought of her imprisoned like a convict.

Slowly he hoisted himself up on one elbow and looked down at her. "What the hell were you doing in the brig?"

"It was my punishment."

"For what?"

She blushed. "I fell asleep during my evening watch."

"So the captain put you in the brig? But you're his sister."

"That's the trouble," she grumbled. "I want to be a sailor, but James won't treat me like one."

"He put you in the bloody brig. I'd say he treats you *just* like one."

"Only because I badgered him into doing it."

He cocked a brow. "You did?"

"Well, I deserved to be punished like any other tar."

He flopped back onto the bed. "Belle—"

"Don't say it, Damian. I know you're tickled to hear I won't be a sailor. You were against the idea from the moment you heard it, but I—"

He squeezed her tight, curtailed the breath from her lungs. "I was going to say I'm sorry, Belle. I know how much this dream meant to you."

He kissed her then. Slowly. Deeply. Never mind that he *was* tickled to hear that she wouldn't be sailing the *Bonny Meg*, that she wouldn't be risking her neck at sea. He just didn't want to fight with her right then.

Damian slipped his tongue between her lips, drinking in her essence. She snuggled even closer to him, wrapped her arms around his neck in a tight hold. Her body felt so good against him, so warm and comforting. He didn't want to let her go—ever.

Damian moved his lips to the line of her jaw. He then licked her neck, tracing the regal contours from her collar to her chin. She moaned softly, digging and twisting her fingers into his hair.

Her breasts were next, the magnificent mounds neglected for far too long. Dipping his head, he cupped a plump breast in his eager palm, and brought the rosy tip to his parted lips.

Her back arched forward, thrusting the tantalizing coral peak deeper into his mouth. He sucked the generous mound, whipping his tongue over the puckering nipple in slow and sensual caresses.

He loved to hear her moan. To gasp. To cry out his name. Every wanton sound filled him with satisfaction. He loved to make her want him. He *needed* her to want him.

After thoroughly laving his tongue over the swollen mound, he moved to attend to her other breast, licking and kissing, giving it the same salacious rubdown as the first.

His lust sated—for now—he could look after any parts of her he had overlooked in their hasty coupling. And he did just that, massaging her backside, then skimming his fingers along her thighs in feathery strokes, making her shiver.

After he'd touched her everywhere, kissed her everywhere, made her sigh in total fulfillment, she rolled onto her stomach, wedging her elbows next to her large breasts. Propped up, she smiled down at him, a seductive smile that made him quiver with a frightening depth of emotion.

"I should be going before James wakes up."

She kissed him. One quick peck on the lips before she moved off the bed to don her discarded garments.

He watched her dress from the bed. Studied her every movement in avid interest. She hopped to get into her tight-fitting trousers, her breasts bobbing. Then she stretched her arms high above her head to slip on her shirt.

He really should look away; this was too erotic to watch. But he did no such thing. He was transfixed. Something stirred deep within him. It rumbled and groaned and demanded satisfaction. Not lust. But . . .

He wasn't quite sure. It was a familiar sentiment, though. Ever since he'd met Belle, the feeling had rooted itself in his gut, growing larger, stronger with each passing day. It alarmed him. It also made him feel almost whole. But he couldn't keep Belle forever. And the constant wish to do so was only a distraction. A hope never to be fulfilled, for even after his mission was complete, he could not take Belle home with him. He was too much like his father—and he would hurt her as his father had hurt his mother. It was in his blood. In time, he would cause Belle great pain. And he didn't want to do that. Ever.

When she was fully dressed, Mirabelle headed for the door, casting him one final, sensual look. "I'll see you tomorrow night, Damian."

And then she closed the door.

Chapter 15

Damian had made a terrible mistake. It was one thing to flirt with a siren like Belle, it was another thing entirely to bed her. She had awakened in him the dormant demon of lust. Now the rutting instinct was so great, he was hard for Belle all the time. And if she didn't visit him each night to slake his lust, he would tear the ship apart, plank by plank, in frustration. He had never felt this way about a woman before. So insatiable.

"Careful, Damian," said Quincy. "The rope isn't furled right."

Damian glanced down to note the bundle of rope sagging in one direction. He quickly adjusted the overlap and continued to evenly roll up the yards and yards of rope.

The captain had deemed him back up to snuff and

able to take on his roster of duties once more. Though no longer plagued by headache and vertigo alike, Damian was still forbidden to tend to the sails or any other chores aloft. Aside from navigational responsibilities, it was simple ship tasks for him. For a while at least.

He was also back in the forecastle, bunking with the rest of the men. There would be no more private rendezvous with Belle. That was a good thing, really. He had to stay away from the woman. He had already risked too much by being with her thus far. And since it was evident he had not the will to resist his enchanting siren, it was fortunate a material barrier was placed between them. One even he could not scale.

Yet the restless rumbling of lust was already howling in his chest, and he knew, despite all sound reasoning, he *would* find a way to be with Mirabelle. He had come to yearn for the peace and fulfillment she offered him in her arms each night. It was an addiction he could not shake—nor did he want to anymore.

"Damian?"

He looked up at Quincy. "What is it?"

"The rope."

Damian glanced back at the rope, lopsided again. He heaved a sigh, and positioned the rope back to its rightful place.

"Something troubling you?" said Quincy, feeding him more of the cord, which Damian accepted and continued to wind.

"No."

"A headache then?"

"No."

"Clipped your tongue when you lost your footing the night of the storm, did you?"

Damian glared at the kid.

But an unabashed Quincy offered him a cheeky grin. "I only want to know what's wrong."

"Nothing's the matter," he said gruffly. "I just don't feel like talking." *I feel like ravishing Belle.* But Damian kept that thought to himself.

"Well, then, I'll talk," a cheery Quincy quipped. "I don't know about you, Damian, but I can't wait to dock." He leaned in closer to whisper, "There's this wench in port, Tilly. She has the biggest pair of—"

"Quincy," Damian cut in, his groin stiffening at the mere thought of a woman's breasts. Belle's breasts. Belle's heavenly breasts. Belle's heavenly plump breasts. "I need more rope."

"Oh, sorry." Quincy offered him more of the lead. "Now where was I? Oh yes, Tilly. A real wildcat. I could diddle away with her in bed for days. She does the most amazing thing with her tongue—"

"Quincy."

"Hmm?"

"Is that a ship on the horizon?"

The kid glanced over his shoulder. "Looks like."

"So that's another one."

"Another one?"

"I've seen a lot of vessels lately," said Damian. "More than usual."

"Really? I haven't noticed."

"I have." Damian twisted the rope. "I rarely come

across more than a couple of rigs during an ocean crossing."

"And on this one?"

Damian thought back. "Maybe five or six sightings in the last three weeks."

The kid quirked a brow. "That many, eh? I bet it's the storm's fault. It threw us for a big loop, more'n likely did the same to other ships. We're all crisscrossing this way and that, trying to get back on course."

"Makes sense to me."

"Why?" Quincy wrinkled his brow. "Were you thinking something different?"

"Just the usual."

"The usual?"

"Pirates . . . Quincy, are you all right?"

"Fine." The kid made some garbled sound. "What makes you think it's a pirate ship?"

Damian shrugged. "We're at sea. It's not impossible to meet a roving band of cutthroats."

Quincy shifted his weight from one foot to the other. "But a ship hunting its prey for three whole weeks?"

"Like you said, the storm threw us all for a loop. Could be the ship took a while to catch up to us."

"Right," Quincy mumbled. "You know, you have a real dire imagination."

You have no idea, Damian thought. "One has to as a sailor. Real dangers lurk the waves."

Quincy presented him with more rope. "Damian?"

"Yes?"

"Have you ever come across a pirate ship?"

He looked up at the kid. "No." But he intended to

change that very soon. "I didn't mean to worry you about pirates, Quincy."

"Oh, I'm not worried," he said stoutly.

"I mean it, kid," he emphasized, in case Quincy's confidence was nothing more than bravado. "The ship is probably passing by, just like you said."

"No, really, I'm not afraid of pirates."

Damian grumbled, "Just like your sister."

"What was that?"

"Nothing, kid. I need more rope."

The rope was handed to him. "You know, Damian, I think it'd be rather adventurous to be on a pirate ship."

"I'm sure you do." It was just like the foolish scamp to think such a thing. Only Quincy wasn't privy to the brutality of the trade. Or perhaps he was, but figured it was overstated to deter young bucks from straying the moral line. Either way, he didn't know what he was wishing for.

"You never thought it would fun, Damian? Being a pirate?"

"No."

"Not even a little?"

"No."

"Oh."

Damian cast him a sympathetic look. "I didn't mean to dash your wild dream, kid. But being on a pirate ship really isn't for you. You're better off here with your brothers."

"I know, but . . ."

"But what?"

Quincy shook his head. "Never mind."

"Cheer up, kid." Damian went back to work. "Think of home . . . and Tilly."

Quincy quirked a half smile, then sighed. "I think you would have made a good pirate, Damian."

"I might have a long time ago—but not anymore."

Damian coiled the last of the rope. He stood up and arched his shoulders back to take out the chink in his spine.

Eyes on the horizon, Damian said, "That ship is awfully close."

Quincy turned around to see for himself. "Oh, that's nothing. You should've been out here a few nights ago. Within a league's eyes of another rig."

"Really?"

"Oh, yah. Never had a vessel come so close, 'cept when . . ."

"When what, Quincy?"

The kid suddenly scanned the deck. "I gotta go find the captain."

"He's down below," said Damian. "What's wrong?"

But Quincy was off. All Damian could do was stare after the kid in wonder.

Mirabelle was on her hands and knees, scrubbing the stairwell with salt and vinegar, when Quincy came bounding down the hatchway. He narrowly missed trampling her fingers, and didn't even bother to pause and apologize. He just kept sprinting toward the captain's cabin.

"Bloody numskull!" she cried. "Watch where you're going."

Quincy didn't pay her any heed, though. He burst into the captain's room without bothering to knock first. "I think we're about to be attacked, James."

Startled, Mirabelle dropped the scrub brush into the bucket and dashed down the corridor. But she was brushed aside when James came thundering out the door, spyglass in hand.

Quincy fell in step behind the captain, and Mirabelle behind Quincy.

"What's going on?" she demanded, following the rushing pair topside.

"A ship keeps appearing on the horizon," said a breathless Quincy. "She looks like she's heading straight for us."

Mirabelle couldn't believe her ears. The *Bonny Meg* was about to be attacked? But she was a bloody pirate ship. No one was suppose to attack *her*. She was suppose to attack other rigs.

Poised on the poop, James lifted the spyglass to his eye and scanned the horizon. Mirabelle did the same, squinting. The other ship was still a good distance away, about five miles, she reckoned. Without a spyglass, though, the vessel was no more than a blot on the horizon, so Mirabelle couldn't be sure of her direction.

"I was thinking, James," said Quincy. "On the night we almost clipped another rig, maybe it wasn't an accident. Maybe she was gunning for us."

The captain didn't say anything, deep in thought.

"I was also talking to Damian," Quincy went on to state, "and he mentioned spotting a handful of ships on the horizon over the past few weeks. What if it's not many ships crossing our path, but *one* ship tailing us?"

Still nothing from the captain.

"It could be the American authorities, James. After escaping the gaol, we might've been followed into port."

Mirabelle watched the captain's inscrutable features in anticipation. After a long pause, he slowly turned toward Quincy. "I'll order the helmsman to keep a safe lead from the other ship."

She recognized that mulish gleam in James's eyes. He was being overly cautious for her sake. He wouldn't dash headlong into battle if he could avoid it—not with her on board.

"In the meantime, let's see if we can scare her off," said James. "Quincy, fetch me the Jolly Roger."

Mirabelle's heart started to pound. "What about Damian?"

"That's right," said Quincy. "You haven't told him who we really are . . . and I don't think he'll be thrilled to find out."

"Why?" James demanded brusquely.

"Oh, just a hunch I have." Then hastily he added, "But remember, James, Damian saved my life. You can't hurt him, even if he doesn't want to join the crew. You'll have to find some other way to keep him from—"

"Lock Damian in the brig."

James and Quincy glanced at her, puzzled.

"It's simple really," she said, heart pounding in her breast. She wasn't sure whether the nausea swimming around in her belly was due to the thrill of a potential fight or simple fear. Fear of what, though? "Lock Damian in the brig and he won't *see* anything. He'll only hear the cannons. We can explain later how we were attacked and defended ourselves. He'll never be the wiser about our true identity."

"Um, not that I disagree with your plan," from Quincy, "but how will we get Damian *in*to the brig?"

"Leave that to me," she assured him.

"And how are *you* going to get Damian into the brig?" demanded James.

Oh, I have my ways. "Just trust me, James."

After a thoughtful pause and much glowering, James gave a curt nod. "See to it."

Mirabelle scampered off the poop in search of the navigator, while Quincy headed for the captain's cabin to retrieve the Jolly Roger.

As of yet, the cry to arms had not been given. First Damian had to be tucked away. Though perhaps a battle cry would not be necessary, she thought. Once the pirate flag was hoisted, the other ship might balk and run. Unless, of course, it *was* the authorities chasing after them as Quincy had predicated. Then a battle was inevitable. She would soon find out.

Scouring the ship, Mirabelle saw no sign of Damian and moved her search below deck.

Her queasiness grew worse. What the devil *was* she so afraid of? Losing her brothers? Bah! The men had been through countless clashes and survived each one. So that couldn't be it.

Losing the treasured ship? Unlikely. The *Bonny Meg* was built like a rock. Mirabelle had confidence in the vessel's strength. The ship had survived scuffles and storms alike and limped to sail another day.

So what was it then? Damian?

Her heart pinched at the thought of losing Damian to injury or to the sea. She had grown rather fond of the rugged bounder, if truth be told. She didn't want to see him get hurt.

But, really, all these jitters just for Damian? Impossible! Wasn't it?

Perhaps she was just anxious about participating in her first real conflict? That had to be it. Surely.

Well, she would find out soon enough, once the ordeal was over.

Mirabelle prowled the galleries below deck, looking for Damian. She turned the corner and smacked right into his chest.

"There you are," she said. "I've been looking for you."

"Have you?" Powerful arms slipped around her waist. "Whatever for?"

But he wasn't waiting for an answer. Ravenous lips pressed hard over hers, twisting her insides into a knot, taking her words and her breath and her wits away.

How she loved kissing him. It was never dull or predictable. It always felt like the first exhilarating time.

Damian broke away from the kiss to whisper raggedly, "I need you, Belle."

She understood his meaning—and that this was her chance to get him safely out of harm's ways.

Flicking her tongue over his lush lips to entice him

even further—for she'd discovered last night that he *really* liked that—she purred, "I know a place where we can go."

His dark blue eyes smoldered with a sensual look she had become all too familiar with. "Show me."

Mirabelle took him by the hand and steered him through the passageway. She hated lying to Damian, really she did. It had never bothered her before, telling a fib. She was quite accustomed to it, considering who her brothers were, but she disliked having to lead Damian astray. Over the last few days a bond had developed between them. Each night she had come to him and trusted him to do whatever he wanted with her, to show her all the pleasurable sides to lovemaking. He had never hurt her. He had never disappointed her. She wasn't sure when it had happened, her trusting him. She supposed it had come on the night he'd confessed his past to her. She had realized, then, that his brooding façade was nothing to be suspicious of, that he was just another lonely soul . . . like her.

Bloody hell. She was becoming too sentimental. She was on a pirate ship, remember? And while her dream of becoming a pirate had all but fizzled away, she should still act like one while she was on board, and do away with maudlin emotions that would only distract her. After all, her tryst with Damian would eventually come to an end. She didn't want a lover or, perish the thought, a husband. She was just having a bit of fun with Damian. Exploring her passionate side. Her heart need not be involved.

Down in the lower levels, she guided Damian toward the brig.

He quirked a sable brow at the sight of the iron bars. "In there?"

"Why not? No one comes down here." Then she gave him a seductive smile. "It's private."

Thick arms circled her waist. "You have very unusual taste."

She snorted. "After what you did to me last night on the table, you call my taste un—"

Mentioning last night got her kissed—and him aroused. Damian was already backing her into the brig, and she had to reach over his shoulder to quickly confiscate the keys dangling from a little hook on the wall.

Once inside, she let his lips roam over her a little longer, lulling his senses—and her own, apparently, for she had to force herself to remember the task at hand.

She broke away from the kiss and pushed Damian up against the wall. "Don't move," she said in a smoky whisper, and started to back away from him, undoing the laces of her black leather vest. "Just watch."

He did, eyes burning, following her every move. Mirabelle kept his gaze occupied long enough to back out of the brig. Once beyond the threshold, she slammed the door shut and quickly locked it.

Damian looked at her, bowled over. "What are you doing?" There was no anger in his voice. He sounded puzzled, really, like this was all part of a game and he had forgotten the rules.

"I'm sorry, Damian." She moved away from the bars. "Captain's order."

His brow furrowed even more. "Why?"

"Well, we have a bit of trouble topside and the captain wants you out of the way."

His expression slowly hardened. "What trouble?"

"I'm not sure yet. This is just a precaution, Damian. The captain thinks you're still not feeling well. He doesn't want you topside in case we have to . . . man the cannons."

He was glowering now and took an ominous step forward. "Man the cannons?"

She nodded. "It seems we're being followed."

His hands gripped the iron bars. "By a pirate ship?"

"The captain isn't certain. But we might have to defend ourselves, and the captain needs all able hands to man the cannons. He didn't think you'd listen to an order to keep out of the battle, and since he can't be sure you won't get dizzy and—"

"Belle!" It sounded more like a bark, his tone. She had certainly never seen him so livid. "Unlock the door. Now!"

"I can't, Damian."

"Belle, you don't understand. I *have* to be there. Now let me out."

"Captain's or—"

"Confound the captain!" He rattled the bars. "Now open the bloody door!"

She shook her head, guilt and regret and all sorts of other unpleasant emotions swirling in her belly. "I'm sorry, Damian. I won't disobey an order."

He was glaring at her, his chest heaving, a whole slew of emotions bubbling in his eyes. Emotions she had never seen before . . . dark emotions.

"You tricked me," he said in a low and unsettling voice, the thought evidently having just occurred to him.

"I had to." She stuffed the keys into her pocket. "Trust me, Damian. It's for the best."

"Belle!"

But she was already heading down the corridor and making her way topside again.

It felt like a cannonball to her gut, the burden of emotions. So cumbersome. So lousy. She *really* hated having lied to him. The look of hurt in his eyes had been a blow she was unprepared to confront.

She didn't think it could wound so greatly, breaking a trust. A tentative trust, but still, the expression of disbelief in his eyes—before the fury had set in— told her plain enough he had never expected her to do such a thing.

But it was for his own well-being, she tried to console herself. Damian could *not* know their true identity. Not yet anyway. It might put his life at risk, especially if he refused to join the pirate crew and keep their secret. And until the captain was certain of his loyalty, it was prudent to keep Damian in the dark about their piracy.

Despite all that sound reasoning, she still felt miserable. But her morose mood didn't linger too long. The muffled blast of cannon fire, aimed somewhere off the rig's stern, snapped her from her pensiveness and sent her sprinting.

Topside, the commotion was under way.

James was strutting across the deck, shouting orders. The other ship was attacking astern, trying to avoid a broadside, aiming for the *Bonny Meg*'s rudder.

It looked like the Jolly Roger hadn't inspired the fear the captain had hoped for.

James was hollering for the helmsman to bring the ship about. The *Bonny Meg* was returning fire, but placed in such a precarious position, it was difficult to aim for the other ship, and most of the cannonballs landed well off their mark.

It looked like a bloody mess, the deck. But everything was in order. Every hollering pirate, every musket firing was designed to distract and intimidate the other vessel's crew.

It was also deafening, the thunder of cannon blasts. Potent, too, as the sting of sulfur invaded her nostrils. Mirabelle choked back on the smoke and fumes. Her ears were ringing. This really was more vivid than she had ever imagined it would be.

"Get off the deck!" James shouted at her.

She ducked as a bullet hit the mast behind her, the wood splintering. Mirabelle did as she was told and got out of the way, but below deck, she was arrested by a tar, who stuffed a powder chest into her arms.

"Fill it with gunpowder!" the pirate ordered. "Get it to the gunners!"

Mirabelle didn't hesitate. She had been asked to help. This was her one chance to redeem herself, she suddenly realized, in the eyes of the crew. Show them she could be of use. That she wasn't a bad omen or a slouch or any other such rot. That she could work with them and help them. And if her brothers and the crew could just come to accept that, then maybe her seafaring dream wasn't dashed after all.

A quick powder monkey, Mirabelle clambered down to the ship's belly where the gunpowder was stored. There were other men already there, each in turn filling their chests and rushing back to the gun deck.

Mirabelle entered the room, lined with copper sheeting to prevent the powder from igniting accidentally. She swiftly filled her chest and secured the lid. Out the door and scrambling back to the gun deck, she headed for the pirate closest to her, who was hollering for more powder.

The man gave her a brief look, as though wondering what she was doing there. But then the blast of a cannonball, tearing through the ship's hull, sending shards of wood flying, snapped him from his reverie.

He grabbed the chest from her and emptied it into the cannon. "More!"

When the chest was shoved back into her midriff, Mirabelle grinned. The crew might just come around and accept her, after all.

Chapter 16

❦

Damian slammed his boot into the iron bars.

Blast it! The cage was secure. With a growled oath, he swung around and prowled the narrow width of the cell.

He couldn't believe Belle had done this to him. That she had lured him into the brig. And why? Because the captain thought he might get dizzy and faint? Horseshit! He was fine. He should be out there right now, aiming a cannon at that bloody pirate ship.

A fist went into the wall and he let out a frustrated roar. To have traveled so far and so long, and then to fail at the end of his journey was unbearable. He had vowed to sink the pirate ship responsible for his brother's death. And there she was, just off the stern, blasting her guns in a frenzy.

Was this what it had been like for Adam and Tess? A hail of deafening cannon fire before the ship slipped under the waves, the couple's screams forever silenced?

Damian smashed his heel into the bars again. The door would not budge, but he needed something to vent his fury on.

A thought struck him then. A hopeful thought. Perhaps this wasn't the pirate ship that had attacked his brother. Perhaps it was another pirate vessel and he hadn't lost the chance to avenge his kin . . . or perhaps he was just being an idiot.

Damian knew, deep down in his gut, the cursed ship and crew guilty for his brother's demise was out there right now—and he was locked away in the brig.

He was a blundering half-wit. Lust had muddled his senses, distracted him from his goal. He had always known that it would, yet still, he had given in to it. He had surrendered to his weakness, granting Belle power over him. And she had used that power by manipulating him into the brig. If only he hadn't succumbed to his old wants and desires. If only his selfish side had not prevailed.

The demons in his head laughing at him, Damian brought his fingers to his temples in an attempt to quell their ribbing. But it did no good. The fiends guffawed and hollered and condemned him for his failure to avenge Adam . . . and all because of Belle.

It was perverse, really. She had trapped him in the brig. He shouldn't give a bloody fig about what happened to her anymore. But he did. He cared more than he should, that was for sure.

A horrifying image soon consumed his thoughts. Belle's limp body drifting in the water, maimed and bloody—and dead.

He suddenly wanted out of his cage for a whole different reason: to save Belle.

The derisive laughter grew louder in his head, reproaching him for his attachment to Belle. Another weakness. Even so, the drive inside him to protect her was stronger than the impulse to abandon her to fate.

Demons be damned, he would *not* allow her to disappear under the waves as Adam had done. Now if only he could get out of the blasted brig!

The cannonball that ripped through the hull just then, sending splinters shooting in all directions, also made a dent in the door.

Having ducked at the sound of the blast, Damian slowly rose to his feet, coughing at the fumes and examining the twisted iron bars.

With one robust kick, he sent the rest of the mangled metal swinging on its hinges.

Free.

Damian shot out of the brig. First, he had to find Belle and get her out of harm's way. *Then* he'd help sink that filthy pirate ship.

Blood pounding in his head, Damian made his way topside.

Clouds of smoke rolled across the deck of the *Bonny Meg*. A sudden gust of wind cleared the area up ahead, revealing William at the helm, the helmsman down and motionless next to the wheel.

Heart thundering, Damian scanned the sea of sailors for a bright blond head. But there was no sign of Mirabelle.

He started to stalk across the deck, amid the roaring cannon fire and pungent stench and whizzing bullets. Searching through the chaos for Belle, his heart throbbed with each second that passed and he saw nothing of her.

The captain shouted an order Damian could not hear, but the sudden lurch of the vessel beneath his feet confirmed it had been a command to bring the ship about.

Damian landed on his back with wicked force, the breath knocked clear out of his lungs. He squinted for a moment, vertigo brushing over him, but it quickly passed, his vision returning.

As the blurry images high above his head sharpened, Damian narrowed his gaze on one black scrap of fabric whipping violently in the wind.

Bewildered, he rolled onto his knees and strained his eyes over the starboard rail toward the other ship, thinking for one brief and ludicrous second he had been blown clear off the *Bonny Meg* and onto the pirate vessel.

But no. He was not looking at the *Bonny Meg* from a pirate ship. He was *on* the *Bonny Meg*.

The world around him faded into oblivion. The bellow of cannon blasts, the bitter scent of sulfur, the holler of men. Damian saw and heard none of it anymore. He sensed only the blood rush through his veins, the roar deafening.

Convinced his imagination had gone awry, Damian glanced back up again. But the skull and crossbones still flapped in the mighty gale . . . as did the winged hourglass. Belle's ring!

Damian suddenly wanted to vomit. He staggered to his feet, the pain in his head throbbing. He caught sight of James strutting across the deck, and for the first time he took notice of that long dark hair, black as pitch, billowing in the wind.

The Black Hawk.

"No," Damian moaned. "It can't be!"

James paused, dictating an order to a tar. No, a pirate. A bloody pirate!

The captain pointed in Damian's direction and the pirate scurried off as bidden, but James's gaze lingered for a moment, connecting with Damian's.

Captain and navigator locked eyes briefly, a silent understanding passing between the two. The *Bonny Meg*'s true identity had just been revealed. Neither was pleased by that.

James looked away, the battle at hand demanding his attention.

But Damian stood rooted to the spot. He could scarce breathe, never mind move, the emotions inside him suffocating.

He was on a pirate ship. The very one he had been looking for. The men he'd shared quarters with, dined with, worked with, were pirates . . . the pirates who had killed his brother.

Muscles hard, rage pounding in his chest, Damian thundered back below deck. So he was *on* a pirate ship instead of firing at one? Fine. It changed nothing. There was still Adam to avenge, and he would do this one thing right, he vowed, even if it cost him his life.

With steely determination, Damian moved down the hatchway toward the gunpowder room. One spark and the *Bonny Meg* would be no more.

But the alarmed cry of a woman, as she smacked into him bounding up the steps, tossed that notion from his mind.

Mirabelle!

She was a bloody pirate.

Damian's heart slammed into his ribs at the realization. This was the woman he had lusted after . . . the woman in whose arms he had found a measure of peace. And all the while she was akin to an enemy. Her brothers had destroyed the only semblance of goodness he'd ever had in his miserable life: Adam. And yet, he could not bring himself to sink the ship. Not with her on board.

"Damian!" cried Belle, her eyes round with evident horror. "What are you doing here? How did you get out of the—"

He grabbed her by the arm and dragged her up the stairs. He wasn't really sure what he was going to do with her. The pain hacking through his heart was distracting.

"Damian, we'll have to discuss this later!"

She wriggled free of his hold and took off running. He bounded after her, determined now to lock her away until the battle was over.

But she was a quick siren, eluding his capture, sprinting through the ship and eventually onto the gun deck, where she handed a gunner her powder chest. The pirate emptied the chest into the cannon and handed the container back to her. She bolted again, intent on more gunpowder, Damian assumed, but she didn't get very far. He hooked his fingers around her arm, stopping her in her tracks.

"Not *now*, Damian!"

He paid her outcry no heed, dragging her away from the gun deck. She struggled to break free. He wrapped both his arms around her waist and was prepared to hoist her over his shoulder when they both heard the jubilant cries.

Damian and Mirabelle glanced toward the portholes in time to see the now badly damaged vessel slowly retreating. Orders were relayed to the gunners to hold their fire. Apparently, Black Hawk wasn't going to finish off the rig as he had on the night Adam had perished. Why? Damian wasn't certain. But then the idea came to him.

Mirabelle.

The captain obviously didn't want to prolong the battle unnecessarily with his sister on board. It would only risk her life further. Damian could think of no other reason that James would abstain from destroying the other vessel, especially since *she* had attacked the *Bonny Meg* first.

As the smoke cleared from the gun deck, the pirates, all congratulating one another with smacks across the back and whoops of joy, slowly quieted down as they noticed Damian standing on deck.

The navigator was privy to their identities. Everyone was suddenly aware of that, even Belle, who cast him a both vexed and anxious look.

Heavy footsteps were heard coming down the

hatchway, followed by the captain's curt command. "Take him back to the brig."

Later that night, Damian was locked back in the brig. The cell door had been temporarily repaired and was strong enough to hold him.

Morose, lost in thought, he sat on the floor, arms curled around his knees. A pirate ship. He was on a miserable pirate ship. He still couldn't fathom how he had found himself in this predicament. After such a long and exhaustive search, for fate to simply toss him onto the *Bonny Meg* was staggering. Even more staggering was his failure to act on fate's boon. He'd had one chance to blow the *Bonny Meg* to hell, and he had failed to take it. He had failed his brother. Again.

Damian let out a growl. Why did Belle have to be here? She had wrecked everything with her presence. But for her, the *Bonny Meg* would be lying at the bottom of the sea right now.

Damian rubbed his eyes, still stinging from the sulfur fumes. He was weak. More so than he had imagined. Like Odysseus, lost at sea, he had fallen under the enchantment of a beautiful siren. He had lusted after that siren to distraction. And now she had thwarted his goal: his vow of vengeance. A vow he had made in earnest to his brother.

The conflict inside him was brutal. The guilt intolerable. It was as though Adam had died a second time when Damian had failed to avenge him. Only this time, *he* had struck the mortal blow, not the pirates.

The creaking wood planks disturbed Damian from his gloomy meditation.

He glanced up to find Mirabelle approaching, lantern in hand. She set the light on the ground, a soft orange glow enveloping her features, highlighting her classic beauty.

She was a pirate. That bowled him over the most. His passionate, fiery temptress was nothing but a cutthroat. A novice cutthroat, but still, she aspired to be the one thing he hated more than anything else in the world . . . and he had bedded her. Over and over again. He had wallowed in debauchery and had loved every minute of it. And the crux of the problem was that he was *still* attracted to the woman, pirate blood and all!

"Quincy will bring you something to eat soon," she said softly. "But I wanted to talk to you first."

He didn't say anything, didn't trust himself to keep a cap on his temper. He might inadvertently confess his true intention, that he was trying to kill her brothers. And Belle, of course, would warn her kin, dashing all his hopes of ever bestowing retribution.

"Damian, I'm sorry you discovered our identity like this. It wasn't suppose to happen this way. James was suppose to make a decision once we reached port . . . well, it doesn't matter now." She sighed. "But you'll have to make a choice soon."

He wrinkled his brow.

"You see," she went on, hesitant, "you'll have to join the crew or . . ."

"Be killed?" he said, not the least bit surprised by his so-called choice.

She nodded.

"I'm not joining the crew." He was adamant. The very thought of it made his stomach churn.

"Damian, please, listen to reason. James can't let you go, knowing our trade, but as a crew member you're bound to him. If he plunders a ship, you are implicated, too. You can't reveal his identity without condemning yourself and—"

"I understand the captain's logic," he cut in, a rough edge to his voice. "I'm still not joining the crew."

"But you'll die."

"So be it."

"Damn it, Damian!" Her arms folded under her breasts. "Life aboard the *Bonny Meg* isn't so bad. You've seen firsthand. Why won't you even consider it?"

"Because—" *Your brothers killed mine, that's why.* "Forget it, Belle."

Uncrossing her arms, she crouched down, their eyes level. "Damian, think about it. The wealth and the freedom. Surely being a pirate isn't so disagreeable?"

He studied her for a moment, wondering why she was trying so hard to persuade him to stay. He finally asked, "Why do you want me to be a pirate?"

"I don't want to see you get hurt," she whispered.

Her words, words of caring, made his heart tighten. "Why?"

"Because you saved Quincy's life—and mine. It wouldn't be fair to take yours away."

He shouldn't have pushed her for an answer. He should have left it alone at *I don't want to see you get hurt.* At least then he could imagine what he wanted, that she actually cared for him instead of feeling a sense of obligation.

Bloody hell, what was wrong with him? That's all he needed, the affections of a pirate. Better that she loathed him. After all, he would kill her brothers as soon as he got the chance.

"Fine, Belle," he growled. "I'll think about joining the crew." *Just leave*, he thought, for he couldn't stand looking at her through the iron bars anymore, knowing he couldn't touch her—ever again.

"Really, Damian?" She dropped down to sit on the balls of her feet, her legs splayed. Though she was covered in her leather breeches, Damian couldn't stop the salacious image of her legs bare and splayed from skipping through his head. And he hated himself all the more for still finding her so irresistible.

"Really, Belle," he returned gruffly. "Now go before Quincy finds us in a compromising position."

Her brow furrowed. "How's that?"

The bloody temptation was more than he could bear. He realized then, if he didn't break off his obsession with Belle, he would never see his plan of vengeance to fruition. She would always be in the way, distracting him. And she would always give him false hope for a life he knew he could never have. A life void of emptiness and pain. A life filled with promise and joy.

He grabbed her through the cage and hoisted her to her knees, so her body was flush with the cold metal bars. One arm wrapped around her midriff, his other hand cupped the warmth between her legs.

She gasped.

He kissed her hard through an opening in the bars.

"If you insist on spreading your legs," he growled, breaking away from the heated kiss, "then I'll insist on ravishing you." With a cruel smirk, he added, "But next time, Belle, you don't have to get down on your knees and beg me like a tavern whore."

The sound crack to the mouth knocked his head back.

Mirabelle pushed him away and staggered to her feet, her amber eyes spitting fire. "You son of a bitch!"

She was gone then, the lantern forgotten.

In the shadows of the brig, Damian sat back against the wall, fingering his tender jaw. *Good girl*, he thought. *Hate me. I deserve it.*

And he did deserve it. He was nothing but a worthless, miserable sod. He couldn't do anything right—except bring out the worst in a person. And that talent had just come in handy. Belle surely despised him now. She wouldn't be coming around anymore, tempting him. He would spend the rest of the voyage alone.

It was bloody better that way.

It really was.

Chapter 17

Mirabelle hammered away. It was dark out. Only a small lantern off to the side provided her with a glimmer of light. It was so dark, in fact, she wasn't even sure she was driving the nail into the right place. But she didn't care right then. If she didn't vent her fury on something, she would have to vent it on some*one*. And as tempting as the idea might be, she didn't think it very wise to smack Damian across the head—even if he did deserve it.

A whore! The bloody ass had called her a tavern whore! To have said something so ruthless, and after everything they had been through. Why? Because he was on a pirate ship? Was he really so angry about it? Would he join the crew now that he knew the truth?

Oh, she didn't give a damn about Damian anymore. She had tried to save his life. First by locking him in the brig, then by urging him to become a pirate. And how had he repaid her good intentions? By insulting her, the blackguard. He had enjoyed their tryst as much as she had. What did that make him?

She snorted. Not a whore, that was for sure. Apparently, only a woman could be saddled with such a stigma. Bloody unfair, really. She couldn't do anything that she desired without being condemned for it. And she was growing sick of all the reprimands. First from her brothers and now from Damian.

The pounding in her chest painful, Mirabelle gritted her teeth to halt the surge of tears welling in her eyes. She had grown to care for the lousy bounder. There was no sailing around that truth. But he apparently didn't give a fig about her. He never had. He'd claimed an infamous reputation. A rogue. She should have believed him.

She was such a fool. A sentimental fool. She bloody well deserved to feel so rotten. This was the very reason she had vowed to never give her heart away. It made her vulnerable. It made her weak . . . It made her miserable.

Well, she had learned her lesson. Never again would she let anyone into her heart. Never again would she rely on anyone for her happiness. It was up to her—and her alone—to find it, fight for it, and keep it. And that's just what she intended to do.

"Belle?"

She glanced up to find James hovering above her. "What is it?"

"Why don't you go below and get some rest?"

She turned away from him. "I'm not tired."

"Then I'm ordering you to bed."

She hit the nail head hard. "Why, damn it?"

"Because I won't have a ship left to sail if you keep trying to fix it."

Brow creased, she stepped back to examine her handiwork, and it was then she realized what James was talking about. The starboard rail did look rather crooked.

She let out a winded sigh. "I'm sorry, Captain."

"Don't be. I know this has been a rough day for you."

You have no idea. "How's the crew?"

"Mending." James crossed his arms over his chest and propped his hip against the rail. "Brice is recovering nicely. He should be up and about soon."

"That's good." Brice, their quartermaster, had been stationed at the helm when a cannonball demolished part of the rail, peppering him with a series of splinters. "And the ship?"

"She'll make it back to England, I'm sure. But she's going to need a minor overhaul once we reach land."

She nodded. "Did you figure out why the other ship attacked us?"

"Not yet. But I intend to. Anything else?"

"What do you mean?"

"Any more questions before I order you to bed—again?"

She made a moue and handed James the hammer. "No." She started to move away from him, took about two steps before she paused to face the captain again. She had vowed to dismiss Damian from her head and heart, but despite that conviction, she said, "What will happen to Damian?"

"Don't worry about the navigator, Belle. I'll take care of him."

That didn't sound too good. She shouldn't have asked. Now she would never get any sleep.

Morning rays filled the brig through the cannon holes in the hull. Damian squinted at the shaft of sunlight creeping over his face, then moved his head to the side to avoid the brilliancy.

With a growled oath, he rolled onto his back. He had never had such a miserable night. Pirates had infested his dreams. He'd ached for Belle in a most wicked way. And now he awoke to a stiff pain in his neck and back and everywhere else for that matter. The result of spending the evening on the hard wood floor.

With a grimace, he slowly sat up. The blood rushed to his head, his temples throbbing.

"Bloody hell."

It was like rousing from a drunken stupor, only he hadn't had a drop of spirits.

Damian swiveled around to press his back against the wall. He had a full view of the room from his vantage point, and so was quick to notice the figure that strode in through the door.

Bile burning in his gut, Damian glowered at Quincy. A dastardly, loathsome, murdering pirate. An enemy.

Squatting, Quincy set the tray of food on the floor. He offered Damian a grim, even contrite expression. "I guess this is kinda my fault."

Damian couldn't stand to look at the kid anymore. Grief wracked his brain. Quincy was nothing but a merciless cutthroat. It almost defied reason. But harrowing as the truth might be, the kid was a villain. And he had to die.

"If I hadn't dragged you along," said Quincy, "you'd be in New York right now. Stranded, granted. But safe."

Damian looked back at him, fiery pain cutting up his soul. "Forget about it, kid."

Quincy was about to say something in return, then quirked a sable brow. "What happened to your face?"

Damian reached for his chin. It was then he noticed the swelling. His lips were puffy, too. A parting gift from Belle.

"Never mind, kid."

Quincy shrugged. "Listen, Damian . . ."

But another large figure appeared in the doorway then, curtailing Quincy's remark.

The Black Hawk.

Damian's muscles hardened.

James took an ominous step into the room. "Out, Quincy."

With a sigh, the kid lifted off his haunches and departed, leaving Damian alone with the pirate captain.

The two men glared at each other for a moment.

Damian was a mess inside. James had murdered his brother. A rabid rancor gripped Damian. A desire to destroy the pirate who had slain his kin . . . but why did *James* have to be Black Hawk?

Damian wanted to howl in agony. So long he had hunted Black Hawk. So many nights he had stood atop the poop of his own ship, staring into the black beyond, wishing for Black Hawk to appear so he could send the piratical swine to the seabed. Vengeance had once seethed through his blood for the pirate captain. Now Damian was in turmoil. The anger still churned in his belly, but it was not easy to think of James as an enemy. Damian had come to respect the captain over the last three weeks. He was a sage commander, who elicited the respect of his crew—a pirate crew.

Damian took in a sharp breath. James was a fiend. He had to remember that. He *would* kill the captain and the rest of the men. Adam's death demanded vengeance.

"Why?" Damian growled, "Why are you a pirate?"

James stepped deeper into the room. "And what else should I be?"

"Anything but a pirate."

"Oh? And what if I want to be a cabinetmaker, like my father?"

"Then be one."

He grunted. "Aye, it sounds simple enough, doesn't it? Marry and have a family and work hard every day of my life, until one day a troop of goons come along and take it all away."

"The press gang."

James lifted a black brow.

"Belle told me about your father."

"Did she?" James moved to stand in front of the

cage. Darkness swirled in his cobalt blue eyes. "Then you should understand why I'm a pirate, Damian. I'm not going to heed law, only to have my life snatched away by 'king and country.'"

A tight knot formed in Damian's throat. "And what of the lives you devastate?"

It was hypocritical, the query, coming from him, considering all the lives *he* had devastated, but Damian needed to know the answer nonetheless.

"And what lives would those be, Damian?"

"The lives of your victims."

He gave a chortle. "Really, Damian, do you think I pillage miserable farmers? What do you care if a lofty merchant or lord looses a few pence?"

Oh, he cared. He bloody well cared a lot.

"Enough of this," said James. "I've decided what I'm going to do with you."

"I thought the choice was supposed to be mine?"

"Not anymore." James crossed his arms over his chest. "Since you saved both Quincy and Belle's lives, I am indebted to you. Therefore, *you* are going to join the crew and I won't have to kill you."

Damian fisted his palms to hold in his temper. "I won't do it."

The captain's voice was cool, considering the fiery subject matter at hand. "Aye, you will."

"I'll escape as soon as we reach England."

James shook his head. "You won't leave this ship for the next year."

Damian couldn't restrain the fury anymore. "You'll keep me in this cage for a bloody *year*!"

Composed, but determined, James returned, "I'll

let you out of the brig once we're at sea—far away from land."

"That's—"

"The way it's going to be," James said tersely. "After a year, you'll be as guilty of piracy as the rest of us. I won't have to worry about you turning us in then. Take heart, Damian, you might even come to enjoy being a pirate."

Damian was about to contest the remark, but then decided against it. He was protesting for the wrong reason. True, he had no intention of becoming a bloody pirate, but he needn't worry about that ever happening. He was going to scuttle the ship, remember? Once Belle was gone, of course. He had only to bide his time. The *Bonny Meg* would soon be home. Belle would be back on land—she had said so herself, that James would never let her join the crew. And then the ship would set sail again, bent on another piratical venture. Since Damian was allowed out of the brig once the vessel was at sea, he'd have no qualms about sinking it. He would see his vow of vengeance to an end, bring his own miserable existence to a close, and he wouldn't have to harm a hair on Belle's head to do it.

More at ease, Damian refrained from any further comment. The captain must have interpreted his silence as reluctant acquiescence, for he gave a curt nod of approval and then unlocked the brig door.

Chapter 18

Home.
    Mirabelle gazed at the shadowy coastline. The remaining journey to England had been without incident. No storms. No sea battles. No tempestuous rows with a certain navigator.

She propped her elbows on the rail, a soft breeze whistling through her hair. It was late. Only the glimmering dots of firelight, poking through the tavern windows, illuminated the ghostly shore. The *Bonny Meg* had dropped anchor a little ways from port. Most of the men had already departed for a brief interlude on land. After a few days of carousing in the taverns, and once all the repairs were made, James wanted the crew to head back to New York and complete the plundering mission *she* had interrupted. She, of course, was not invited to come along.

Mirabelle let out a heavy sigh. She had tried, she really had, to convince the captain she would make a good seafarer. She had done her work without complaint. Volunteered for any of the more laborious, even odious, chores. But her efforts had made no impression on the captain. He'd never once mentioned she might be able to join the crew. There was nothing left to do but pack her belongings. It was time to go home.

She abandoned the bow and headed for the captain's cabin. James was already inside, hunched over a table, shuffling through a stack of charts. He glanced up at her.

"I've just come to gather my things," she said quietly, heading for her side of the room.

James cocked his head, following her trek across the cabin. "You're not going to beg me to let you stay?"

She stuffed a shirt into her carrying case. "No."

"Why?"

He sounded genuinely confused and she turned around to confront him. "Why should I? I don't need to hear—again—how I don't belong here. I'm bloody well sick of hearing it."

James crossed his arms over his chest. He propped his hip against the desk and studied her curiously. "You concede defeat then?"

"Yes," she gritted out, jamming another garment into her bag. Was he going to be a blasted nuisance about all this and rub defeat in her face? "Do you want to hear me say it? Fine. I give up. There, will that do?"

He nodded. "It's settled then."

She shrugged. "I suppose it is."

Mirabelle continued to collect her things. She dreaded going home. It was going to be lonely, the house all quiet, eerily so.

For some absurd reason, Damian came to mind at the thought of loneliness. She remembered how she had felt in his embrace—anything but lonely. Bah! She shook her head to dismiss the haunting vision. It was all in her head. She really belonged right here, aboard the *Bonny Meg*. If only there was some way for her to stay . . .

Oh, forget it. Why dwell on the impossible? She would go to London and visit her friend Henrietta Ashby. That would help offset the loneliness.

James didn't say anything for a while, then: "The men have been talking."

"About what?"

"You."

She stiffened. "What about me? No, wait. Don't tell me. I don't want to hear about how unlucky I am or other such rot." She crammed her hairbrush into her sack.

But James ignored her request for silence. "Apparently, you were very helpful on the day of the battle."

"I was? I mean, of course I was." She narrowed her gaze on James. "The crew told you this?"

He nodded. "It seems you did everything right that day. The men were . . ."

"Impressed?" she said hopefully.

"Surprised."

"Oh." She continued to stuff her breeches away. "I guess that's better than angry or appalled."

"It looks like you're not the bad omen many of them suspected you would be."

"Well, lucky me." She dropped the sarcasm, though, when another, more pleasant thought hopped into her head. "James, are you trying to tell me something?"

"Like what?"

"Like maybe I can stay aboard the *Bonny Meg*?"

He snorted. "No."

She jammed another shirt into her already stuffed sack. "Then why the hell are you telling me all this?"

He shrugged. "I thought you should know."

"Well, now I do. So thank you and good-bye."

She was strutting for the door when James grabbed her by the arm.

"You've got a bloody bad temper, you know that, Belle?"

Her amber eyes flashed. "And you have a stubborn streak that would put a mule to shame. What of it?"

He let go of her arm and heaved a deep sigh. "Nothing."

"James," she drawled, "are you sure you're not thinking of letting me stay?"

"Yes . . . maybe."

Her heart missed a beat. "Really? Oh, James—"

"*Maybe*." He was glowering at her as if she'd done something wrong. "The men aren't so opposed to you joining the crew anymore. That doesn't mean I'm going to let you stay, but I guess you don't have to pack your bag just yet," he groused. "We're here for a few days and we'll talk about it some more in that time."

She could barely contain her joy. Oh, what the hell! Mirabelle dropped her bag of belongings and flung her arms around her brother's neck.

"Thank you, James."

He was reluctant at first, but then he returned her embrace. "I'm not making any promises, Belle."

"I know," she whispered and kissed his cheek for good measure. "But thanks for giving me the chance."

He grunted. "Are you going to hate me if the answer still turns out to be no?"

She contemplated that for a moment, then said, "I could never hate you." And it was true, she couldn't. Even if he was an obnoxious lout sometimes.

"Good." He pulled away from her, looking somewhat discomfited at having teetered on the edge of sentimentality. Swiftly he composed his features and gave a curt nod. "Now off with you, Belle. Cook needs help in the galley with inventory."

A grin on her face, Mirabelle kicked her bag in a corner and all but skipped from the room. She couldn't believe it. She might yet be able to stay. Stay with her kin and . . . with Damian.

She paused in the corridor, her merriment ebbing away. Damian was going to join the crew. She had forgotten about that. He was trapped aboard the *Bonny Meg* for at least a year, according to James. And if she joined the crew, she would have to spend time with the bounder. It was unavoidable. She was going to be reminded, over and over again, each time she saw him, of what he had done to her—the good and the bad.

Bloody hell.

Damian shifted in his cage. He was back in the brig now that the *Bonny Meg* had reached shore. And all he could think about was Belle. She was going to leave the ship soon. He was never going to see her again. That had been the plan all along, to break away from her, yet he wanted to tear the blasted iron bars apart with his bare hands. A great need overwhelmed him. A need to see her, talk to her . . . kiss her one last time.

"You're going to be stuck in there for a while, you know?"

Heart pounding, Damian looked up at the familiar sound of a husky voice to find Belle standing in the doorway.

He took in a deep and measured breath. She was a vision in black, breeches and tight leather vest. And she could still stir the flames of his passion just by being. He need only glance at her, hear one sultry word from her, and he felt alive, invigorated.

He was going to miss her.

It appeared Mirabelle wasn't going to venture farther into the room. She remained by the door, arms crossed in a defensive manner. Her catlike eyes were masked by shadows, yet he could *feel* her fiery stare. It warmed his blood, sent his heart thumping even faster, the primal look she gave him.

"Are you leaving now, Belle?" It hurt to say the words. Cut right down to the bone.

"No, I'm not leaving."

After a few thoughtful moments, he furrowed his brow. "Right now, you mean? But you are leaving the ship soon, aren't you?"

She shrugged. "It looks like I'm staying right here."

"What?" he rasped, a welter of emotions rising in his chest.

"James is going to consider letting me join the crew."

"That's madness!" he suddenly blasted. "You have to get off the ship!"

He could see the muscles in her arms flinch. "I don't have to go anywhere, Damian. By and by, if I stay, *you* are going to keep away from me. Got that?"

"You're not staying, Belle." It was a firm remark, said more to soothe the panic in his breast than anything else, for Damian did not have the authority to make such a decision. The captain did. And if James was daft enough to allow his sister to remain on board, then Damian's pledge of vengeance was dashed. He could never sink the ship with Belle a part of the crew.

"The captain will come to his senses," said Damian. "He *won't* let you stay."

"We'll just see about that."

And then she sauntered out of the room.

With a hard jerk, Damian kicked the iron bars opposite him, the metal ringing out in vibration.

What the hell was he going to do now? He had to get Belle off the ship. But how? She was a bloody stubborn wench. She would never leave unless he dragged her off. But no. That wasn't a good idea. She would just swim back to the ship, he was sure.

Damian slumped his brow in his palm and rubbed his throbbing temples. Perhaps James would find his wits and forbid her to stay . . . or perhaps not. Damian couldn't take that chance. He had to get Mirabelle off the *Bonny Meg*. He had to keep her safe. It was an instinct so primal, it consumed his mind.

He growled in frustration. It had all gone amok, his vengeful intentions. He had trained and primed for every conceivable circumstance over the last two years. But meeting Belle was the one happening he had never prepared for, the one glitch in his scheme he could not have anticipated. And if he didn't find a way around the predicament of her being here, he was going to fail in his mission.

So what to do? How to get Belle off the ship *and* keep her off?

Put her under lock and key, that's how, he thought, disgruntled. But the only way he could do that was if he kidnapped her . . .

Damian lifted his head. Was it possible? Could he abscond with Belle and still achieve his vow of vengeance? The thought slowly took root.

If he kidnapped Belle, he'd get her off the ship. That was one problem solved. And if he took her back to his castle, her brothers would surely follow—right to the dungeon. That was two problems solved. He'd keep Belle safe while exacting revenge on the pirates who had murdered his kin. Not all the pirates, granted, but the ones that mattered for sure, the ones in charge of the venture—Belle's brothers.

Damian mulled over the idea a bit more and decided it was a sound plan. There was no other way around the quandary. He couldn't risk letting the *Bonny Meg* weigh anchor and set sail with Belle on board. He had to do this. He had no other choice.

Quincy strode in, tray in hand.

"Brought you some dinner, Damian." He set the fare on the ground. "How are you doing?"

Damian didn't say a word.

"Sorry to hear that." The kid scratched his head. "It's only for a little while more, you know? James will let you out just as soon as we're at sea."

Still nothing.

"Well, I'm off now," said Quincy. "Most of the men are already in port. I'm going to join 'em." He grinned. "Off to meet Tilly, and all. I'll be back in the morning—or maybe noon. But don't worry, I won't forget about you."

Quincy lifted off his haunches.

Damian stood as well.

A sound crack between the eyes silenced the kid. He hit the floor with a cumbersome thump.

Damian crouched down and shifted Quincy's body so he could better reach the trouser pockets. Arms stretched, he groped along the kid's leg, feeling for the keys.

It didn't take long to locate them. He pushed Quincy's body away from the door, then unlocked it.

Once free, Damian grabbed the kid under the shoulders and dragged him into the brig. He was about to secure the door, but paused. Quincy might wake up and holler for help before Damian had a chance to smuggle Belle off the ship. Maybe he should kill the kid now and be done with it?

But a sharp pain in his chest dissuaded him from that idea. Instead Damian tore at Quincy's shirt, making two long strips of cloth. He secured the kid's wrists with one strip and fastened a gag over his mouth with the other. That should keep Quincy quiet for a while.

Locking the brig door, Damian turned and walked away. There was no reason for him to bloody his hands now. Shortly, he'd have all the brothers caged in the dungeon of his castle, and then he'd have his revenge.

Dismissing the uncomfortable ache still in his chest, Damian focused on the task at hand, prowling the passageways, making his way toward the captain's cabin. Fortunately for him, the ship was virtually deserted, so he could skulk along the dimly lit corridors without much risk of discovery. He was in need of a certain provision before he abducted Belle. A provision he was sure the Black Hawk possessed.

Damian reached the captain's door. It was closed. He pressed his ear to the wood, listening. No movement within.

Carefully he opened the door. A quick peek confirmed the room was indeed empty. He slipped inside and went straight to work.

Under lamplight, Damian scavenged for gold. Ironic, really, considering he didn't want to be a pirate. But without blunt, he'd never get home. There was clothing to buy and transportation to arrange, and throwing his ducal name around was no assurance he'd get everything he needed. Townsfolk might not believe he was the Duke of Wembury, after all. He certainly didn't look the part, with his long black hair and scruffy beard. Why, he looked more like a . . . pirate.

He thrust that disturbing thought aside. Rummaging through the captain's things, Damian searched for coins. He looked in trunks and in burlap sacks. Nothing. He explored the bed. But all he found was a stunning dagger. There had to be money somewhere. Every captain had a stash. Damian had always stored his valuables in a safe aboard his ship. But where did James hide his?

The glimmer from the shaving mirror captured Damian's eye. Secured to the wall, the oval glass had titled just enough to reveal a crack in the wood boards.

He walked over to the mirror and pushed it aside. A round opening in the wall, big enough for a fist, presented itself. He stuck his hand in the hole.

Damian smirked. Out came a small, but heavy sack.

Treasure.

Now to find Belle.

But first, he headed for the captain's desk. Leafing through the stack of papers, he recovered a clean, crisp sheet. Quill pen in hand, he inked in flowing script: *Duke of Wembury*.

Damian then picked up the dagger he had found

under James's bed and pierced the parchment to the
desk.

That should get the captain's attention. And by
the time James and his brothers figured out the
duke's identity and address, Damian would be
home—waiting for them.

Quietly Damian vacated the captain's room. Topside, he scanned the deck. The *Bonny Meg* appeared
to be a ghost ship. Apparently everyone had gone to
port to cavort with wenches. Had Belle gone, too?

Bloody stupid question. Of course she hadn't. So
where the devil was she?

Squabbling voices drifted up the hatchway.

Damian quickly ducked behind a mountain of
rope. James emerged topside first, followed by . . .
Belle?

Damian blinked. Once. Twice. Bloody hell. What
had happened to her? She looked wondrous.

Decked in a powder blue frock, his seductive siren appeared almost angelic. Almost. The thrust of
her bountiful breasts indicated she wore a corset. A
tight-fitting—and revealing—corset. And the way
she sashayed across the deck exuded confidence no
virtuous miss would posses. She had a loose bun secured atop her head, a few stray wisps of shimmering hair flapping in the breeze. The tresses trapped
between her flush and rosy lips, and she brushed the
straggling strands aside.

Damian gawked at her. He couldn't believe the
transformation. Gone was his tempestuous Belle,
decked in tight leather breeches. In her place stood a

more refined—though no less alluring—woman. He wasn't sure if he liked the new Mirabelle, though. He had grown accustomed to the old one. He hadn't realized how much until now.

"I want you back in an hour, Belle."

"I know, James," she huffed.

"You're to get everything that Cook needs, then—"

"Head back to the ship." Her hands went to her hips. "I'm not deaf, James. I heard you the first three times."

The captain let out a disgruntled growl. "I can't believe *everyone's* left the ship."

She quirked a smile at that. "The men's breeches are on fire, Captain, and need a good dousing. But don't despair, I'll see to the task."

At her bawdy humor, James shot her an appalled expression.

Mirabelle laughed. A smoky laugh that made Damian's blood burn with desire.

"Where the hell is Quincy?" James grumbled and looked around the deck.

But an impatient Belle was already climbing over the rail, a flash of black leather beneath her skirt's hem.

There was a warmth in Damian's chest at the familiar sight of her black leather boots. His old Belle was still there.

"Quincy's late," said Belle, "so he'll just have to wait another hour or so to get his breeches doused."

"Belle!" the captain barked, his hands gripping the starboard rail. "Get back here. You are *not* going into port alone."

"Don't worry, James," was heard a distant holler. "I'll be fine."

"Belle!"

But the captain's command went unheeded.

James slammed his palms against the rail and let out a curse. He turned and stalked away, bellowing for Quincy.

As soon as the captain disappeared below deck, Damian sprinted to the starboard rail. He looked down to the murky black water. No boat. He looked ahead, and sure enough, Belle was rowing toward shore.

Damian let out a curse of his own. That was the last of the boats. And he wasn't in it.

So much for a flawless abduction.

Damian glanced back at the hatchway. James would discover Quincy soon. But it would take a while to free the kid from the brig since Damian still had the key. That gave him enough time to get to shore—and to get Belle.

Damian swung his leg over the rail and scaled down the rope ladder. He was going to have to swim to shore.

He needed the exercise.

Chapter 19

Mirabelle counted off her fingers. Six chickens. Check. Three barrels of smoked and salted meat. Check. Another six barrels of beer. Check. Two firkins of wine for the captain and lieutenant. Check. Four barrels of oats. Check. One hundred pounds of—

"Bloody hell." She stumbled over a muddy hole in the road. Bunching the fabric in her fists, she lifted the hem off the ground. A bit grubby, but she'd tend to the stain later. The dress was also shabby and too snug in the bust, but she refused to discard the garment. It had been tailored for her years ago, at her father's behest, and she would keep it always in memory of him. It was useful, too. She had packed the garment for just such a venture. Prowling the streets in search of supplies in her breeches would attract unwanted attention. At least in a dress, she wouldn't garner scandalized looks or remarks.

Now where was she? Chickens. Meat. Beer. Wine. Oats. And? Oh yes, one hundred pounds of flour. Check.

Mirabelle beamed. Within the allotted time—and without a chaperone—she had arranged for all the provisions to be collected in the morning. She was quite proud of herself, and she expected the captain to be pleased as well—albeit grudgingly. James loathed to admit he was beat.

She bustled through the port, amid muffled jeers and hoots of laughter and bubbly music, making her way back to the dock where her boat was secured.

A horse snorted.

Startled, Mirabelle whirled around to confront the figures skulking in the shadows.

"Good evening, Belle."

She gasped. "Damian!"

He broke through the blackness, dressed in riding gear, his long ebony mane secured at the nape of his neck. But with his scraggly beard concealing much of his features, and his captivating sapphire eyes glowing in the firelight, he appeared like a devil emerging from the darkness.

Swiftly he clamped his palm over her mouth, stifling her scream. He scooped her in a mighty embrace and set her on the gelding's back, straddling the seat behind her. Nudging the steed's flanks, he set off at breakneck speed.

She gripped Damian tight, hollered for him to stop, but the blackguard didn't even slow down. He was riding the animal for all it was worth. Hooves thundered in her ears like drumbeats, as did her heart. The man must be mad. What did he think he was doing? And how the hell had he escaped from the brig?

After a long and pounding ride, Damian finally brought the great black beast to a steady canter.

Nerves tattered, she took in a few gulps of air to steady her throbbing heart, then let her fury rip forth. "What the hell is the matter with you, Damian!"

His sultry breath skimmed the rim of her earlobe, making her shiver. "Ironic words, coming from a pirate."

Stomping her jitters right down to her toes, she griped, "*Why* did you take me?"

"You witnessed my escape. I had to take you or you would've warned your brothers before I had a chance to get far enough away."

Mirabelle was suddenly all too mindful of his grinding hips, moving exquisitely into her backside with each gentle lurch of the horse. And to dismiss the erotic sensation, she tried to fix her thoughts on the situation at hand. "Someone will notice the empty brig soon."

"I'm well aware of that."

"And my brothers are going to come after you—and me."

"I know."

Now why did that sound so ominous? Mirabelle shook her head. "So why bother to escape?"

"I won't be a pirate."

"You don't have a choice in the matter."

"I beg to differ."

His words, so cutting, chilled her. There was something different about Damian. Something dark, even calculating. He had betrayed her brothers by escaping. But why? Why risk his life? James was going to come after him. So why run away? Was being a pirate really so hateful? Was being near her such a chore?

Mirabelle dismissed the sentiment at once. She was a bloody fool, letting the mawkish thought into her head. But still, it stabbed at her heart, knowing Damian was trying to escape the ship . . . and trying to escape her.

Bah! She should not be so sentimental. She should be more furious with the navigator. Already an hour had passed since she'd left the *Bonny Meg*. James would be irate. And once he discovered the empty brig, he'd assume she and Damian were together, that she was in some sort of peril.

"You've ruined everything, Damian!"

"How so, Belle?

"I should be back on the *Bonny Meg* right now. James will be livid."

"Your brother's always livid."

"Yes, but now he'll think I'm nothing but trouble and never let me join the crew."

"You are nothing but trouble, Belle."

"I like that," she huffed. "*You* kidnapped me, remember? I'd say you're the troublemaker here."

He didn't reply to that. Instead, he said, "Why do you want to be pirate, anyway?"

"Why shouldn't I be a pirate? My father was brutalized by the navy. Pirates saved him and set him free, and I intend to follow in his path."

"No wifely duties for you?"

She snorted.

"Still, Belle, you don't belong on a pirate ship."

"I'm not the first woman to be a buccaneer, you know?"

Smugly he wondered, "And how did your fellow brigands fare?"

She didn't say anything.

"Not well, you say? At the end of a rope, you say?" At her prolonged silence, he grunted in satisfaction. "As I said, Belle, you have no place aboard a pirate ship."

She made a moue and decided to change the subject. "How did you get the clothes, Damian? The horse?"

"I stole the money from James."

She stiffened.

"Something the matter, Belle?" He nuzzled her temple, the throaty whisper gushing into her ear. "Is stealing wrong?"

She jabbed her elbow into his ribs. "Let me go, Damian."

He jerked slightly, but didn't ease his hold, the obnoxious lout. "I don't think so, Belle."

After an uneasy pause, she snapped, "So what are you going to do with me?"

"Just . . . keep you around for a while."

Thunder rumbled in the distance.

The fine hairs on the back of her neck spiked. "What do you mean, 'a while'?"

"I can't let you go, Belle. Not yet."

She craned her neck to better look at him. A gust of

stormy wind ruffled his midnight black hair, and she found herself utterly mesmerized by the brooding dark devil. "And why not?"

He said not a word. She had to nudge him in the ribs again to encourage his reply.

Those enchanting blue eyes delved deep into her soul. "It's too soon, Belle. I'm not ready to let you go."

Even in his warm embrace, the chill on her spine was biting. "So I'm to be your prisoner?"

"That's a harsh word," he whispered. "Maybe I'm just fond of you and don't want to say good-bye."

She snorted. "Don't pretend like you give a damn."

"Oh, but I do," he said quietly, gruffly.

She humphed and stared ahead. She didn't believe him. Really, she didn't. He was just trying to cajole her. Make her agreeable to this whole miserable abduction.

To dismiss the shiver tickling her spine, she needed a distraction, and said, "So how did you escape?"

"Quincy let me out."

"You're lying," she said flatly.

He shrugged. "It took a little convincing, but the kid did set me free."

Her back grew rigid. "You didn't hurt Quincy, did you?"

"He'll live."

"Blast you, Damian! My brothers will trounce you all the more for this."

He drawled in a husky voice, "And you care because . . . ?"

"I don't care, of course," she huffed. "But this debacle of an escape was all for nothing."

"Not for nothing, Belle. I assure you."

She quivered again. "What do you mean?"

"It doesn't matter."

Her heart pattered. "You're going to turn them in, aren't you?"

"I have no intention of turning your brothers in to the authorities."

She let out a quiet sigh of relief. "Then what do you intend to do?"

"Kill the demons inside my head."

Puzzled, she looked back at him. "What?"

Dark and turbulent eyes stared at her, burrowed into her. And strong arms gripped her even harder. "Never mind, Belle."

The man had lost his wits. How was she supposed to ignore that cryptic riddle?

She wanted to press him further, but curiosity yielded to thoughts of self-preservation. She *had* to escape and make her way back to port. Then James would see she could take care of herself, that he need not worry about her stumbling into danger and being trapped. If she didn't prove her abilities to her brother, he would never let her join the crew.

Without a second thought, she put her father's pugilist training to good use. A quick jab to the solar plexus and Damian grunted, relaxing his hold on her waist, giving her enough room to wriggle free.

She hit the ground and sprinted.

Damian cursed up a storm behind her.

She did a little cursing of her own. Blasted skirt!

What she wouldn't give for her breeches right now.

Hiking the dress up over her knees, Mirabelle dashed through the willowy blades of grass. She didn't hear the thunder of hooves behind her, though. Damian was hounding her on foot.

Blood pumping in her ears, chest sore from the exertion of the chase, Mirabelle soon sensed heavy breathing on her neck.

Her escape dashed to bits, she let out a frustrated scream as two burly arms circled her waist.

The couple toppled to the ground; smashed into it was more like it. Damian took the brunt of the fall, landing on his back, air whooshing into her face.

She hit his chest with a hard thump, letting out an "Ooof" in exhale before ranting, "You son of a—"

Her affront stifled, Mirabelle found herself on her back. A firm and muscled thigh wedged between her legs. Hot lips devoured her.

It was like a punch to her gut, the kiss, filling her belly with heat that swarmed her senses. Damian moved over her in sensuous waves, his body grinding against her limbs, his mouth burning and wild.

There in the quiet meadow, the scent of fresh blooms in the air, the moment seemed enchanting, like a dream.

A chained feeling in her heart threatened to break its restrictive bonds. The clanking manacles resounded in her head, the emotion demanding to be released.

Like hell she'd let it out! This was the man who considered her nothing but a tart, remember? The man who had betrayed her brothers and injured Quincy. And he would hurt her, too. Break her heart if she let him get too close. He cared nothing for her. He would ravish her and be done with her. Again.

The more Mirabelle pounded such unseemly thoughts into her head, the more she hushed the other, rather frightening sentiment inside her.

Beating on Damian's shoulders, she struggled beneath him.

He broke away from the dizzying kiss.

"Get off me, Damian!"

"Belle," he whispered her name in such a gruff way it made her quiver, then took her lips in his once more.

She bit him.

He winced.

She wouldn't let him lull her senses. It didn't matter how good it felt to be in his arms. It wasn't right. And she damn well wasn't going to give him the satisfaction of using her again; of assuaging himself of his lust, only to throw her another barb.

"I mean it, Damian. Get off me. I won't be your whore tonight . . . or will you take me even if I fight?"

Dark emotions twinkled in his eyes.

For a moment he stared at her—hard. Quickly, though, Damian got up and yanked her roughly to her feet. He dragged her through the meadow, over to the horse, and tossed her into the saddle.

Mounting behind her, he steered the gelding back onto the road.

Neither said another word to the other.

Chapter 20

"What the hell do you think you're doing, Damian?"

"Hold still," he barked, lacing her wrists to the bedpost.

Belle struggled against the winding rope. "You're mad!"

Damian stepped away from the bedside, inspecting his handiwork. The knot should hold his tempestuous siren.

A lamp already burning, the chamber had been prepared at Damian's behest. Fresh linens, cooked fare, a steamy tub—but no brig. The rope would have to suffice. He couldn't risk Belle sneaking away in the middle of the night.

A spark of lightning filled the room, followed by the distant boom of thunder.

They would rest here, at the Drunken Horse tavern and inn until dawn. Come morning, the storm would pass, and the journey to his castle in Colchester would resume—as would his plan of vengeance. For now, Belle grudgingly accepted the reason for her abduction: to shield his escape from her brothers. But soon she would know the truth. Soon she would despise him even more.

"Are you hungry?" he asked.

She stuck her nose in the air and sat down on the bed.

"I guess not." He settled in a chair and leafed through the contents of his plate with a fork and a curious eye, then muttered, "Stubborn wench."

"You mean whore!" she sneered.

Damian sighed and dropped his fork on the table. She *really* hated him. But that had been his intention all along, to evoke her wrath, thus severing the bond that had been forged between them, and making what he had to do to her brothers all the more bearable. And he had succeeded in getting her angry. Splendidly. So why did he feel as if he had failed?

The rickety chair legs scraped along the hardwood floor. Damian picked up the plate and fork and headed over to the bed.

He sat down next to her.

She scooted closer to the headboard.

He stabbed the fork into a roasted carrot and stuck it in front of her mouth. "Eat, Belle."

Lips clamped shut, she just stared ahead.

"Eat," he growled.

Still nothing.

He leaned closer to her, whispering, "If you're not hungry, perhaps we can finish our interrupted kiss?"

Her lips parted, but her eyes never met his.

He thrust the carrot into her mouth, then picked at the potatoes. She wouldn't touch him, or look at him . . . or kiss him. She didn't want anything to do with him. She was still angry with him for calling her that foul name. And she would stay angry for a long time. She would come to loathe him even more once he killed her brothers. She would seek vengeance, he knew. And he would let her have it. Once his oath to Adam was fulfilled, Damian didn't care if Belle slit his throat. To die at her hands was a better fate than to live a life of misery.

He finished feeding her the meal. Evidently she *was* hungry. There was nary a morsel left on the plate by the time she shook her head, indicating she was full.

Damian went to set the empty dish on the table, then proceeded to the tin tub at the far end of the room. Steam still drifted from the water. His muscles ached in anticipation of the hot bath.

Mirabelle twisted her neck to better look at him, slender blond brows arching. "What are you doing?"

He discarded his riding coat and set to work on the buttons of his shirt. "Taking a bath."

Her lips pursed. "Now?"

"Yes, now." He tugged off his boots, then attended to the buttons of his trousers. "Care to join me?"

"No," she said tightly. "And you can't take a bath. *I* don't want to look at you."

"So turn your head." After nights spent relishing sinful pleasures aboard the *Bonny Meg*, chivalry seemed rather hypocritical.

He whipped off his trousers.

Mirabelle gasped—in outrage, he assumed—and faced the wall again.

"Aren't you being rather prudish, Belle?"

Her back stiffened. "For a whore, you mean?"

Damian hardened. He hated hearing her say that word. He hated even more being reminded that *he* had said it first.

Rain pounded on the shingles overhead, the patter filling the silent void between them.

Damian settled in the balmy tin tub. He picked up the soap and worked up a lather. He hadn't had the luxury of a bath in weeks, and despite the warmth of the water bathing his muscles, he found no pleasure in the diversion.

He watched Belle. With only an oil lamp in the room, lanky shadows painted the walls, and even though she wasn't facing him, she could still see everything he did just by looking at the shadows—if she wanted to. Did she? Damian wondered. Was she studying him as keenly as he was her? Probably not. He had dashed any regard she might have sheltered for him. He had to accept that . . . yet he was tempted to make amends. Again.

Damian smeared the soap suds over his chest and shoulders. He couldn't make the same mistake twice. He had come close to begging her for forgiveness tonight in the meadow. What a mistake that would have been, thwarting all his own efforts. To have engaged in one more passionate tussle with Belle would only have strengthened their bond. And he was trying to sever it.

A dull ache throbbed in his chest. It was better that she despised him, really it was. He didn't need her affection. He didn't need the comforting heat of her body. He had lived twenty-eight years of his life without Belle. He could go on without her for a few more days.

The ache in his heart tightened. To hold Belle in his arms, snug against him, to feel her faerie breath tickle his skin, was a calm unlike any he had ever experienced. He could close his eyes when with her and not dream of demons. He could close his eyes and hope. Hope for a life worth living.

But it was a false hope, he knew. He was too much like his father. Even if he abandoned his quest for vengeance and made Belle his wife, he would still hurt her one day. It was in his blood, the need to destroy, to devastate the lives of those around him. He could never have a real life with Belle. And it hurt like hell to admit it.

Damian suddenly felt as if he were drowning in the tin tub. He quickly stood up, water sloshing all over the floor. He grabbed the towel draped over the chair and started to dry himself.

His hasty movements must have startled Belle, for she whipped her head around to glare at him. She was a delightful sight. Pouting. Hair escaping her loose bun in an unruly mess. He wanted nothing more than to strip her locks of pins and comb his fingers through the mussed and silky strands; to twist his palms in her wild tresses and lose himself to her like a fortress lost to ivy long ago.

"Finished so soon, Damian?"

He wrapped the towel around his waist and stepped out of the tub. The weight on his chest was crushing. An intense feeling of loss gripped him. The loss of Belle. She was only a few yards away from him, and yet he sensed she was gone. Gone from his life and from his heart.

It was suffocating, the thought. A darkness came over him, blanketing him in despair.

"Damian?" Her brow furrowed. "Are you all right?"

He moved to the window, staring out at the thrashing storm beyond. Lightning cracked in the distance. Thunder roared. The glass panes rattled under the fury of the whirling winds. It was like standing in front of a mirror. The tempest reflected his inner being to perfection. Pure mayhem. What he wouldn't give to have the pain, the loneliness, the chaos inside him stop.

He headed for the bed.

Belle's eyes widened. "What are you doing, Damian?"

But he didn't say a word. Roughly he yanked at the knotted rope, setting his siren free.

She bounded to her feet. Alarm and outrage flashed in her amber eyes. She looked ready to have an emotional snit, but he didn't give her the chance . . .

Mirabelle gasped.

Damian's hot mouth crushed hers in a wicked kiss,

the tempestuous movements taking her breath—and her wits—away. Hell's fire, but the man could whip her insides into a frenzy. About to rail at the blackguard for tying her up like a convict, she was suddenly lost for words. She could only feel the maddening passion he impressed upon her, arousing her, stirring her heart . . .

Oh no you don't!

The oaf had her in a mighty hold and she couldn't break free, so she pounded on his chest, desperate to get away. She would *not* give in to him, no matter how delicious the experience. The bloody bastard had called her a—

"Forgive me, Belle, for what I said."

His whispered words, so sultry and sincere, made her heart pinch in forgiveness. Oh, cursed heart! So weak and—

"Don't deny me this, Belle."

Those beautiful blue eyes, so stormy, so needful of her, cut up her soul. There was such agony in his heated gaze. For just a moment, she could see inside his heart. And she saw a man in pain, vulnerable.

She didn't resist when Damian took her lips in his once more. She kissed him back and let the warmth of his touch bathe her, burn through her flesh, scorch her to her very soul.

"Oh, Belle," he breathed and dropped to his knees, burying his face in her midriff.

Damian reached under her skirt and tugged at her boots. She splayed her fingers over his moist back, holding him close, and lifted one foot, then the other. Soon both her feet were bare. She sighed in pleasure as he massaged her toes, her ankles, her calves. Slowly he moved his hands along her legs, his fingers raking her fevered flesh, hoisting the garment up to her waist. Quickly she pulled the dress over her head, dropping it to the floor in a crumpled heap.

Damian was still on his knees. He reached around to fumble with the laces of her petticoat. Yanking the garment to her ankles, he then tossed it aside.

She clutched him in a passionate hold as he pressed kisses to her belly. Smoldering hot kisses. She twisted her fingers in his hair and curled her toes when he licked her belly button in a lazy caress. Then kissed. Then licked again.

Mirabelle shuddered. She was naked from the waist down, the chill of the room mixing erotically with Damian's balmy wet kisses and warm palms.

Suddenly she couldn't breathe very well. The corset clutching her breasts seemed too tight. She wanted out of the restrictive garment. Now!

Fortunately, the apparel laced up the front, so she quickly set to work to rid herself of the suffocating nuisance.

But Damian stopped her.

"Let me, Belle."

She shivered again. Her name had never sounded so carnal before, like a seductive growl.

Blue eyes fiery and intent, Damian slowly unlaced the meddlesome corset. She was anxious all of a sudden. She wanted him to go faster, but she could tell by his easy pace he intended to take his time. To torture her with exquisite pleasure.

Damian must have sensed her impatience, for he

dipped his head to kiss her midriff in appeasement. Carefully he unworked the corset, Mirabelle quivering in anticipation. With a hard jerk, he broke the last of the troublesome bonds, her breasts springing free.

She let out a half sigh, half moan of relief, and thrust her sore breasts forward, searching for more of Damian's soothing kisses.

He obliged her. Still on his knees, he captured one rosy hard nub between his lips and gently sucked.

Mirabelle shook with abandon and want. Her nipple ached in Damian's mouth, not with pain but with throbbing pleasure. She held him tight to her breast, leaned against him for support, for she sensed her balance tipping.

Reverently he licked and kissed and sucked the sensitive mound, evoking a whimpering groan from her lips.

She closed her eyes and bowed her head forward, lost to the blissful sensation. It felt so good, being with Damian. So powerful. So right. Her heart pounded in her breast. Her skin prickled and danced. Her body hummed with desire. And all because of one man. One man who made her feel such wonderful things.

She wanted Damian. To be with him always. To feel him inside her whenever the need arose. She wanted it more than . . . being a pirate.

Damian leisurely got to his feet, leaving titillating kisses all along her frame. With a flick of the wrist, he discarded his towel, and their bodies pressed together. The warmth between them was intoxicating.

Mirabelle opened her mouth to the hot thrust of his

tongue. Rocking on her tiptoes, she took in the heady scent of him, the taste. She was a mess inside. On fire. She was eager to be with him. But he, the dratted man, was in no hurry.

"Damian," she purred, trying to entice him, "I want you."

But he made no effort to quicken his pace.

"Now," she all but growled in frustration.

He chuckled softly. Gruffly. Making her tremble with delight. "I want to take you slow this time, Belle."

He pressed his sex, already hard and throbbing, against her belly and gently undulated, the erotic movements mesmerizing.

She was growing wet with need. When his hand slipped behind her buttocks to stroke the dewy flesh between her legs, she all but crumpled onto the floor.

Firm fingers fondled the sensitive area, rubbing in quick and fluid strokes, whipping her loins to a pulsating frenzy.

He withdrew, his fingers moist with her essence, and trailed his hand along her hip and thigh. She groaned in disappointment, wanting his wanton caresses to go on forever. The bounder! Was he intent on making her beg?

"Damian—"

"I'll give you what you want," he cut in hoarsely, kissing her between words, taking the pins from her hair until her locks rained free. "I promise."

You'd better, was all she could think. And when he finally started moving her toward the bed, she wanted to quip, "About bloody time." But his devouring lips prevented her from making the rejoinder, so she simply held him tight, making sure he really *did* take her over to the bed and ravish her thoroughly.

He set her down and moved to nestle between her thighs. It was thrilling, the pressure between her legs. A tantalizing torment. And she wriggled and squirmed beneath him until she could better feel his long, engorged organ pressed hard against her quivering flesh.

He kissed her over and over again, cupping her breasts, swirling his thumbs over the puckering nipples, so sore and sensitive and begging for more.

She ached inside for him. A burning need consumed her. She couldn't stand it anymore.

"Damian, if you want me to forgive you, you'll take me now."

He groaned at her words. A groan of sweet surrender. No sooner had she made the demand than he slipped inside her in one piercing stroke.

Yes! she wanted to scream. But his mouth crushed hers, so she moaned instead. He moved within her. Swift and steady plunges. Hips grinding, he rocked her body in ecstasy.

Mirabelle sensed the tension building at her apex. She lifted her legs higher, taking in more of his eager thrusts.

"Oh yes, Damian. Don't stop."

He hooked his arms under her knees, holding her in place, so he could push deeper into her.

She groaned. Each hard thrust was more titillating than the last. The strain between her legs intensified, twisted. She could feel the explosion coming.

She cried out. A sound of gratifying pleasure as the muscles in her loins throbbed, squeezing him deep inside her. Damian gave a guttural cry of his own, shuddering, spilling his seed into her. He had never done that before. But it was such an intimate moment, to feel him climax inside her.

Slick with sweat, Damian rested atop her, supporting his weight on his forearms so as not to crush her. He remained imbedded inside her for a little while. She didn't mind. She liked the feeling.

Heart still thundering in her ears, she could feel Damian's stomping against her breast.

"That was wonderful," she praised weakly, stroking his damp and mussed hair.

He kissed her softly. "You stubborn"—another kiss—"impatient"—another kiss—"demanding siren." He slipped out of her heat and rolled onto his back, taking her with him. "I wanted to take you slow."

"And let me go up in flames?"

He gave her another tender peck on the lips. "I would have put out the fire in time, Belle."

She snorted. "Why did you want to take it easy? You've never been slow about it before."

He looked up at her, a pained and troubled expressions in his heavenly blue eyes. "I just didn't want to hurry this one time with you."

"Because it's our last night together?"

He didn't say anything.

Mirabelle sighed. He was going to let her go now, it seemed. But what else was there for him to do? He had escaped her brothers. He need not haul her through the countryside anymore. But she didn't like the thought of being let go. It had a downright wretched effect on her, twisting her heart in the most wicked way.

"Where are you going, Belle?"

Squirming in his arms, she paused to look down at him. "To get my clothes. I have to get back to the ship."

It hurt to say the words. It hurt even more to separate herself from the sizzling warmth of his body. But she had to go. The longer she stayed with him, the harder it would be to say good-bye.

The warm light in Damian's eyes disappeared, a cold darkness taking its place. "I can't let you go, Belle. Not yet."

Her brow wrinkled. "But why?"

"I need you."

"For what?"

He rolled out of the bed and stalked over to the window. He just stood there, in the buff, glowing in the misty candlelight. God, how she yearned for him. It was a pain in her breast she cared not to dwell upon, the thought of losing Damian. Of living the rest of her days without him. Even the allure of the sea and the soothing creaks of the *Bonny Meg*'s deck could not inspire within her the fierce emotions that Damian did. The more time she spent with him, the more she came to accept that truth. Did he feel the same way? Was that why he didn't want to let her go? Did he want to be with her, here on land?

Her heart pinched at the thought. A thought not so unappealing.

She asked again, her voice fluttering, "Why do you need me, Damian?"

But he still didn't answer her.

Perhaps he needed a little incentive . . .

Mirabelle scooted off the feather mattress and set about collecting her clothes. "Well, I'm leaving. You can roam the countryside all you like . . . whoa there!"

Well, her motion to leave had certainly provoked a response in Damian. Only not the one she had intended.

He grabbed her by the wrists, and with rope in hand, dragged her over to the bedpost.

She thrashed all the way. *"Damian!"*

But it did no good, her cries. Once more, she was secured to the bedpost. And naked at that!

"You bastard!"

Gathering her garb, Damian placed the bundle on a nearby chair. He then picked up a blanket and draped it over her.

He didn't say a word. He just turned away and slipped back into his breeches.

It was suffocating, the turmoil inside her. A great welter of disbelief—and disgrace. She tried to pound the tears into submission. The fiend! He had tricked her. Made her think he was truly sorry for what he had said to her, that he cared for her. But no, he'd just wanted to rut about, to relieve himself of his burdensome lust. He was going to prolong the miserable abduction. But why? Did he hate her that much? Hate that she was a pirate?

And then the dreadful truth came to her. Damian intended to escape her brothers *and* torment them by kidnapping her. A reprisal, of sorts, for the time he'd spent confined aboard the *Bonny Meg*, immured in the brig.

Mirabelle took in a deep and shuddering breath, careful to hide her face in the blanket so the black devil would not see her grief.

Bloody hell, it hurt. Squeezed at her heart and crushed the bones in her chest, the betrayal . . . but it also made her cold.

Soon the tears stopped coming. Soon the pain was numbed. And as Damian lay quietly on the bed beside her, she vowed the bounder forever her enemy.

Chapter 21

In the faint light of the breaking dawn, Mirabelle
sat on the bed, her legs curled and tucked under
her chin, her eyes fixed on the devious navigator. Still
strapped to the bedpost, she could do little but watch
Damian scrape away the last vestige of stubble from
his chin. It was such an intimate moment. So private.
Something a doting couple would do.

She snickered. A doting couple? With her tied to
the bed like a slave?

Damian set the shaving blade aside and dipped his
palms into the washbasin. Splashing water across his
fresh-trimmed face, he then patted it dry with a towel.
Decked in riding gear, he sported a close-fitting,
double-breasted coat, copper brown in hue. Black
leather boots, scuffed and smeared with mud, cupped
strong, thick calves, and supple suede breeches masked

hard-muscled thighs. Thighs that had moved against her last night and given her incredible pleasure . . .

Mirabelle took in an unsteady breath. Shame still burned in her belly. She couldn't believe she had considered opening her heart to the bounder. Of spending the rest of her life on land with him. What the devil had happened to her last night? She had vowed to keep away from the scoundrel. He had betrayed her brothers by escaping. Of course he would betray her, too. So why hadn't she realized that last night? Why had she accepted his hollow words of contrition?

Because she was a sentimental fool, that's why. She had wanted Damian to have feelings for her. To need her . . . as she needed him.

What rot! Feelings of caring only brought pain. Her mother was proof of that. Mirabelle should have guarded her heart better.

"We have to go, Belle."

No mushy words of remorse from him. Last night he'd espoused regret . . . but last night he'd had an itch in his pants.

Damian moved across the room, gathering her clothes. He placed the garments on the bed beside her. "Get dressed."

She didn't budge, even after he tugged the binding rope loose. "Why? So you can watch me? Humiliate me even more?"

Mirabelle gasped as a hard and handsome face swooped in to press close to hers. The soapy scent of him swirled around her, arousing her senses. And that look in his sea blue eyes, so scorching! Her nipples turned stiff and pointy under his ravenous stare.

"Get dressed, Belle. Now! Or I'll dress you my-self."

He headed for the door and rested a sturdy shoulder against the barrier, blocking her escape route. But he also turned away from her, giving her privacy.

The blackguard! How could he *still* make her feel all warm inside? Aroused, even? Could hate and lust really live in harmony? Apparently so.

Mirabelle snatched her apparel. With the blanket still draped around her shoulders, she sprinted to the corner of the room. There, by the window, stood a rickety changing screen.

She busied herself getting dressed, peeking around the partition to see if the bounder was still facing the door. He was.

She snorted. A little late for chivalrous conduct, wasn't it? Where was the rogue in him now?

Oh, blast him! He had ruined everything. Even her dream of becoming a pirate was dashed to bits. James was surely beside himself with worry. He would never let her join the crew now. He would never let her near any sort of danger again. She was doomed to live a lonely life on land. And all because of Damian.

The rotten scoundrel! Well, if he wanted to get even with her brothers for locking him in the brig, she wasn't going to help him.

Mirabelle eyed the window in assessment. A snug fit, but still, she reckoned she could wiggle her posterior through the opening.

Quietly she inched her way over to the window, shuffling about to make it sound as if she were still getting dressed. A clandestine peek through the glass revealed a thatched roof one floor below, protecting the main entrance. It wasn't the softest spot for a landing, but it was better than the ground. She could easily clamber down from there, and be off. Damian would never get his wide shoulders through the narrow slit in the wall. He'd have to storm through the inn to get outside. And by then, she'd be gone.

Pulse thumping loud in her ears, she carefully lifted the pane of glass . . .

Bloody hell! The squeak echoed like a trumpet blast. Without pause, she threw up the sash and dove out the window.

But two robust hands clasped her booted ankles and roughly yanked her back inside the room.

Stout arms circled her waist, crushing her ribs. And a livid face dropped to mesh ominously with hers.

"Going somewhere, Belle?"

He kept one hand secured to her hips, and used the other to shut the window. It slammed closed, the glass splintering.

Her heart missed a beat. "You have no right to keep me here, Damian."

"Oh? I wasn't aware a pirate had any rights."

Confound him! He was going to make her suffer all the more. Keep her near him, make her remember over and over again how wonderful it'd been to be in his arms. And how devastated she had been to learn it all a ruse.

With a sharp edge to her voice, she charged, "I know why you've taken me, Damian."

He seemed startled by her assertion, then demanded darkly, "Why?"

"You want to get back at my brothers for locking you in the brig, don't you?"

A dark flame burned in his delft blue eyes. He didn't confirm her assumption, though. He didn't have to. The truth was evident.

"Just let me go!" She struggled in his embrace. "You've punished my brothers long enough by keeping me all night."

He gripped her tighter. "Not nearly enough, Belle."

She stopped flailing to demand, "How long are you going to hold me? Days? Weeks? Do you intend to drive my brothers mad with grief?"

He hauled her across the room and laced the rope over her wrists again.

"You bloody scound—"

He pressed his lips close to hers, his warm breath bathing her skin, sending shivers dancing down her spine. "Do you want a gag, too?"

She fell quiet, then gritted out: "I hope my brothers find you and thrash you soundly."

"Until then, why don't you come along quietly, like a good little girl?"

She kicked him.

He growled. "Fine, then."

"Damian!"

Whisked in the air, she found herself slumped over his sturdy shoulder and carted out of the chamber.

She made a fuss all the way to the kitchen, then hushed once she realized the two of them were not alone. She didn't want to draw attention to herself.

She didn't want to risk her pirate identity being revealed.

Her tousled mane in her eyes, Mirabelle blew at the wisps of hair to better see who was in the room.

A serving maid. And she didn't seem the least bit stunned. What, did this sort of barbaric behavior happen often at the inn?

The girl handed Damian some freshly cooked fare bundled in a cloth. He nodded in acceptance of the baked goods, which Mirabelle eyed with only mild interest, her thoughts preoccupied with a certain rogue navigator holding her captive.

But her fury was forgotten when the serving maid bobbed a curtsy.

What the devil did she do that for?

"You're welcome, Your Grace," said the girl.

Mirabelle's brows stitched together, but before she could ask the girl what was going on, Damian hauled her out the door and over to the stables.

"What was *that* all about?"

"Nothing," said Damian curtly. "A mistake in identity."

Bloody hell, he should have known this would happen. Once he had shaved his beard, it was more apparent who he was, and being so close to home, it wasn't unreasonable to suspect the locals might recognize him. Hell, he might have wandered into that pub at some point in his drunken existence, even met the serving wench, without realizing it.

"She mistook you for a *duke*?"

"Humorous, don't you think?"

His steed ready and saddled by a rather drowsy stable lad, Damian mounted the beast, hoisting Mirabelle into his lap.

He set out quickly, impatient to leave the Drunken Horse tavern and inn behind. He didn't want anyone else to recognize him. He didn't need this abduction to go even more awry. If Belle discovered his true identity before it was time, she would only fight him all the more, struggle even harder to get away—and warn her brothers.

Belle cocked her head to the side and eyed him shrewdly. "You don't look like a duke. Why would she think you one?"

He shrugged, trying to sound dispassionate. "Perhaps the girl was half asleep and didn't see me very well."

Belle snorted but didn't say anything else. Good. He needed a silent moment to correlate his wayward thoughts.

He had done it again, bedded Belle. The memory of it burned in his blood. He shouldn't have done it. He shouldn't have given in to his despair and sought comfort in Belle's arms. Now he wanted her all the more. And it would hurt all the more to lose her.

Damian pressed his arm firmly against her belly, holding her snug, inhaling the heady musk of her sea-doused locks. She stiffened in his hold. She was back to hating him. He supposed it was better that way, but still . . .

He gave an internal sigh. Nothing had gone as planned, not even last night's coupling. His slow seduction had turned into a wild romp in bed. He had spilled his seed into her, too. That had not been his intent. Not at first, anyway. But once he was buried deep inside her, rocking against her pulsing core, the consuming need to possess her, to brand her as his overwhelmed him. He'd poured himself into her with exuberance, cherishing the earth-shattering moment as divine. Now she was his. In some small way at least.

And if he got her with child? He had not considered the consequence last night . . . or perhaps he had. Perhaps the thought of her enceinte had had some appeal. For it would truly make her his—forever. No matter how much she came to loathe him after the deaths of her brothers, there was one eternal part of him she could never resent—his child. Damian sensed in the bowel of his gut she would never hate his child—their child. He would be with her always then.

And that was the only way he could ever be with her, for now he had a mission to complete. And he needed Belle as bait. He had to stop looking at her with a tender eye. He had to stop being a hen-hearted ninny, as his father would say. Emotions made one weak. Already his shifty little pirate had tried to escape him. She'd almost succeeded, too. He had to keep a better watch—and hand—over her. He had to be strong for Adam's sake. Cold, even.

"Damian?"

He gathered his resolve, abrupt in his reply. "What is it, Belle?"

At his brusque query, she paused. He could hear her teeth grinding. She was annoyed with him. And rightly so. After all, he had kidnapped her. What right did *he* have to be in a dark mood? she likely wondered. Little did she know he *had* to be in a dark mood just to get through the rest of the journey. He was growing too soft, too fond of Belle. And such feelings posed an intimate threat to his mission.

After a short rest, she said, "Why don't you want to be a pirate?"

"I don't care to be a cutthroat."

She scoffed. "My brothers aren't cutthroats and you know it."

Was she daft? . . . Of course not. She adored her brothers. She thought them "honorable" pirates. And they, scheming brigands, would not disabuse her of that belief. Why, Damian himself had at one time supposed James a fair and righteous captain, the crew a merry lot of brotherly tars. How wrong he was! So it was no great mystery, Mirabelle's devotion to her kin.

"Admit it, Damian, the real reason you don't want to be a pirate."

She wanted truth, did she? Fine. He'd give it to her. "I made an oath to my brother."

"What? Not to become a pirate?"

"No, I have a vow to fulfill. And I can't do it trapped aboard the *Bonny Meg*."

Especially with you on board! he thought.

She humphed.

"You don't believe me, Belle?"

"Well, what were you doing in New York then?"

Looking for your brothers.

"Like I said, Belle. I had an oath to fulfill."

"In a gaming hell?"

"I was cleaned out. I needed the money."

A snort from her. "You were prepared to spend the night wagering, deep in your cups, weren't you?"

"I don't drink, Belle, or gamble for pleasure."

"*You* not drink? And you *don't* have fun gambling? What kind of a rogue are you?"

"A reformed rogue."

That had her snickering. "Aye, I see how well you've reformed. Kidnapping me and all."

"You, a pirate, expect fairness? I think your moral compass is a little off."

"As is yours. So you see, Damian, you would make a fine pirate. Which brings me back to my first question: why won't you join the crew?"

"I already told you."

"Sticking to the oath story, are you?"

"And what do you want to hear, Belle?" He pressed his lips to her ear, to whisper roughly, "Spit it out, for I'm tired of this inquisition."

But she wouldn't tell him her mind. Not that it mattered. Just then, Damian was held rapt by the distant figure on horseback that appeared over the hilltop.

He squinted at the dark shadow, but could not make out the face. One of Belle's brothers already? No, it couldn't be. James was a clever captain, but still, it would take more than a night—a stormy night, at that—to pick up their trail. A highwayman maybe? At the crack of dawn, though? Damian didn't think so. Then who?

But Damian didn't get to study the mysterious

figure very long, for soon the shadowed horseman disappeared back behind the hilltop.

The sparring with Belle had to stop. It was too great a distraction. Potential danger lurked everywhere, and he'd best remember that.

Chapter 22

~~~~~~ GO ~~~~~~

The large London square was bustling. Harlequins in bright costumes danced. Giants and dwarfs mesmerized little children with their antics. A theatrical booth in the center of the square delighted spectators with a rowdy Punch-and-Judy show.

A fair.

"Bloody hell." Damian dismounted first. "We're going to have to wend through on foot."

And so they did. Damian steered the horse through the crowd with one hand and gripped her bound wrists with the other. He was careful to keep her close to him, so no one would see her tied wrists—and so she couldn't escape.

Her dire predicament forgotten for a moment, Mirabelle was enraptured by the enchanting spectacle. Minstrels piped their jigs. Vendors peddled their wares. She passed a gingerbread stall and inhaled the spicy richness of the freshly baked fare.

She even smiled a bit. She had not been to a fair in years. Father had always loved to attend such festivities. Going to the Goose Fair had been his favorite pastime. Each year he would take her and Quincy and Eddie along, until the boys grew too old to attend the event—or care, as it were—and then it was just she and Father who'd amble out into the countryside to partake in the merriment.

Mirabelle glanced around the revelry. It was a pleasant reminder of days gone by.

Damian cut through the masses, past the furniture sellers and silversmiths. Beyond the muslin dealers and toy makers.

She finally thought to ask: "Why did we come here?"

"Because it's quicker to cut through the city."

"To get to where?" she wondered.

"To get to my . . ."

"Your what, Damian?"

Silence.

She huffed. Of course he wasn't going to tell her. He was going to drag her across the country, make her brothers fret, then abandon her in some remote village with neither knowledge nor means to get back to the *Bonny Meg*. He was just that kind of a devil, she was sure. Not a trace of honor in his soul.

Why, he wouldn't even admit to the real reason he'd absconded from the *Bonny Meg*. Oh sure, he'd tried to convince her of an "oath" to his dead brother he had to fulfill, but really, did he think her so daft? The navigator wanted his freedom. He wanted to roam the land, the sea. Whatever suited his fancy. He wanted to cavort with wenches and frolic in gaming hells. And being imprisoned on a pirate ship for a whole year would put a pesky wrinkle in his pleasurable pursuits. Damian was not the kind of man to stay in one place for very long—or be with one woman for very long.

She suddenly felt a flutter of unpleasant emotions and suppressed the ache to demand, "I want to go home, Damian."

He steered her round a dancing harlequin. "Not yet, Belle."

"Then *when*?"

"Soon, Belle."

She twisted her bound wrists. "Damn it, Damian, let me go! You've punished my brothers long enough. Even you, scoundrel that you are, can't be this cruel."

He stopped and whirled around, his lips so close to hers, she could feel his words brush her skin. "Oh, but I can, Belle."

The chill on her spine was biting. The rogue. He was going to be spiteful. And to think, she had once considered him a kindred spirit. She had once empathized with him, deeming him another lonely soul like herself. She had fretted over him. She had lusted after him . . .

Mirabelle took in a deep and measured breath. She had a lot to regret. And she was going to spend a lifetime nursing those regrets, she was sure.

"Move that cart!"

Mirabelle started and peered over Damian's

shoulder. A fruit cart blocked the street, and the obstinate vendor refused to budge, thumbing his nose at the navigator.

A row erupted then, the two men bickering. The commotion proved timely, as Mirabelle struggled for freedom. But of course the lout of a navigator had a grip on her like an iron manacle.

Too engrossed with her fight for liberty, she didn't notice the buxom flower girl strutting through the square. Not until the girl walked right past her, that was, and broke the bond with the navigator.

Mirabelle blinked in surprise.

Free.

She backed away.

Damian grasped behind him for a wrist. He grabbed the flower girl's instead, too distracted by the heated quarrel with the vendor to notice he had the wrong woman.

"Let me go!" the flower girl demanded, twisting her wrist this way and that.

Damian held her fast, squabbling with the fruit seller, oblivious to the stranger he had snared in his grip.

Steadily retreating, Mirabelle cast Damian one final, watery glance. Blasted tears! What the devil was she sad about? Certainly not that she was going to miss the scoundrel of a navigator.

Wiping the moisture from her eyes, Mirabelle turned on her heels and ran.

Twilight hovered over the city of London.

Wrists free of rope, Mirabelle hugged herself as she

made her way through the misty cobblestone street. She was hungry and tired and she wanted to get back to her brothers. She wanted to forget all about Damian.

A little voice inside her snorted. *Forget the navigator? Not without a magic wand and a sprinkle of faerie dust.*

Nonsense! The man was a cad. A scoundrel. She would dismiss him from her mind, right quick at that, and go about her way . . . but what was her way?

For a brief and ludicrous second she had believed her fate was with Damian. But then he had betrayed her, the blackguard. Clearly her destiny lay elsewhere.

So where was she to go? Home? Tend house and garden, and wait for her brothers to return from yet another buccaneering adventure?

Like hell! She belonged on the *Bonny Meg*. And she wasn't going to quit her ambition so easily. She was going to fight for it. She didn't care how much James protested or how many times she had to stow away, she *was* going to be a sailor. She wouldn't let Damian devastate her seafaring dream . . . as he had devastated her heart.

Mirabelle gathered her resolve and moved through the twisting alleyways, making her way over to the West End. Good thing it was dark. In her smudged apparel, she wasn't fit to be seen in such a lofty part of town. But it was her only recourse. She had to see her best friend, Henrietta Ashby.

Mirabelle turned a corner and found herself on a familiar path. She could still remember the route to

Baron Ashby's home. She had come many times before to visit with her comrade. Secretly, of course. And she was so close now. If only the blasted vehicles would get out of the way, she could better see the grand houses.

Craning her neck over horses and town coaches alike, Mirabelle peered through the gaggle of masked females, searching for that proverbial iron gate.

Ah! There it was . . . and the gaggle of females were traipsing through it in throngs.

"Oh no," she groaned.

A ball.

A bloody masquerade ball!

Mirabelle ducked into the shadows. Chattering ladies in resplendent gowns waggled up the steps, feathers and ribbons adorning their features. The gents were no less brilliantly attired in evening wear, with masks of dark silks and jewels.

All ages and shapes streamed into Baron Ashby's summer home—and Mirabelle cursed the lot of them.

Huddled in the darkness, she listened to the thrumming instruments and counted the number of arriving guests. Twenty-seven in just the last few minutes.

Blast it! How was she going to get inside the house to see Henry? She certainly couldn't waltz in uninvited. She might be friends with Henry, but no one else in the family had ever met her. And clad as she was, Mirabelle couldn't parade around as just another masked visitor. She would be carted into the street before she got past the threshold.

She twisted her lips, put out. She would just have to

wait, she supposed, for the ball to get well under way before she could put her piratical skills to good use.

And she waited for nigh an hour before tiptoeing from the shadow of her sheltered nook and slinking into the Ashbys' yard. The ball was in full swing, the guests all crammed inside. And in the darkness of the night, no driver took heed of her skulking figure, the servants too engrossed with their own festive gathering in the street to pay her any mind.

Amid the jeers and laughter of the coachmen, Mirabelle made her way with stealth skill through the courtyard, into the back garden where the old gnarled tree stood.

She scanned the terrain first, to make sure no one was peeking, then hiked her skirt up over her knees and clawed her way to the treetop with ease. Good thing she'd practiced climbing the ratlines aboard the *Bonny Meg* or she just might have ended up in a pinch right about now.

But getting out of the tree in her skirt was another matter altogether.

Lips pressed in determination, she slowly inched her way along the prickly bark. If she was in her breeches, she would just leap the rest of the way, but in a skirt, she had not the dexterity to spread her legs wide enough to make the jump.

Reaching for the balcony ledge to better support herself, she stretched and stretched and . . . lost her grip.

Mirabelle toppled off the branch, landing on Henry's balcony with a hard thud.

She winced at the pain in her side. What an

inelegant tumble! Good thing she wasn't aboard the *Bonny Meg*. Otherwise her cheeks would be glowing apple red right about now.

Hoisting herself to her wavering feet, she ducked into Henry's room.

Closing the glass door behind her, a frazzled Mirabelle stepped into the bedchamber—and tripped.

Fortunately a ball of satin cushioned her fall this time.

"Bloody hell," she grumbled, staggering to her feet once more.

Mirabelle peered around the dimly lit room. An oil lamp on the dressing table was still burning and provided enough light to illuminate the ghastly sight.

Gowns tossed everywhere. On the floor. On the bed. One frock was even perched high on a bedpost. Masks littered the tables, too. The chairs . . .

Crunch.

The floor.

Mirabelle flinched and peeked under her boot. Some things never changed, like her comrade's penchant for disorder.

Picking the peacock feathers from her heel, Mirabelle pondered her friend's scatterbrained disposition. Henry was never one to make a decision until the very last possible moment, and even then, it wasn't always the wisest choice. After tearing through a half-dozen gowns, Mirabelle couldn't fathom what her friend had ended up wearing. It wouldn't be a stretch to assume the girl was late even for her own parents' ball.

She smiled. She'd really missed Henry.

Mirabelle got right to work, rummaging through

the frocks. It would be so simple to swipe something from Henry's room, hawk it, and get back to her brothers. But she wouldn't do such a thing. Not to Henry. She would ask Henry for help. For money. Just enough to get her back to the *Bonny Meg*. It was too difficult to plunder the streets of London with no tools or weapons for defense. And there was the added risk of being caught rifling. No. It was much easier to request Henry's assistance.

"This should fit," she murmured, holding the dress up to the light. It was a coral peach in hue, with short puffed sleeves and a long flowing skirt.

Well, there was only one true way to find out.

Mirabelle set the frock on the bed and wiggled out of her blue dress. Henry was like her in size and stature, so the dress should fit.

She slipped into the evening gown, roomy so far. But she hit a snag when it came time to fasten the buttons on the back. She couldn't reach the bloody things!

With a frustrated huff, she took the button hook from the dressing table and did something akin to a dance, as she twisted one way, then the other, trying to get the last of the buttons in place.

Finally, she sighed. The bodice was a bit too tight. But it fit.

She dropped the button hook back on the table and massaged her aching neck. Working out the chinks, she turned her attention to shoes. Slippers, really. Dainty satin slippers. She found a pair, but footwear, it seemed, was one thing she and Henry did not share in common. She could not cram her foot into Henry's slipper without tearing it. And what good would it do her then?

Mirabelle tossed the slippers aside and yanked on her boots. She looked down to see if black leather peeked out from under the hemline. It did.

Oh well, she needed to talk to Henry for just a little while. Maybe no one would notice.

Now for the locks. Mirabelle sat down at the dressing table and shoved the ribbons and masks aside, combing through the paraphernalia in search of hairpins. She found a dozen or so scattered across the tabletop and set to work on her coiffure, twisting it and pinning it as her governess had taught her.

A half hour or so later, she was ready. Peering into the mirror, she examined her attire. The gown fit well, the satin a bit crumpled from Henry's neglect, but not too apparent. The waistline was below the bust, unlike the former empire style of the regent years. Her locks were whimsical-looking enough. All she needed was a mask.

Swiping one off the bed, Mirabelle held it to her face and concluded she was presentable. No one would suspect she was anything but an invited guest.

She hoped.

Now to find Henry.

The bedroom door creaked open and Mirabelle peeked into the dimly lit passageway. Empty. She slipped out of the boudoir and treaded softly through the corridor, down the stairs, and through the causeway.

Wait!

What was she doing, slinking through the winding

halls like a thief? She was a guest, remember? She looked the part; now she had to act the part. If she continued to think like a pillaging pirate, she would only attract suspicion.

Mirabelle paused and straightened her shoulders. She lifted her nose a notch to appear a bit hoity, and then strutted with confidence all the way to the ballroom doors.

But as soon as she reached the shiny threshold of the grand arena, she faltered.

What a dazzling sight! Yellow silk draperies . . . crystal chandeliers . . . ferns . . . tapestries . . .

A whirl of color danced by Mirabelle, the resplendent satin gowns capturing the flickering candlelight like a rainbow.

She blinked back the sheen and pressed her palm over her quivering belly. She suddenly felt sick. The heat from the room doused her like a torrent, the melted candle wax tickling her nose. The twirling frocks made her dizzy. She was hungry and tired . . . and apprehensive.

Maybe this wasn't such a good idea, after all?

"May I have this dance?"

Mirabelle started and stared at the gentleman holding out his hand. He wasn't dressed like the other gents at the ball, arrayed in black breeches and tinted vests and elegant tailcoats. He looked more like a coachman. Oh, his attire fit him well, tailored to his height and breadth of chest, but it lacked the ornamentation the other dandies seemed to adore. And his mask! Why, it didn't match the rest of his ensemble at all. It was as though he had picked up any old headdress to put across his face. Even so, there was something familiar about him. Something about his eyes, so cold and lost . . .

"Thank you," she said, "but I don't care to dance."

Mirabelle backed away, bumped into the statue of some Roman god, almost tipped the statue over, then, flustered, scurried away.

Bloody hell. She had to grab hold of Henry. Soon! Balls were not her forte. She would rather be aboard the *Bonny Meg* amid a hail of cannon blasts than trapped in this peculiar wonderland.

Keeping to the wall to avoid any more mishaps, she was having a devilishly hard time breathing with so much stuffiness in the air and a tight bodice to boot. *Where* was Henry?

Mirabelle scanned the crowd of a hundred or so with an eager eye. But it was hard to pinpoint one woman among so many. And all of them holding masks!

A kerfuffle near the lemonade bowl captured Mirabelle's attention and she peered between the waltzing couples to see a vexed female feverishly plucking feathers from a distraught lady's mask.

Henry!

Mirabelle all but vaulted onto the dance floor, quickly weaving through the throng of whirling partners.

She reached Henry without calamity, grabbed her by the wrist, and yanked her away from the simpering female who didn't have a mask anymore.

"I say, unhand me," griped Henrietta.

But Mirabelle dragged her all the way to the

other side of the ballroom and pushed her behind a fern.

"What the devil is the matter with you?" Henrietta demanded, then, curiously: "Who are you?"

Mirabelle lifted her mask.

"Oh, Belle!" Henrietta gasped, and right away flung herself at the other woman.

With squeals of delight both females hugged and hopped for a while. It ached deep inside, to be with Henry again. She had missed her comrade so much. Tears of joy could not be squashed and Mirabelle sheepishly wiped the moisture from her eyes before Henry took heed.

"What's the matter, Belle? Are you hurt?"

Henrietta dropped the frayed mask to the polished wood floor and removed her own bejeweled headpiece. She looked just as lovely as Mirabelle remembered her. Stunning red locks. Not the unfashionable flaming red some girls were cursed with, but a dark russet red in hue, like autumn in full glory. Her dark, bay brown eyes shimmered with warmth and mischief and laughter. And her voice had a richness to it that made Mirabelle long for her kindred company. And she had need of a friend now more than ever.

There was such sincerity in Henry's gaze. Mirabelle sensed she could confide in her chum and not fear censure. But she swallowed her fury and heartache instead. She had to return to her brothers. And she needed her wits intact to do it. If she surrendered to her misery now, she might never get back home.

"I'm all right." Mirabelle took in a shuddering breath to ease the flurry of emotions in her breast.

She needed a moment to gather her unruly thoughts, and pointed to the shabby mask on the floor. "What was *that* all about?"

"Oh, Cat's a conniving little witch."

"Cat?"

"Catherine . . . never mind." Henrietta waved a hand. "The girl *was* my friend up until a minute ago."

"What happened?"

"Catherine was suppose to tweak Viscount Ravenswood's nose and get the man to notice *me*. She wasn't supposed to set *her* cap for him." The baron's daughter huffed. "As if Ravenswood would ever flirt with a mousy little thing like her."

"Viscount Ravenswood?"

"I told you all about him. Don't you remember?"

"Vaguely."

Mirabelle's indifference triggered yet another gasp from Henrietta, who promptly took her by the arms and spun her about.

"*That* Ravenswood."

Henrietta pointed over her shoulder, through the ferns, to a dashing gentleman at the far end of the ballroom. A bloody big gentleman, Mirabelle mused, with dark black curls and a sinister aura about him that she didn't find too appealing. He wore a red silk mask that sensually offset his lush—and she suspected kissable—lips.

Ravenswood was conversing with Baron Ashby— or listening to the elder gent prattle away, was more like it. He didn't seem the least bit interested in what the baron had to say, though. Instead, he was engrossed with a particular fern—one concealing two mischievous cohorts.

Mirabelle shivered under his piercing gaze. "He seems rather dangerous."

"He's blind."

"Oh, the poor man."

Henrietta made a noise of disgust. "Blind about me, the blackguard." She stared at Viscount Ravenswood with steely determination. "I've been in love with the fool ever since his brother Peter married my sister Penelope. It's been eight years and *still* he treats me like a child."

Mirabelle glanced back at Ravenswood. The dark glare in his eyes didn't seem all that innocent. "Are you sure he thinks of you as a child?"

"I'm *very* sure."

It looked as though Mirabelle wasn't the only one in the world with troubles of the heart. "Then you are still unwed?"

An inelegant snort. "Of course I am. No one but Ravenswood will do." She sighed then. "Although Mama is convinced I will die a spinster and insists on throwing these troublesome balls to help find me a mate."

"You're only twenty."

Henrietta shrugged. "Mama thinks I'm difficult. This is my third season without a husband and she's sure I'll have many more."

"And what does your father think?"

Although Mirabelle recognized the baron—for Henry had pointed him out at public assemblies like Vauxhall and Ascot's—she didn't know the man personally. Or any of the Ashbys for that matter. She and Henry had a clandestine friendship. Oh, Henry had wanted to introduce her to her kin, but Mirabelle had been apprehensive. It was obvious, despite the tutelage of her governess, that she was no aristocrat. And she didn't want to embarrass her comrade with her common lineage. Lofty lords and ladies always looked down on anyone in trade. And to remark that her father was a "merchant" would send brows skyward.

Henry thought the whole thing rather droll. *Her* parents, lofty. "It was a contradiction in terms," the girl had always said. But Mirabelle could sense, even with the Ashbys' eccentric disposition—like naming their youngest offspring Henry—the couple still adhered to propriety. One didn't want to risk the ignominy of being shunned by the *ton*, not with five daughters to marry off. Well, one daughter now. If memory served, the four eldest Ashby girls were already wed.

"Papa doesn't think much on the matter of my marital state," said Henrietta. "He's quite content to marry off four girls and keep me around for good."

Mirabelle smiled. "He loves you that much?"

"He likes to be in the company of his only *son*. And while I adore Papa, I'd rather spend the rest of my years with Ravenswood." Her lips pursed, deep in thought. "I'm going to have to do something scandalous to get Ravenswood's attention."

Mirabelle suddenly felt sorry for Viscount Ravenswood.

"Scandalous?" She eyed Henry's accouterments. "You mean like wearing a *very* revealing gown?"

Henrietta glanced at her apparel and sighed again. "Can you believe it? Rose silk, deep ruffs, a heart-shaped neckline, and still the dratted man won't *look* at me. He tells me to put on a chemisette; the impudence. I'm not a debutante."

Mirabelle had a sudden desire to goad her comrade. "It is a bit too charming, shall we say?"

"Don't you start that, too." Henrietta looked at her with reproach. "Besides, your dress is just as risqué . . . I say, isn't that my dress?"

"Yes, well, I had to sneak into the house and borrow the dress to come and talk with you. I didn't bring along my dancing clothes, you know? I didn't know you were having a ball!"

"Oh, that's right." Henrietta pulled her back behind the fern. "Why are you here, Belle?"

"I'm stranded," she said bluntly.

"What do you mean?"

Oh, I was kidnapped by a rogue sailor, who trampled my heart, and now I'm all alone in the streets of London.

"Tell me, Belle."

The soft coaxing did the trick. All those cumbersome sentiments Mirabelle had tried to stomp down into her toes raised their loud and pesky heads, and she was rapt with the intense desire to confide her troubles to her friend. "I'm a fool, Henry. I very nearly gave my heart away to a rogue."

Henrietta perked up. "Ooh, really?"

"Really. I even thought I could share a life with him. But I was wrong. I can't be with him."

"Why, Belle?"

Because he doesn't care about me. He doesn't want anything to do with me or my brothers or the Bonny Meg. "I just can't have him. Trust me, Henry."

"I do, Belle. Hush. It's all right."

Mirabelle took in a steady breath, to quiet the jitters in her belly. "I have to get back home to my brothers, Henry."

"Say no more." The girl put up a hand. "I know were Papa keeps a stash of coins hidden from Mama."

"Thank you." Mirabelle smiled in appreciation. "I'll send the money back to you as soon as I get home, I promise."

"Oh, rot. What's a few farthings between friends?" Henrietta took her firmly by the hand. "Are you going to be all right, Belle?"

"I think so." She sniffed. "Henry, I know he's an undeserving rogue, but still . . ."

Henrietta offered her a thoughtful look. "Still what, gel?"

"It hurts," she whispered.

A look of understanding passed between the two women.

"Oh, Belle!" Henrietta gave her a tight hug. "Don't I know it."

Chapter 23

A peck on the cheek and Henry was off. "I'll go and get the blunt."

"I'll wait for you out on the terrace."

Henrietta nodded, secured her mask, and skirted away.

Camouflaged by the fern, Mirabelle spied her comrade wend through the mob of dancers and disappear into the corridor beyond. Once she was gone, Mirabelle moved to the open terrace doors and peeked outside.

She had only the moon and the stars for company, it seemed. A good thing, too, for she wasn't in the mood to converse with strangers.

Mirabelle moved to the edge of the terrace, intent on the shrubs and garden paths. Her eyes wandered over the ghostly terrain, to the knotty tree she had scaled a short while ago, and on to the twinkling heavens.

It was such a beautiful night, the moon glowing in full brilliancy. A soft breeze kissed her skin in a cool and soothing gesture, stimulating her otherwise bereaved spirit.

She should not have said anything to Henry about Damian. Even the smallest reference to the navigator made her heart quiver with woe, evoked memories she would rather have stifled.

But this was just her penance, she supposed, for letting Damian so close to her heart. She had vowed to keep the bounder at bay. To ignore his charms . . . his kisses. But she had faltered in that resolve. Now look what had happened. The knave had injured her. It was only a prick. She would get over it. Really, she would. But still, he had hurt her. And it was a miserable thought, knowing she had given Damian clout over her, even a little.

"Good evening."

Mirabelle whirled around to confront the large figure lurking in the shadows. There was something familiar about the sound of his voice. She screwed up her face in contemplation, but soon quit trying to remember. She wanted to be alone.

"Good evening," she returned stiffly, hoping to discourage the gent from further conversation. But her cool demeanor didn't appear to dampen the bloke's desire for chitchat one little bit.

He stepped out of the shadows and approached. *Now* she recognized him.

"You again?" She didn't bother to hide her displeasure. "I already told you, I don't want to dance."

He placed a hand to his heart. "You wound me, madam."

She snorted softly. The man might be dressed like a coachman but he was clearly a member of the peerage. His diction was superb. His grace and flirtatious manner polished. He even swaggered like a noble.

She wasn't comfortable in his presence. He still wore his mask, and she felt quite naked standing beside him without hers. But it would be foolish to secure her mask at this stage, so she simply held the headpiece in her hand and flitted it in the direction of his chest. "I'm sure your heart will mend soon enough. You men have a way about you when it comes to such matters."

"Not all men heal after a broken heart."

Mirabelle sensed her own heart pinch at his murmured words. She suddenly wondered if Damian would recover from their affair quickly. Would it take him months to forget her? Or just a few days? And *why* did the thought of being forgotten by the blackguard make the bones in her breast ache so?

The somber subject was set aside in favor of more light banter. "Aha! I see why you do not want to dance, madam."

Mirabelle stomped her bewildering grief into the bowel of her belly. "And why is that?"

"You have misplaced your dancing shoes."

She blushed. Carefully, she slipped her booted toes

beneath her hemline. "And you, sir, have misplaced your dancing clothes."

He laughed softly. A deep and husky rumble that unsettled her. "Touché. We are both mismatched, you and I."

He was funning with her, she knew. But there was something devious in his manner and tone of voice.

"I left my dancing shoes at home—intentionally," she quipped. "I do not want to dance."

"Not want to dance?" He took another step toward her. The fine hairs on her arms bristled. "A beautiful miss like yourself?"

Mirabelle squirmed in her spot. He really was making her uneasy.

"Is your heart broken?" Dark and shadowed eyes pinned on her. "Is that why you're not inclined to dance?"

"No," she said curtly, and then to maintain her pretense of nobility, huffed, "And it's very rude of you to ask."

"My apologies, madam. I am only concerned with your well-being."

"Rot!"

"You mistrust my sincerity?"

"I have four brothers." She held up four fingers to prove her point. "I know exactly what men are like, always searching for innocent girls to woo."

His voice was smooth and unquestionably wicked. "Are you an innocent girl?"

She took in a sharp breath. The impertinence! "*What* are you implying?"

"Well, I'm convinced it is not your brothers who have instructed you in the ways of the heart . . . but a lover." Then in a hushed voice, he said, "Unrequited love, is it?"

She gnashed her teeth. "I told you, there is no one."

"Come now, madam," he drawled, eyes luminous like a prowling cat's under the moonlight. "What young woman would come to a ball and not want to dance? Unless she was pining?"

A finger went to her chest. "This woman."

Mirabelle twirled about and headed for the terrace doors.

"So he does not care for you?" a call resounded after her. "The scoundrel."

She paused and turned around to glare at him. "He is none of your concern."

Her maddening companion quirked a half smile. "So there is someone?"

"Oh, you are a persistent devil," she charged, scowling.

"No, just a curious one." He knotted his arms across his strapping chest. "Did he leave you?"

"I left him."

"Bravo, madam!" Soft clapping was heard. "Abandon the knave, as he justly deserves."

"He's not a knave!"

Mirabelle started. Now where the devil had that assertion come from? Of course Damian was a knave. He had betrayed her. So why in heaven's name had she just defended the blackguard?

"Oh?" said the stranger. "He cares for you then?"

He doesn't give a fig about me, she thought, but couldn't quite admit the truth aloud. There was a deafening roar in her ears and a throbbing in her chest, making the words too difficult to enunciate.

Not that her silence dulled her companion's dogged curiosity. "Well, if he cares for you, madam, he will come after you."

"He won't come after me." She was sure. Damian didn't care for her, wretched as the truth might be. He didn't even know where she was!

"We shall see about that, madam."

Mirabelle stared at the masked figure with scrutiny. She wanted off the topic of Damian, and noted the bandage secured to the man's palm.

She quirked a questioning brow. "What happened to your hand?"

"It's nothing." He glanced at the wound with indifference. "A botched duel, I'm afraid."

"You lost?"

"A stalemate, actually. But we will have another go at it soon."

"I have two brothers just like that," she said in disgust. "Always fighting."

"It's a matter of honor."

"Slaying an opponent over a misunderstanding or slight? Restitution not enough?"

He said softly, darkly, "Sometimes an apology won't do."

She shivered. She had had enough of the peculiar man's company. "Well, sir, I hope you fare better the second time around." She lifted the side of her dress to skirt away. "Better yet, I hope you come to your senses and forget all about the ridiculous duel."

But when she glanced back to impart those words of wisdom, she found the stranger was gone.

What an odd gent!

Mirabelle smoothed her wrinkled brow and looked ahead to find Henrietta dashing toward her.

She was thankful to see her comrade and let it be known by the noisy sigh she exhaled. "What took you so long, Henry?"

"Well, I had a devilishly hard time getting past Ravenswood. The rogue trapped me in Papa's study to scold me about what I did to Cat's mask." Henry huffed. "Lud, the man is impossible. He notices everything I *don't* want him to see and pays no heed to everything I *do* want him to see."

"Like your gown?"

"Exactly." Henrietta let out another frustrated burst of air. "Here." She handed her friend a small velvet sack. "This should be enough to get you back home."

Mirabelle cradled the hefty bundle. "More than enough. Thank you."

The girls looked at each other, then hugged.

"I have to go," whispered Mirabelle, voice choking.

"Must you?" Henrietta broke away from the embrace, her eyes filling with tears. "You've only just arrived. Can't you stay and chat for a little while more?"

"I'm afraid not."

"But it's been more than a year since I've seen you."

"I'm sorry, Henry, but my brothers will be worried if I don't get home soon."

The girl nodded in reluctant approval. "Oh, very well. If you must." She squeezed her shoulders. "But promise me you will come back and visit soon."

Mirabelle wanted to, she really did, but she intended to go back to the *Bonny Meg* and she didn't know when she might get the chance to journey back to London. And she didn't want to make a promise she couldn't keep. Not to Henry.

"I will try, Henry," she said instead, amid a puddle of tears in her throat. "I have to go back upstairs and change."

Henrietta nodded and took her by the hand. "I'll come with you."

The two girls headed back inside the ballroom.

Mirabelle took only a few steps before rooting to the spot.

He stood across the room; big, beautiful, and dressed in riding breeches. He wore a mask, but such a sexy and towering figure could never blend in among an ordinary crowd. And he didn't. Voices whispered and fingers pointed as soon as he appeared in the doorway. Not that Mirabelle paid the commotion any heed. Oh no. She was far too busy trying to keep from hooting with joy.

Stormy blue eyes scanned the horde and lighted on her. All other thoughts faded from her head as he marched through the parting mob of dancers—heading straight for her.

Heavens, he had never looked so perfect . . . so passionate . . . or so livid. But she didn't mind his temper just then. He had come for her. And she was too dazzled by the flurry of giddy sentiments stirring in her breast to speak or blink or even breathe.

"Is *he* the one, Belle?"

Somewhere in the recesses of her mind she heard Henry's voice and nodded.

"Oh, I say, Belle, I don't know why you think you can't have him. He seems quite determined to have *you*."

Damian thundered across the dance floor. Fury filled him.

The shifty little witch! She had left him. Abandoned him in the street like a grimy urchin. He had turned his head, and *poof*, she was gone. Vanished. Lost to him for good.

He shuddered at the morbid memory and struggled to contain the frenzy of dark emotions roiling in his gut.

He was going to shake her. He was going to throttle her. He was going to spank her . . . He was going to kiss her wildly.

It hit him with the might of a berserk horse, the desperate joy rattling in his chest at the sight of her. Could she look more devastating, more wanton, in that shimmering coral frock? The bodice so low and tight it made his heart pinch in sympathy for her generous breasts, stuffed so snugly. Her glorious gold locks sat in a mound of twisted knots atop her head, her slender neck exposed, so delectable. The warm glow of her cheeks, the bright fire in her sensuous amber eyes, the rosy pink lushness of her lips . . .

A gloved hand popped in his face. "How good of you to come."

Impotent passion wracked Damian. He couldn't get to Belle. A bloody pest was in his way.

"Henrietta Ashby," the girl clipped out. "I'm delighted to meet you."

Henrietta "Henry" Ashby? It was then reason intruded. Music shifted in his head. Voices, too. He stared at the offered hand and recognized it as a saving grace, for he'd been about to set off a rumpus by mauling Belle—or something akin to it.

With much restraint, he accepted the gloved fingers and kissed the back of Miss Ashby's hand.

He then moved over to a bewildered Mirabelle, and with quiet firmness said, "Outside. Now."

He cupped her elbow and steered her toward the terrace doors.

"What a delightful idea," Henrietta chimed behind them, loud enough for the guests to hear. "A stroll sounds charming. I shall chaperone."

In the shadows of the garden, Damian tore off his mask and pressed his lips to Belle's with a carnal hunger he had never suffered before. The blood hastened through his veins, pounded in his head. He devoured the taste of her, inhaled the rich musk of her, smothered the warmth of her against him. He gripped her with strength and tenderness and wild abandon. Fingers ripped through her hair, groped her lush behind. He couldn't breathe. He didn't care. She was filling his soul with hope and joy. He was awash in the promise of her comfort, of her ability to slay the demons in his head.

It was some time later he broke away from the kiss. Belle slumped into his arms with a satisfied sigh. Lips swollen, lids heavy with heady passion, she appeared a sultry wanton. A siren, beckoning him. And he heeded the enchanting call.

With the pad of his thumb, he stroked her puffy lips and kissed her softly. Blood still rushed through his limbs, and he all but gasped for air, but slowly, steadily, the passion subsided, and Damian could think with clarity once more.

And the first thing he noticed was the lone figure perched on a stone bench a little ways off. Henrietta. She was fanning herself with her mask and looking on in apparent fascination . . . and envy?

"Oh, I say," she murmured. "I'd give my baby toe to be kissed like that."

Damian spared her a curious glance before he peered around the rest of the terrain. Deserted. Good. He didn't want anyone to recognize him and reveal his identity to Belle. It was too soon. Henrietta was no threat. He had never met the girl before . . .

No. Really, he hadn't. It was hard to remember the adolescent, even adult, years of his life after so much drink, but he was sure he had not encountered the innocent Miss Ashby before. He doubted very much her father the baron would have allowed it.

With that resolved, Damian took Belle by the hand. "Let's go."

Mirabelle blinked. "Go where?"

He dragged her.

She dug in her heels. "Tell me, Damian."

It was then he heard the clinking sound. He paused

to look her over, wondering what she had on that was causing so much racket. He spied the bundle in her other hand.

"What's that, Belle?"

"Nothing." The bundle disappeared behind her back.

He reached around and grappled with her for the small sack. When she didn't relent, he kissed her—hard. Knocked the wind from her lungs; his, too.

In the chaos of the stormy kiss, she lost her grip on the sack and it plunked into his palm.

"Scoundrel," she hissed.

He quirked his lips. Weighing the velvet bag in his hand, he concluded it was blunt. "Going somewhere, Belle?"

She huffed. "I was trying to get home."

"Not yet, I'm afraid." He tossed the bundle back to a waiting Henrietta. She caught it in the darkness of the night without fumbling. Impressive. He looked back at Belle. "I'm not finished with you yet."

There was more promise in his voice than threat. And when she shivered in his embrace, he rebuked himself for sounding like a seductive lover. He couldn't dally with Belle anymore. He damn well knew it. He had come for her to take her back to his castle. He needed her to avenge his brother. He could not have a wonderful life with her. It was as simple as that.

He took Mirabelle through the garden.

"Good-bye, Henry!" she cried.

"Bye, Belle!" Henrietta hastened to the garden edge. "Let me know how it all turns out."

It was going to turn out miserably, that's how, he

thought. Damian pushed back the twisting grief in his belly and pressed on.

"How did you find me, Damian?"

Good. Something other than pending doom to think about. "It wasn't hard," he returned gruffly. "You told me about Henry, remember? And how she was the daughter of Baron Ashby."

"Oh, that's right," she murmured, thoughtful.

"I just figured you would go to her."

Through the courtyard and out into the street, Damian hauled his wily pirate over to the stationed gelding. He hoisted her into the seat and straddled the beast behind her.

"What, no rope to bind me?"

He nudged the horse onward. "Don't tempt me, Belle."

She made a noise akin to a huff. "Why are you here, Damian? Why did you come back for me?"

"Like I said, I'm not finished with you yet."

She stiffened. "You mean you're not finished torturing my brothers?"

He didn't say anything.

"You scoundrel!"

She thrashed in his arms.

He clamped her body close to his, giving her nary an inch to move.

"I should have known you didn't care!" she cried. "A rotten bounder like yourself!"

Lips close to her ear, he whispered, "Did you want me to care, Belle?"

She fell silent then, her body trembling with suppressed emotion.

At least she was back to hating him. He had made an asinine blunder in kissing her just a short while ago, arousing passions better left dormant. But his fiery temptress had so frazzled him with her hasty desertion that he'd all but lost his wits. Now he had her back; his wits, too. And it was time to return to the mission at hand. There would be no more kisses or passionate strokes or amorous words. From this moment on, there would be only death and despair.

Chapter 24

❧

"Who lives here?"

Nestled amid a lush green valley stood an old and imposing edifice. Two soaring, round towers framed the ancient dwelling, the spire roofs disappearing in the late afternoon mist.

After a night of respite and another long day of riding, they had come upon the striking fortress, the castle resting like a solitary tomb on a forgotten burial ground. The swirling fog only darkened the already grisly gray walls. And with no light flickering through the stony slits, the structure appeared all the more uninviting.

"I live here," said Damian.

"*You?*" Mirabelle twisted her neck to confront the navigator. "I thought you were a sailor?"

"I take to the sea when I must." He was staring

straight ahead, shadows churning in his sapphire blue eyes. She had seen that look before, long ago, aboard the *Bonny Meg*, when he had spoken of his father. The castle must remind him of the man, and in a very ghastly way. Had his father been a servant there, too? Was that why Damian looked so sullenly upon the place?

Mirabelle had loved her own father dearly. She couldn't imagine what Damian was feeling. It was such a bizarre sentiment to her, the dislike of a parent.

"What do you do here?" she said. "Work in the stables?"

"Not exactly."

"Then what?"

"It doesn't matter, Belle."

The low timbre of his voice sent quivers through her limbs, and she had to think hard to remember the words. "Where are you taking me, Damian?"

"Home."

She gestured with her head to the castle. "In there? But why?"

He didn't say anything.

"Damian?"

Still nothing.

Mirabelle was mystified. Why had he brought her here? Surely he must realize she would tell her brothers where he lived. So what the devil was going on?

He doesn't want the affair to end yet, silly.

Mirabelle mulled over the thought. Was he keeping

her to delay the good-bye? Just one more night of sweet passion?

The man must be mad. Did he think her a wanton ninny? The arrogant blackguard! He had betrayed her brothers, dragged her across the country, and he thought her daft enough to submit to his savvy charms—*again*?

She snorted. Well, if he attempted to seduce her once inside the castle, he was going to get a mighty sore lip—again.

But then another, more disturbing thought raided her mind. Why was he riding so slowly?

Mirabelle puckered her lips. If her instinct was spot on and the man wanted another tussle, why wasn't he tearing up the grassland to get to the castle? Why the steady canter? It just didn't make any sense.

They approached the fortress, so inhospitable. Not even ivy blanketed the walls to offset the barrenness. Modifications had been made over the years, though, for it was not an iron gate that greeted them but a set of tall, well-polished wood doors. The front doors?

"Damian, shouldn't you be steering the horse round back? To the servants' entrance?"

Not that she intended to dally with the navigator. Certainly not. But still, if he wanted to seduce her, he damn well couldn't haul her through the front door and introduce her to the master! Damian would have to be more clandestine than that.

"Blast it, Damian! If anyone sees us we'll surely be in trouble."

But he still said not a word, the dratted man.

She let out a growl in frustration just as the steed came to a halt. Damian dismounted and dragged her down from the saddle, tucking her under his arm. He had been doing that a lot of late, the oaf!

He didn't bother to knock or announce himself. He simply opened one of the illustriously carved doors and stepped into the entranceway.

"Have you lost your wits?" she hissed, fearing to attract any notice. But the castle appeared to be as lifeless on the inside as it was on the outside. Dark, too. Nary a candle was in sight. Just two elaborate sconces on the far wall provided illumination. Low burning at that.

The shadows in the room were impressive. The gargoyles, too. Four sat perched above her head in hideous poses, each facing a compass direction. Curtains, heavy and dingy, bloodred in hue, concealed the windows and much of the stone façade. There was a mammoth brick fireplace embedded in the side wall, so big, she was sure she could step inside it without the need to stoop. It was lit, but mere embers glowed in its gaping mouth.

Damian stalked down the corridor with her in tow. He moved along the passageways like the master of his domain. The arrogance. He didn't so much as flinch when a maid scurried by. Mirabelle did, in trepidation. Caught! But no, the maid hurried off without even protesting the intrusion. She seemed in even more of a fright than Mirabelle. Odd. Then again, it was an odd home. So gloomy and hostile. The staff must be skittish of everything and every-

one. She certainly would be if she was cooped up in
here.

After twisting through one hall, then another, she
demanded, "Where are you taking me, Damian?"

He didn't answer. No surprise there. But then, he
didn't have to. A staircase appeared at the end of the
causeway—going down.

Mirabelle rooted her heels in the runner. Something
was dreadfully wrong. Servants dwelled in the upper
levels, didn't they? Usually in the attic space. Only the
kitchen resided underground—or a dungeon.

Despite her resistance, Damian easily carted her
down the winding staircase.

The alarm in her voice was evident. "What the hell
do you think you're doing?"

Down and down they went. Into the depths of hell
it seemed. The air grew rank. The light grew scarce.
And Mirabelle couldn't hear the rats for the thumping
of her quivering heart. What was this place? Why was
Damian bringing her here?

The ranting panic in her breast encouraged her to
send her booted toe into Damian's shin. The man
didn't even cringe. In one deft swoop, she found her
rump perched over his shoulder.

She pounded on his back with her fists. "Say something, damn it!"

He didn't.

She squirmed.

He grasped her even harder.

Damian had lost his wits. Surely there was no other
reason for his ludicrous behavior.

But she couldn't fret over his abrupt spiral into madness for very long. Hinges squealed, and she frantically swished her head from side to side to better see where he was taking her.

Everything was upside-down. And dark. Nothing but stones and a door and . . . chains.

Damian set her on the ground. She bolted. He grabbed her by the waist and hoisted her in the air. She shrieked and thrashed all the way to the wall.

"Damian, please," she begged. "Don't do this!"

Manacles clapped around her wrists: a loud and deafening closure of iron. The sound boomed throughout the empty chamber. No. Dungeon. It boomed in her heart like a death knell, too, foreboding nothing but misfortune.

"Why?" she croaked through her tears, her voice raw and faint from screaming.

She was secured to the slimy stone wall, the dampness chilling to the bone. But the chill in her soul was even more insufferable. And Damian's tender words made it all the worse.

"I'm sorry, Belle."

Chapter 25

⌒◯◯⌒

Damian burst into his bedchamber and marched straight over to the bed. He yanked the opulent coverlet off the mattress and tossed it to the floor, spreading out the corners. He grabbed the pillows off the bed next and dropped them into the center of the blanket. He then stalked around the room collecting lamps and other knickknacks.

He paused. Weeping resounded in his head. Deafening sobs that crippled him. Belle's sobs. He could not blot out the hurt, the bewilderment he had heard in her voice. He could not dismiss the grief reflecting in the amber pools of her eyes. Grief so poignant, so cutting, his own heart ached in a way reminiscent of the time Adam had died. And Belle's imprisonment was a death of a sort. The death of hope.

Interminable darkness clouded his mind. It

swallowed his soul and let out a grunt of satisfaction in having had him for supper. He was lost to that darkness now. He would never be able to find his way out of the bowels of despair without Belle. And she would never offer him a saving hand. Not once he killed her brothers.

He was truly alone now. He had always believed with Adam's death his solitary existence was complete. But after meeting Belle, he'd realized there was still joy in life, though he would never get to feel that joy.

It was a grief he had not imagined. It was a grief he had not known he could feel. But feel it he did. A fiery wound pulsing in his heart. And the more he reflected on the torment awaiting him, the more his movements grew stagnant, his breath more laborious. He was sweating with fear. The fear of losing Belle. Of knowing he would devastate everything good left in his life by hurting her.

It ripped through him with twisting agony, the realization of what he was about to do. How could he destroy Belle like this? How could he just surrender to the darkness?

"You're home."

At the sound of his mother's dispassionate voice, Damian glanced toward the door, a welter of emotion stirring in his breast.

Emily stepped into the bedchamber, adorned in mourning garb. After all this time, she still retained her macabre attire. He suspected she always would.

She moved to the center of the room. "How long will you be staying this time?"

He cast her a quizzical look. Long ago, she had grown accustomed to his frequent sea trips. The pestering questions about his whereabouts and activities had ceased the night Adam had perished. She had disentangled herself from his life completely. Two years ago, he had wanted her to do that very thing. Today, though, he wouldn't mind her attention.

But she would never again show interest in him. Some time ago, he had resigned himself to a life without his mother's company, which made her current query all the more baffling.

Damian swallowed the knot of icy grief in his throat, and set the amassed trinkets in the middle of the coverlet. "I'm staying for good, Mother."

She made a wry face at the word "mother." It didn't hold much meaning to either of them now . . . though perhaps that wasn't entirely true.

Damian sensed the pressure on his heart at the memory of his mother. After the death of the former duke, Emily had tried to repair their tattered relationship, but by then, he'd had no desire to form a rapport with her, and had brushed aside her conciliatory efforts with scorn. She had persisted in her attempts to mend their bond for years, until Adam had died. Then she withdrew into her woe, the world and everyone in it lost to her—even him.

Emily glanced down at the bundle of paraphernalia in the center of the blanket. "Then why are you packing again? Or are you just redecorating?"

"Redecorating," he said firmly. *The dungeon.* But he refrained from saying that part aloud. He intended to return to the dungeon. He wouldn't leave Belle in there alone—as he had been left alone.

Emily dismissed the odd accumulation on the floor and walked over to the window. She had aged much these last two years, he reflected, appearing well beyond her seven-and-forty years. Her dark black hair pinched in a tight chignon, thick gray wisps streaked her coiffure. The darkness in her eyes, under her eyes, around her lips, gave her an even greater appearance of age. An ancient wraith prowling the corridors of the keep, that's what she looked like. Destined to haunt the castle causeways for an eternity, grief grounding her in an empty existence.

She stopped at the window and gazed out into the blackness. "I heard a scream."

Damian stiffened but otherwise didn't express any emotion. "A maid must have seen a mouse. You know how skittish the staff can be."

"Especially with you for a master."

He studied her small frame thoughtfully. "Why are you here?"

She looked back at him. "Do you know what day it is today?"

"No."

"Two years ago today Adam and Tess drowned at sea."

His heart shuddered. Was it really two years to the day? He had never counted anniversaries before. Time had had no meaning for him. The quest for pirate blood was endless. No deadline by which to achieve his goal. But now the two-year anniversary of his brother's death would mark the end of Damian's quest. It would also mark the end of Damian's life, for he would lose Belle tonight.

"I had Jenkins dim all the lights in remembrance," said Emily.

Damian hadn't even noticed. Doubtful thoughts about what he was doing to Belle had congested his mind, still congested his mind. But when he considered his mother, her bleak and soulless stare strengthened his resolve. An ideal source of inspiration, she reminded him of why he had to realize his plan of vengeance. Adam had been the one constant goodness in both their lives. Sentimentality could not distort Damian's sense of justice. He owed his brother more than that.

"It's hard to believe he's been gone this long." She moved away from the window and came to stand across from him. "I've had the chapel in the west wing restored. I'm going to go and light a candle for Adam. Will you come with me?"

He stood so close to her, within arm's reach. He was alone with her, too. He had never been allowed to do that while Father was alive. But near to her as he was, it made no difference now. He might as well be back on America's shore for all the intimacy there was between them.

"I can't come with you," he said. *I have pirates to round up.*

She nodded and headed for the door. "I thought I would ask."

He watched her go. So many times in the past he had watched her go and abandon him. Turn her back on him and leave him to his father. All the anger, all the resentment inside him welled in his breast at that moment. He hated to admit it, but it hurt what she had done. He loathed to confess to such a sniveling and pathetic weakness, but the agony of one lonely and forgotten boy suddenly stabbed him in the chest, and even he, the cynical "Duke of Rogues," could not ignore the embedded blade.

"You've never thought to ask before," he said tightly, holding back the bitter howl he wanted to spit forth. "In the past two years, you've never asked me anything about Adam. Why now?"

Emily paused in the door frame and turned to confront her son. "You weren't home during the first anniversary."

"But *why* ask me to commemorate the second?"

"It was the proper thing to do."

He snorted. "You've never done the proper thing before." He crossed his arms over his chest. "I think we both know that, Mother."

Emily's apathy cracked, her bottom lip trembling. "This coming from you? A man who has desecrated every code of decency."

"And the code of decency *you* desecrated?"

"Such as?"

"You left me with *him*!"

There. He had said it—or shouted it, as it were. He had wanted to say it for most of his miserable life.

Something glistened in her eyes. "I tried to save you from him, Damian, you know I did."

He did know. He remembered the night she had come to the dungeon to comfort him. He also remembered how she got beaten for it.

"Why didn't you *keep* trying, Mother?"

She made a mournful grimace. "I tried to get you away from your father, but he guarded you like Hades guarding the damned at the gates of hell. I couldn't get anywhere near you. Don't you remember? The castle was filled with his minions. His so-called friends. All wretched, leering, drunken louts. They watched my every move when your father was away."

Aye, Damian remembered them, too. "The Henchmen," as Father had christened them. Villains of all sorts prowling the keep at every hour, engaging in orgies and drunken brawls and fiendish pursuits—tormenting him, for one.

"So why didn't you take me away from here and run?" he demanded.

"And go where?" Her sharp voice cracked. "I was the wife of a duke. No magistrate would listen to my pleas. No church would give me sanctuary. I was to live with my husband, as was proper. I *belonged* to him. There was no place I could hide where he or his 'friends' could not find me. Not even my family would take me in once the wedding vows were spoken. I was *his*. There was nothing I could do."

That truth didn't ease the turmoil gushing around in his breast. It didn't take away the years of agony or silence the ranting demons in his head. No one could do that, save Belle.

"So you just left me." Shuddering grief gripped him. "Is that it, Mother? Traded me for Adam?"

"I couldn't save you both." Her voice quivered, her eyes brimming with tears. She wasn't so dead on the inside, after all. "You are my biggest regret in life, Damian."

"Birthing me?"

"No." She shook her head. "My regret is that I couldn't save you."

Her words came late. Crushingly late. He was about to turn Belle forever against him. He should not be trying to resurrect old wounds now. It would do him no good. He could never heal them. He was hopelessly lost—or he would be soon.

"Go and light your candle, Mother."

Damian pinched the ends of the coverlet and swung the bundle over his shoulder. He picked up a candle and headed for the door.

Emily blocked the entrance. "Why didn't *you* change? Once you were older and your father was gone?"

"I was lost," he said simply. "And I couldn't find my way back."

He brushed past her, leaving her in the entranceway to fight back her sorrow, and traveled though the dimly lit corridor, making his way back down to the dungeon.

Chapter 26

~~~~~

Mirabelle crouched in the corner of the dank dungeon cell, her mind a whirl. She had already dismissed the notion that Damian had lost his wits. The man had apologized to her after snapping her wrists in chains. He was perfectly sound of mind. He knew what he was doing, and he knew it was wrong. That brought her both comfort and distress. Comfort in that he wasn't a madman on a rampage. But distress in that a reasonable navigator was committing a most *un*reasonable act.

Why?

What did he expect to gain by imprisoning her? Was this her penance for abandoning him at the fair? Was the man really so enraged about the desertion? It seemed ridiculous, really. But nothing made sense anymore. Unfortunately, this was one quandary only Damian could resolve.

The dungeon door burst open.

In the doldrums and distracted, Mirabelle scrambled to her feet in surprise, the chains clattering in her haste.

Damian made his way inside the cell, setting a candle on the ground. He proceeded to unfurl a blanket, all sorts of trinkets spilling forth.

Squinting, her vision adjusting to the light, Mirabelle eyed the bundle curiously, then quickly demanded, "Damian, what's going on?"

He picked up a pillow, handing it to her.

She grabbed the feathered cushion in frustration and tossed it to the ground. "Why are you doing this?"

He headed back to the pile of knickknacks.

"Tell me!"

"I didn't have time to prepare the dungeon properly, Belle. You were an unexpected guest."

"Not about that! Tell me *why* you've locked me in here?"

He picked up a second pillow and dropped it at her feet. Something comfy to sit on? She had a terrible suspicion he was trying to make her at ease. But for how long?

"I need something from you, Belle."

Was that all? Bloody hell, did he have to put her in chains to get her to cooperate?

"Then ask me for it, Damian."

His voice deepened to a husky timbre. "I'm afraid you won't give me this if I make a request."

"Just tell me what you want, damn it!"

He stared at her, fiery grief etched in his expression. "Your brothers."

She bristled. "What do you want with my brothers?"

He didn't answer her. He moved back to the coverlet and retrieved two oil lamps, using the burning candle wick to ignite the duo. He then placed the glass orbs around the dungeon, brightening the space.

Pulse thumping, she demanded, "Tell me, Damian!"

Still nothing.

"You promised not to hurt my brothers."

He collected a mantel clock and set it on a stone ledge, the ticking hands in sync with her own ticking heartbeat.

"I promised not to hand them over to the authorities," he corrected.

Quibbling over words! Was he daft? "Are you miffed because they tried to force you into piracy? You got away, Damian. Isn't that enough? Why the petty retaliation?"

He folded the blanket into a neat pile and placed it at her feet. "There is nothing petty about my dealings with your kin. I'm afraid they owe me something precious."

"What?" she all but cried, panic welling in her breast.

"Blood."

Crippling pain squeezed her chest. Damian wasn't making any sense. She hated to think it, but what if he *was* mad, even a little? What then? How to reason with a man who wanted blood?

"I know my brothers locked you in the brig," she said, frantic, "but you don't need to take their blood, Damian. They never hurt you!"

"Oh, but they did, Belle. A long time ago. In a way I can never forget."

Something flickered in the deep pools of his steely blue eyes. Something unsavory. It made her shiver, the bleakness in his gaze. And what was this "long ago" hurt? Damian had met her brothers only a month before. No great length of time. So just *what* was he talking about? Unless there was another matter at hand, one more sinister? Had the rogue navigator been scheming for a while now?

She cut him a grave stare. "Who are you?"

"You already know my name."

"Who are you really?"

He stepped back and gave a sweeping bow. "The Duke of Rogues, at your service."

She gasped. "A duke? Then the serving maid at the inn . . ."

"Was not mistaken," he said crisply. "That's right, Belle."

She shook her head in disbelief. And she had deemed him a stable hand! The man *owned* the bloody castle.

"But what were you, a duke, doing aboard the *Bonny Meg*?" she demanded.

"I needed to get home. I'd lost my ship, my blunt, all thanks to your brother Quincy."

Her eyes widened. "Is that what this is all about?" A spark of hope flickered in her breast. Lost wealth? That was easy enough to repair. "Damian, my brothers will make restitution, I swear. You don't need to hurt them. Whatever you lost on that venture, I'll make sure they repay you."

"This has nothing to do with money."

Hope withered, snuffed out. "Then what?"

"I already told you." He turned around to adjust the flame in the lamp. "Blood."

She hated that word coming from him. It downright chilled her to the bone. "Damian, please, whatever you think my brothers have done, they don't deserve to be entombed in here . . . neither did you."

He whirled around to confront her. "*What?!*"

She nodded to the corner of the wall. There, in child script, was his chiseled name. She had not noticed the carving until a moment ago. After he'd tweaked the light, illuminating the space even more, it had captured her attention like a lightning strike in a midnight sky.

"Your name is scratched in the stone," she said. "This is where your father put you when you misbehaved, isn't it?"

Damian stared at the name in intense concentration, all sorts of passionate emotions flickering in the dark depths of his eyes.

He broke his gaze away from the crudely fashioned handwriting, his attention back on her. "It's the pathetic scrawling of an eight-year-old boy."

The ache in his voice was heart wrenching. She

knew he had been mistreated by his father, he had told her so, but she had never realized how brutally until now.

The agony he must have endured as a child. *She* was skittish being in such a gloomy and foreboding place. How it must have frightened him, a mere babe!

Compassion replaced her anger and fright, and she wanted to reach out to Damian, to make him understand he was not alone anymore. He need not suffer with childhood torment. He need not go through with whatever ghastly plan he had configured.

"Listen, Damian, this can all be resolved—"

He slammed both palms on either side of her head.

Mirabelle took in a quick breath, stifling a cry. She delved deep into his troubled expression. Anguish twisted his features, contorted his soul. She could see it clearly, the battle within him. *What* battle, though? What was he fighting against with such desperation?

But then his eyes sparked. Red hot anger. Pain transformed into determination, and his breathing steadied. "It can only end one way, Belle."

She shivered at his cold words and took in a hefty draft of air. "But how are you going to get my brothers to come to the castle? They don't even know who you are."

He moved away from her, dragging in a deep breath of his own. She heard it clearly, whistling between his teeth. A hand went to his hair. "I left a note for James."

So many emotions struggled inside her. So many conflicting sentiments. Head throbbing, heart hammering, she had to focus hard to keep her thoughts in line.

Fear for her brothers, mingled with the ever-present need to stop Damian from this madness, prompted her to quip, "And do you think my brothers are going to accept your 'invitation'?"

"Of course."

"Why?"

He paused and stared at her. "Because I have you."

She lunged for him, the chains shrieking, taut with tension when the iron rings reached their maximum length. "I *won't* help you!"

"You already have."

There it was, the dreaded truth. It cut to the bone, the twinge in her heart suffocating. "You used me." The chains clattered against the wall as she fell back, astounded. "All those nights aboard the *Bonny Meg* . . . at the inn . . . the kiss at the ball. It was all just a ruse? To get me to come with you without protest? You wanted me to care for you so I would follow you here."

But you never cared for me, not even a little.

She lifted her hands to her face, the chain links cold and biting against her skin. Oh God, it hurt, the realization. A gash so deep she could barely breathe. She had always suspected the truth, that he felt nothing for her, but she hadn't realized it *all* an illusion until now. Every tender word and sultry touch aboard the *Bonny Meg* a dastardly ploy.

Damian wavered, a look of confusion and uncertainty flashing in his sapphire blue eyes. "I never meant for you to be here, Belle, but you were so stubborn, and I needed to get you off the ship before . . ."

"Before what?" she said weakly, breast smarting. "I still don't understand. There are forty pirates aboard the *Bonny Meg*. What were you going to do? Wrestle each one to the ground?"

"Nothing like that."

"Then what?"

"Sink the ship."

"No!" she cried. "You wouldn't have dared!"

"Not with you on board."

She shook her head frantically. "But you would've killed them all."

"That was the intention . . . it still is."

Mirabelle's screams followed Damian out the door. The din pierced his skull, like nails driven through the bone.

He paused in the shadows of the corridor and slumped back against the wall, taking in a long and shuddering breath.

Both fists slammed into the stone behind him. Cursed fate! To give him Mirabelle, balm to his ravished soul, and then make *him* destroy her was a mocking cruelty.

He let out a wretched howl. He was trembling, wracked with regret and pain. He couldn't move for a long while. Dead inside. So still.

Belle's wails made him sick to his gut. Damian finally pushed away from the wall, leaving the horrid commotion behind him, each step ponderous, a grave reminder of all he was about to lose.

Instinct urged him to set Belle free; a sense of duty to Adam compelled him to continue with his plans.

Duty prevailed.

Thrashing his woe into submission, Damian marched onward. He had much to do. Candles to light, servants to dismiss to bed. The final confrontation with Black Hawk would occur within his keep's walls. Although Damian had trained and schemed for a fiery sea battle, an end was an end. And he had already plotted another demise for the piratical brethren.

He would confront the brothers alone. To enlist the aid of his servants might be disastrous. The footmen weren't trained in combat. The maids would only scream in hysterics. In a moment of panic, someone might even scurry off to fetch the magistrate. And Damian hadn't come this far in his mission to allow his efforts to sour.

He mounted the steps. They would be here soon, the brothers. Damian was sure of it. James was too shrewd to fumble through the countryside, searching for the Duke of Wembury. The captain would know where to go for information. He would know where to look for Damian. And he would bring his brothers along. Not the whole crew, for it would take too much time to gather together forty horses. But the four brothers would come. And soon. There was no doubt of that in Damian's mind. The four adored their sister. Thinking her life in peril, they would ride like mad to get here. And Damian would be waiting.

He needn't go to any extraordinary efforts to capture the pirates. One didn't dawdle outside a keep, mulling over plans, arguing about potential hazards, when one's sister was interned within the walls, perhaps being tortured, perhaps already dead. One simply acted. On instinct. On emotion. And Damian would ensure their siege of the keep an easy one. No walls to scale or gates to ram down. A candlelit path to Belle was all it would take to get the brothers down into the dungeon. Then one flick of the wrist on his part and it would be over. The men would be trapped.

An advantage, Damian supposed, that the last confrontation would take place within his home. He knew the castle well. Every dark corner and secret passage. Every weakness and every strength. Unprepared and driven by a reckless desire to rescue their kin, the brothers would finally meet their end. Damian would have his vengeance. And Belle would be lost to him forever.

Chapter 27

⎯⎯⎯⎯◦◦◦◦⎯⎯⎯⎯

An explosion rocked the castle.

Even in the depths of the dungeon, Damian could hear the blast. He didn't move, though. Perched high above the sandy walk, concealed by shadows, he hunkered on the wide stone ledge. Waiting.

A twinkle of firelight dotted the dusty dungeon floor. Candle after candle formed a straight path to an open cell door—and a shackled Mirabelle.

She had cried out his name at the sound of the boom. He had not answered her, though.

She was quiet now. Only the ringing rattle of chains, as she moved restlessly in her corner, resounded throughout the cavern.

The brothers were inside the castle, their arrival announced in a most vociferous way. But the explosion would only distract the servants. A good thing, too, for Damian didn't want anyone wandering down into the dungeon—when the screaming started.

Whispers seeped in through the cracks in the stone. Footsteps treaded faint. Soon a head emerged from the doorway. Three more followed.

The candles flickered gently as the dark figures moved stealthily along the corridor.

Damian observed the pirates from his vantage point, high above the door frame. He could imagine in great detail their thoughts: *The orchestrated commotion up top will surely foil the duke's trap. Now's the time to sneak inside the castle and rescue Belle.*

Now was indeed the time. Two years ago, Adam had been murdered. Tonight his murderers would perish.

The brothers ignored the other dungeon doors, following the lighted trail instead.

Keep going, thought Damian. *Just a little farther and you're mine.*

The chains stopped knocking. "Damian, is that you?" said Belle.

A "shhh" from James was intended to hush her, but it only provoked her cries.

"James!" The chains banged together in Belle's haste to get closer to the door. "Get out of here! It's a trap!"

But the brothers only moved faster, closer.

Love. So predictable. Belle's kin would never leave her behind.

As soon as the four men were in place, just yards away from the dungeon door, Damian straightened and yanked the lever embedded in the wall.

The chains came crashing down. One could hear the rush of metal scraping along the rough stone walls. Two wooden doors in the floor gave way, and the pirates dropped into the oubliette.

Mirabelle screamed.

Damian picked up the ladder resting on the wall beside him and lowered it to the deeper level. He descended the steps and moved nearer to the pit's mouth.

Two pistols sat tucked in his trousers. He caressed the handles in preparation. So many nights he had imagined this moment. So many dastardly schemes of death had passed through his mind. And now the time for vengeance was upon him . . . and he did not care to make the pirates suffer. He only wanted the ordeal at an end. A few shots should do it.

A cloud of sand, roiled by the swinging trap doors, engulfed the opening of the abyss. Damian could not see down the hole yet, but he could hear the grunts and groans. It was a deep pit, and inescapable, dug like a well, with smooth round walls. No corners to hide in, no rough edges to scale. A construction from the civil war period, where traitors were dropped in and starved.

"Damian, *please*, don't do this!"

Mirabelle's frantic cries pierced his skull. He crouched down, a little ways from the pit's opening, careful to avoid poking his head over the edge, for the brothers were surely armed and his head would make an ideal target right about now.

"I'm sorry, Belle." The cell door wide open, Damian peered into the dungeon. Firelight caressed her features, the glow reflecting across her cheeks, all glossy wet with tears. "I have to do this," he said tightly, fighting back the chaos in his soul. He didn't think it would be so hard. To murder a band of heinous pirates. He had planned for this day for years. And yet his hands shook right now. He could not grasp the pistol's handle with certainty.

Belle swished around in her corner, her voice trembling with emotion. "Please, Damian, stop."

He looked down at the weapon cradled in his palms. "I owe it to Adam."

"What does your brother have to do with this?"

"Everything. He's the reason I sail the high seas . . . looking for pirates."

She stopped pacing. "You're hunting pirates? But why?"

"Not pirates, Belle. The Black Hawk. Your brother. All of your brothers."

She was bewildered. It was evident in her tone. "Damian, what's going on?"

He stared at the pit, his mind wandering into the past. "Two years ago, the *Bonny Meg* raided a passenger vessel, taking everything of value. The other ship was unarmed, but still the Black Hawk aimed his cannons for the hull, sinking the rig." He glanced back at Belle. "Adam was on that ship."

She gasped. "I know who you are. The papers reported the Duke of Wembury's brother had perished in the sinking." Mirabelle shook her head wildly, long wisps of her golden locks whipping from side to side. "But Damian, you're wrong. My brothers never destroyed that ship."

"I know you think the world of your kin, Belle, but they have to die. Adam deserves justice."

"No!" The chains clamored as Belle yanked at her bonds. "Listen to me, Damian. The papers were mistaken."

"The cabin boy survived the wreckage, Belle. *He* reported the tale before a fever took his life. And he claimed it was Black Hawk who fired at the ship."

"Damian, my brothers plundered the ship, that much is true. But James did *not* murder a vessel full of defenseless passengers."

"You want me to believe the cabin boy was lying? You would say anything to save your brothers. I know that."

Damian lifted the pistol.

"Stop!" She shrieked and struggled against her chains. "Think back to that awful night, Damian. There was a storm, remember?"

He gathered his brow, thinking back to the news article in question. "What of it?"

"It was the storm that destroyed the vessel, not my brothers."

"I don't believe you. The boy said—"

"The boy was delirious!" She took in a ragged breath. "After my brothers rifled the ship, they sailed away. A wild tempest hit. Even the *Bonny Meg* was crippled and almost drowned that night. The cabin boy confused the two events. The excitement of a pirate raid, the fright of a storm mixed together in his fevered mind."

"But he *saw* the cannon blasts," said Damian.

"He *saw* lightning. He *heard* thunder. He muddled

up the two, thinking pirates were firing on the ship. But it *never* happened."

Heart throbbing, Damian stood up and moved away from the pit, walking in circles, his mind a welter of thoughts.

"You're lying, Belle."

"I'm not lying, Damian. I swear."

"You would say anything to save your kin."

"But it *is* the truth."

"According to whom? Your brothers?" Damian tucked his pistol away and marched into the dungeon. "You weren't there, Belle. You don't know what really happened. Your brothers told you that story so you wouldn't think them villains."

She took an undaunted step toward him. "You can't kill them, Damian."

"I have to." His voice softened. "You would do the same if our places were reversed."

She reached for the weapons. He grabbed her by the wrists and forced her hands behind her back, drawing her snug up against him. He took in a deep and lingering breath, cherishing this one last touch.

"What will you do if I kill your brothers?" he whispered in wretched grief. "Seek vengeance?"

She gritted her teeth, her eyes luminous with tears.

"You *will* come after me, won't you, Belle?"

"Damian, please," she begged weakly. "Don't do this."

He pressed his lips to her brow in a tender kiss. "I have to, Belle." He let her go. "I must have justice for my brother . . . just like you must have justice for yours."

He moved back toward the oubliette.

"But this isn't justice," she sobbed. "My brothers didn't kill Adam!"

"Then why aren't they defending themselves?"

Damian stared at the pit's entrance. It was silent down below. No groans. No grunts. No curses. The brothers were still. Listening. Waiting.

"Why should they defend themselves?" she rejoined. "You've condemned them as murderers. They probably think it a waste of time to argue with you."

"But you don't think it a waste of time, do you?"

"No!" she cried. "I know you Damian. You're not a murderer. If you kill my brothers, you'll regret it."

He would regret many things later—the loss of Belle most of all.

"That may be true," he said, "but I still have to honor Adam's memory."

"And is this what Adam would want? For you to kill four men innocent of murder? It was an accident, his drowning. Not a crime."

Damian wavered. His fingers went to his temples to hush the demons ranting inside his head, goading him to shoot the pirates and be done with it. *Avenge Adam!* It was relentless, the chanting. Haunting. Unbearable.

"Damian, you know my brothers." Belle broke through the madness in his mind. "They're *not* monsters. Please, don't do this," she sobbed. "It'll destroy me!"

And with those words, something cracked inside Damian's heart. A hard shell that splintered, then shattered.

The twinge in his breast throbbed, making it hard to breathe. He loved Belle! So much it hurt. He could *not* go through with his plan of vengeance. He could not devastate Belle like this—even for Adam.

A fist went into the stone wall. Damian's knuckles cracked, the blood spurted forth, but the pain shooting through his arm helped to counter the cumbersome ache in his chest.

He slumped against the wall and let out a desperate sigh.

Mirabelle twined her sweaty fingers. She *had* to get through to the duke. She couldn't lose her brothers. Not like this. Not all at once.

Torment gushed in her breast, invaded her throat. She tried to swallow her grief, but the tears flowed freely, thickly.

She shuffled in her corner, cursing the chains that bound her. If only she could get to Damian, shake him, make him see reason.

Damian suddenly moved away from the wall, heading for her.

She wiped her tears on the back of her hand, heart hammering. "Damian?"

He said not a word. In determined strokes, he removed a key from his shirt pocket and unlocked her chains.

The metal clattered to the ground, the sound ringing throughout the quiet chamber. Even her brothers had heard it, for a great murmur arose from the depth of the oubliette.

Damian grabbed her by the wrist and ushered her out of the dungeon. She didn't protest. Hope sprouted in her breast and clung to her heart in a fierce embrace.

Had she finally changed his mind about letting her brothers go free?

"What's going on?" came the thunderous demand from the darkness.

"It's all right, James," she shouted back. But she wasn't so sure. A moment ago Damian, mad with grief, had tried to slay her kin. Now he was hauling her through the dungeon, away from her brothers. And she had yet to determine where he was taking her. Or why.

An uproar echoed behind her. Her brothers were furious. Scared, too, she reckoned, believing Damian might hurt her instead. But Mirabelle didn't have time to think about her own safety. She *had* to make sure Damian didn't harm her kin.

Whisked down the corridor, past the pit's opening, Mirabelle was dragged up the stairs. Her brothers would have to wait in the oubliette awhile longer. She still had to convince Damian to let them *out* of the hole.

The duke climbed the steps two at a time. In great haste, too. She stumbled once, then twice. Muttering under her breath, she snatched the side of her dress and yanked it up over her knees.

Round and round they went, ascending to the ground floor of the castle. Truthfully, Mirabelle didn't care what happened to her so long as her brothers were all right. And she intended to convince Damian to *keep* clear of her kin for good. Just as soon as she could draw breath.

Bloody hell, the man was in a hurry. Not even the smoke in the passageways deterred him from his brisk pace.

Smoke?

Mirabelle wrinkled her nose.

The explosion! That's right. Her brothers' doing, of course. A distraction to get inside the castle unde-tected.

The causeways reeked of sulfur. She coughed back the fumes and brought her wrist to her mouth to hinder most of the heavy smoke.

"Your Grace!"

Damian paused.

Mirabelle smacked right into him.

An aging figure approached—the butler, Mirabelle presumed—all decked out in sleeping gear. His robe disheveled and soot-ridden, he paused before the duke and took in a few deep gasps.

"What is it, Jenkins?"

Jenkins appeared startled by the terse demand. "Your Grace, the castle is under attack."

"Yes, I know," Damian clipped. "Is the fire under control?"

"Yes, Your Grace."

"My mother?"

"Safe in her room."

"The rest of the household?"

"Frightened, but fine."

Damian nodded and started off again.

"Your Grace?"

This time in exasperation, "*What* Jenkins?"

The man bristled at the master's tone. "The magistrate has been summoned. He would like to speak with you about the—"

"Tell the magistrate to go home," was the duke's curt command. "Then open the windows and let out the smoke. Fix whatever needs fixing tonight. In the morning, call for a foreman to oversee the rest of the repairs."

Jenkins rasped out, "And those responsible for the fire?"

"I will take care of them."

The attendant spared Mirabelle a curious glance before nodding to the duke in obedience. "Yes, Your Grace." Twisting on his heels, he disappeared into a cloud of smoke.

Damian pulled her quickly along.

Mirabelle let out a cough, her throat parched and sore from the fumes. Up on the second floor, though, the corridors were relatively clear of smoke. Evidently the thick stone walls served as good buffers against the fumes.

Damian opened a door at the end of the hall and pushed her inside the chamber.

Lamps already burning, Mirabelle glanced around the cavernous space. It was gloomy. Cold. Lifeless. No color at all, except for the bloodred curtains that framed the balcony doors. And those gargoyles! Perched above the hearth in hideous poses, jaws gaping, wings fanned.

She shivered at the ghastly sight. "What is this place?"

"My bedroom."

She made a grimace. "It's awful."

"I know."

He stalked over to the writing desk and discarded the two pistols.

Mirabelle let out a shuddering sigh, relief and joy and thankfulness all billowing in her breast. But soon the anger came back, swelled in her veins.

"*How* could you think my brothers murderers, Damian?"

"I'm not so sure they're innocent, Belle."

So he *still* had his doubts? Well, she had to quash those right quick.

"James would never give an order to sink an unarmed ship. You know him better than that, Damian."

He ripped a shaky hand through his tousled mane and strutted across the room. "I know no such thing."

Angry and restless, he was acting as if he'd made a terrible mistake in sparing her brothers.

A tickle of fear gripped Mirabelle, and, frazzled, she demanded, "Then why let my brothers live?"

He thundered up to her. "Because I couldn't hurt *you*!"

Something snagged on her heart. A nameless sentiment of frightening intensity. It warmed her. It comforted her. But she shooed the emotion away. She had one angry duke breathing over her head, and she had to soothe his agitation before she could even think about what she was feeling.

"Damian," she said in a more even voice, wheedling him to settle down. "You made the right choice."

"Did I?" Dark clouds of torment swirled in his sea blue eyes. "You're a pirate. If *you* think it's the right thing to do then it must be wrong."

She made a noise akin to a snort and marched over to the marble-top washstand. "Even pirates adhere to *some* laws." She immersed a towel in the washbasin. "We're not all uncivilized cutthroats."

He grunted behind her.

Mirabelle took in a rather shaky breath. She had to calm the implacable duke. If he continued in this erratic manner, he might reconsider letting her brothers go. And she couldn't let that happen. She couldn't let her brothers die . . . and she couldn't let Damian sink into despair, become a murderer himself. It was not in his nature, she was sure. He was wounded, in horrific pain. Grief for his brother had blinded him to the truth. She had to make him see reason. She had to make the hurt inside him go away.

Squeezing the excess water from the towel, she sauntered up to the duke. "You don't believe me?"

He was staring at her—hard. Such a piercing stare, full of agony and conflict. "I don't know what to think anymore."

She grabbed his wrist.

He jerked slightly, then sighed in acceptance.

Mirabelle guided his hand to the towel and dabbed at the blood smeared across his knuckles. "You know exactly what to think," she countered with confidence. "You're just stubborn."

"Damn it, Belle, I'm—"

"Hold still!" She gripped his wiggling fingers firmly. "You're reckless, too."

"This coming from *you*?"

She caressed his injured hand, washing away the bloodstains, mesmerized by his robust fingers and the power surging through them. Fingers with enough strength to crush a man's throat. And yet gentle enough to evoke the most divine pleasures.

"A reckless pirate is a dead pirate," she said after a thoughtful pause. "There's nothing reckless about me. Or James, for that matter." She met his troubled gaze. "Can't you see that, Damian? It would be *reckless* to sink a passenger ship and enrage a whole nation. It would be *reckless* to provoke the navy into a cat-and-mouse chase."

"I thought scruples stopped your brothers from sinking the ship?"

"They did, but *you* don't believe me."

"So if you can't appeal to my emotion, appeal to my sense of reason? Is that it?" He laced his wounded fingers with hers. "You would say anything to save your kin."

The low timbre of his voice made her quiver. "You don't want to believe the truth, do you, Damian?" She gave his bloody hand a tender squeeze. "You want someone to blame. To hate."

A strapping arm slipped around her waist, holding her snug. She made a noise of surprise, as she was pulled so close, she could see more intimately the chaos in his eyes, his soul.

Damian's brow touched hers. In an aching voice,

he whispered, "But there is someone to blame, Belle . . . me."

"I wholly agree with that."

Mirabelle gasped.

A cloaked figure stepped into the room, knife drawn. She recognized that voice right away. It was the masked stranger from the ball!

Even more disquieting was the tortured expression on Damian's pale face. His next utterance was no less disturbing.

"Adam."

Chapter 28

Damian took in a ragged breath, lost, the chaos in his soul blinding. "You're alive."

"Am I?" Adam stepped deeper into the room and yanked off his hood. "It doesn't feel like it."

Coal black hair disheveled, features burned and toughened by the heat of the sun, Adam had lost his youthful glow. His slender figure, too. The man before Damian *was* a man. In strength. In physique. A broad chest, bulky stature, Adam was more akin to Damian's size. And apparently to Damian's temperament, too, for the renowned sincerity in his delft blue eyes was gone—replaced by a burning hate impossible to ignore.

Shoving his bewilderment aside, Damian quickly noted the shimmering blade in his brother's hand, the metal luminous under the resplendent lamps.

Aware of the warm body pressed snug against him, Damian whisked Belle across the room, and all but shoved her onto the balcony.

The key snapped in the lock.

Belle pounded on the glass.

Damian turned to face his brother once more, tortured disbelief still stinging in his breast—and yet joy. Trickles of joy seeped through the cracks in his hardened heart at the sight of his brother. Alive.

But how could this be? "I thought you had died at sea."

"Oh, but I did." Adam kicked the bedroom door closed with the heel of his boot. "I died on the night Tess perished."

Twisting pain beset Damian's senses at the mention of his sister-in-law. Teresa had been young, not yet one-and-twenty, on the day of her wedding. And vibrant, too. Full of life and laughter. Damian could understand the horror of losing one so dear. His thoughts shifted to Mirabelle, still pounding on the balcony doors, and he shuddered at the morbid image of her limp body floating atop the waves.

"Adam, where have you been?"

"In hell." Unhooking the clasp at his neck, Adam allowed the cloak to slip free. "All thanks to you."

A flash of grief choked the duke. "Adam, please, tell me what happened."

"Why? You don't give a damn."

Oh, but he did. Damian cared a great deal. He always had. He had just never said it aloud to Adam. Now his brother was back. Ironic, but it seemed too late to tell Adam how much he cared.

"Please, Adam, tell me. I have to know."

"Do you, now?" Adam moved closer to the writing desk. "Very well, then. A wretched storm hit, sinking the ship. I washed ashore on a little island off the coast of Wales, where a group of monks living in an isolated monastery looked after me. For more than a year I had no memory of who I was or where I had come from. And then one night, during a brutal storm, a burst of lightning hit the holy dwelling and my memory came back."

Cumbersome sorrow nestled in the duke's gut. "So it wasn't pirates who destroyed your ship?"

"Pirates? No. It was you."

In the haunting stillness that followed, old wounds, still rankling, swelled in Damian's heart. He realized his brother's intent then, and he did nothing to dissuade him from his goal, for the shuddering agony swirling in Damian's gut, the tortured regret, crippled him in a way no mortal wound could. *He* had done this to Adam. *He* had taken away his brother's wife . . . his soul.

Adam picked up one of the pistols on the table. Armed with both knife and gun, he resumed his steady advance on Damian.

The duke didn't retreat, icy torment hindering his steps. He merely shifted from his spot, away from the glass balcony doors, so if Adam fired and missed, the bullet would not strike Belle.

"It's your fault she's gone." Dazzling fury beamed in Adam's eyes. "I had to sail home to drag you from your filthy existence. I had to wallow in muck for most of my life, lugging you out of whorehouses and gaming hells—and I lost Tess because of it."

The squeezing ache in Damian's chest made his sorrow all the more bitter. What he wouldn't give to grab his brother in a tight hold. To celebrate his return. To shout with joy. But no. He stood rooted to the spot, shivering with despair, taking in the wild rage Adam pounded him with.

"You." Adam pointed to him with the knife, the blade trembling in his shaky hand. "You've destroyed everything good in your life—and mine. You're no better than Father."

Damian could scarce find breath to speak. It was true. So true. He whispered, "I'm sorry, Adam."

"Oh no." Adam shook his head vehemently. "That paltry and insincere gesture isn't going to absolve you of what you've done."

Damian knew that, but he had to say the words nonetheless. And he *was* earnest in his repentance. He would gladly forfeit his own life if it would bring Tess back. Not that Adam would believe him.

It was a mocking cruelty, the family reunion. Adam, always serene and brimming with laughter, was now a twisted soul filled with grief—the very loneliness and despair that had plagued Damian for much of his life. An unsavory thought, but it seemed both brothers were now destined to dwell in hell.

Damian could feel the tears burning his eyes. Tears! He had not shed a drop since he was a babe.

Wracked with conflicting emotion, Damian stared at the knife in his brother's bandaged hand. Comprehension suddenly filled him.

"It was you in the prison courtyard," said Damian,

his voice taut with stress, memory of that night welling in his mind. The night he had met Belle for the first time. The night she had shot a pistol from a prison guard's hand—Adam's hand—and saved *his* life.

"And I almost had you, too," affirmed Adam, taking another step forward. "You've been a bloody nuisance to track this past year, always disappearing at sea. I'd traced you as far as New York—to a gaol, no less." He sneered, "You can't keep your despicable habits under control in any country, can you?"

Damian knew it was a moot point, but the fiery pain in his breast compelled him to admit the truth: "I was looking for the pirates who I thought had killed you."

"*You* giving a damn about someone other than yourself." Adam snorted. "I don't believe you."

Damian didn't expect him to. The "Duke of Rogues" changing his ways? It was rather hard to swallow. But it was the truth nonetheless. "So you followed me home?"

Adam nodded "I wasn't going to let you out of my sight again."

"Then it was you who tried to sink the *Bonny Meg*?"

"It wasn't my intent—at first. I had no wish to devastate what I thought was a simple merchant ship. I only wanted *you*," he said with deafening purpose. "I got too close to the ship one night, trying to keep up with you, and almost clipped the vessel. I strayed behind a bit after that, but when I saw the pirate flag hoisted, I decided to try and sink the ship. I figured I'd get rid of two pests at once."

Adam came to a halt before him. He must have realized by then that Damian wasn't going to attack him or even try to defend himself, for he lowered the pistol to his side—though he still maintained a tight hold on the knife.

Mirabelle banged away on the glass, frantic, her muffled screams piercing to the heart.

Adam finally peeked her way. "She appears to care for you a great deal."

An icy knot of despair choked the duke, for he knew those words could not be true. She couldn't care for him, not after what he had done to her and her brothers. She was frightened, was all. And wanted out of the room. Away from the madness unfolding before her.

"And I suspect you care for her, too?" Eyes filled with venom, Adam glanced back at him. "I followed you both to London, and then I followed *her* to the ball. I didn't want to lose sight of her. I sensed she meant a great deal to you."

A pang of fear sprouted in Damian's chest. "What are you going to do?"

"I'm going to set things right," said Adam, seething. "In memory of Tess, I'm going to take your place as the next Duke of Wembury and put an end to the dynasty of misery you have wrought . . . or I was. But I've changed my mind. I think there's an even better way to make you pay for what you've done."

Adam suddenly lifted the gun and aimed it for the glass doors.

Mirabelle stumbled back in surprise.

Damian roared, *"No!"*

The duke pounced on his brother and both men crashed to the ground with a tremendous thump.

Struggling for the weapon, Damian blasted, "You will *not* hurt her, Adam! She is as innocent as Tess. Your strife is with me!"

Adam stopped fighting. He glared at his brother, chest heaving.

The pistol hit the rug with a muffled thud.

Bitterness flickered in Adam's eyes. "You're right."

Damian gasped at the stinging pain, as cold metal sliced through warm flesh and blood.

"I think it's time your wicked ways come to an end, brother." Adam pushed the knife in deeper. "You've disgraced this family long enough."

Mirabelle screamed.

The blade thrust deep in his chest, Damian sensed the strength withering from his limbs and slumped forward, gripping Adam by the arms.

In one swift movement, Mirabelle kicked up her leg and sent her boot through one of the small windows in the balcony door. Knocking away the broken fragments of glass still embedded in the frame, she reached her hand through the opening and desperately fumbled with the key in the lock, trying to open the door.

On his knees, Damian watched her. He wanted to shout to her to stay on the balcony—away from Adam—but he had not the voice to do it. Blood gurgled in his throat and he could not get the words out.

Adam shrugged off his brother's hold and stood. He yanked the knife from Damian's chest and lifted it high above his head, ready to take another stab at the duke. He was trembling, his eyes wide and luminous in the dimly lit room. "Why won't you fight me now!?"

Damian gripped the gash in his chest, blood seeping between his fingers, and managed to croak, "Because I love you."

The blade hovered in the air.

The room was still, but for Mirabelle's weeping and hysterical struggle with the door.

The moments ticked by; the knife flickered in the light. Finally, after a long and tense pause, the blade clattered to the floor.

Adam dropped to his knees, opposite Damian, and raked his fingers roughly through his hair. Eyes fresh with tears, lips quivering, he stared at the duke, a heavy mist of confusion evident in his tortured gaze.

He suddenly grabbed Damian by the sides of the head and leaned in to whisper wretchedly: "Why did it have to be like this?"

Damian could not answer, blood suffocating him.

Adam was back on his feet, stumbling toward the door. He opened it just in time to collide with his mother, who clutched her breast and took a staggered step back.

Adam paused briefly, just long enough to touch his mother's cheek in tender regard, before he disappeared into the corridor.

That was the last thing Damian saw before darkness clouded his mind.

Chapter 29

~~~~~GO~~~~~

Mirabelle jerked the key in the lock.

The balcony doors burst open. Blinded by tears, her heart wedged in her throat, she rushed to Damian's side.

"Damian!"

He was limp. A mountain of a man sprawled on the floor. Blood was gushing from the wound in his chest, and she clamped her palm over the lesion to halt the flow. It did no good, though. The thick red liquid oozed between her fingers, over her wrist, and pooled onto the carpeted floor.

Eyes darting to the doorway, Mirabelle noticed a woman, entranced and flabbergasted. She looked a great deal like Damian, and it didn't take long to conclude she was his mother.

"Do something!" Mirabelle shouted at her.

The duchess, startled, snapped her attention to the duke. Her already pale features withered even more, and for a moment, Mirabelle feared she might faint. But in the next instant, she hollered, "Jenkins!" and in quick steps, dashed to kneel beside her son.

Clasping her hand over Mirabelle's, she tried to stave off the flow of blood.

Damian wasn't breathing right. Harsh, rasping sounds. Something akin to a hiccup, too, as he tried to gasp for breath.

The butler scurried into the room then, aghast.

"Grab his feet, Jenkins!" ordered the duchess. "We have to get him to the bed."

The butler did as directed, while Mirabelle and the duchess hoisted Damian by the arms. The duke was a big man and it wasn't easy to shift him, but between the three of them, they managed to make their way over to the bed and set him atop the feather mattress.

The bandages came out next, collected by Jenkins. When Damian's wound was temporarily bound up, the duchess ordered for the doctor to be fetched post-haste, and the butler disappeared from the room in a jiffy . . .

Making her way through the castle, Mirabelle wandered a bit, searching for the spiral steps that led to the dungeon. The doctor was with Damian now. There was naught more she could do for the duke, but wait. Wait to see if he would live.

She glanced down at her dress, smeared with blood—Damian's blood—and took in a shaky breath. She was still trembling; she couldn't stop. The attack

on Damian, so brutal, churned in her mind. Over and
over again, she remembered the heated exchange between brothers, such anguish in both their voices.
And she remembered the moment the knife had
pierced the duke's chest. It was an image she would
never forget, for her heart had all but shuddered to a
stop at the ghastly sight.

Mirabelle paused and closed her eyes, trying to
banish the wretched memory. But it haunted her still.
Even more haunting was the fiery expression of grief
in Damian's beautiful blue gaze, just before he'd been
stabbed . . . before he'd saved her from Adam's mis-
guided wrath.

The tears gathered, and Mirabelle let the briny
beads soak her cheeks. Damian had dropped to his
knees and surrendered his life to Adam in place of
hers. He'd been prepared to die for her. Scant time
ago, she'd deemed him a cruel despot. Chided herself
for her folly, for getting so attached to such a devious
rogue. But now a great welter of warm sentiments
stormed her breast. Now she prayed that the duke
would live.

Sniffing back the tears, Mirabelle resumed her
search. She had to find her brothers and set them
free. She had whipped through the keep earlier that
night, when the passageways had been clouded with
smoke, so she didn't remember the exact route. But
it wasn't too long before she recognized the curved
stone entranceway to the castle's depth, and the
winding stone steps that spiraled into the darkness.

Mirabelle scooped up a candle along the way and made her steady descent, lifting her frock to prevent tripping.

Once on the sandy walk, she set the candle down and grabbed the ladder next to the door, hustling it over to the pit.

"It's me, James," she assured him before she stuck her head over the hole. Knowing her brothers were armed, she didn't need them mistaking her for a foe.

"Belle!" chimed a chorus of desperately relieved siblings.

The scrambling started below. Feet shuffling. Bodies knocking. Shouts erupting.

"Here comes the ladder," she said, and carefully eased the wooden structure into the pit.

"Thank God," from Quincy.

" 'Bout bloody time," grumbled Edmund.

"Let's all get out of here," encouraged William.

"Just as soon as I kill the navigator," admonished James.

Mirabelle paused. "What was that, James?"

"Nothing, Belle," he griped. "Now drop the ladder, will you?"

She quickly hoisted the ladder out of the pit.

"What do you think you're doing?" cried Edmund.

"You're *not* going to hurt Damian," she shot back into the darkness below.

"He tried to *kill* us, Belle," growled the captain. "You think I'm going to let that—"

"You know exactly why he *tried*," she cut in. "He believed you'd killed his brother. You would have done the same if anyone had hurt Will or Eddie or Quincy. Besides, Damian didn't go through with it, did he?"

"Drop the ladder, Belle."

"Not until I have your word, James, that you won't hurt Damian."

Silence.

"Fine." She set the ladder on the ground. "I'll come back in the morning. Perhaps then you'll have an answer for me."

She started to walk away.

"Don't you dare leave us down here, Belle!" bellowed James.

"Get back here, Belle!" from Edmund.

"She won't come back," quipped Quincy. "She's as stubborn as the rest of us."

"Promise her, James," said William.

Mirabelle kept moving.

"Belle!"

She paused and looked back. "Yes, James?"

It was quiet for a moment, then: "I promise."

She sighed in approval. She would accept her brother's word. James might be a pirate, but he had never lied to her.

"Good." She marched back over to the oubliette. "Now you, Will."

"Me what?"

"It's your turn to promise."

He let out a winded sigh. "Oh, all right. I promise."

Mirabelle picked up the ladder. "Quincy?"

"I promise, too," said the youngest.

"Edmu—"

"I promise," he said tersely. "Now drop the blasted ladder!"

Confident in the sincerity of all four declarations, however begrudgingly given, Mirabelle slipped the ladder back down the hole.

"Leave the same way you came," she said. "And *don't* cause another fire."

"You'll ride with me," James shouted up to her.

She paused again.

"What now?" groaned Edmund.

Mirabelle lifted the ladder up a bit, so her brothers couldn't quite reach it. "I'm not going with you, James."

"Like hell!" came four unanimous objections.

"I mean it," she said. She would tarry long enough to see Damian well, to hear the steady breath in his lungs once more, to glimpse the smoldering fire in his eyes. Then her frazzled temperament would be satisfied. Then she could go home.

A sharp pinch on her heart at the thought of leaving the duke had her vowing, "I'm staying right here with Damian."

"I order you back to the ship, Belle!"

She snorted. "I don't think so, James."

"The navigator or duke or whatever the hell he is, is mad!" James stormed. "You are *not* staying here."

"Damian isn't mad," she contested. "He was upset about the death of his brother . . . who isn't dead anymore."

"What?" said James.

"Never mind." She waved a hand and almost lost her grip on the ladder. She now better understood why Damian had kidnapped her. Why he had needed her to lure her brothers. Crushing pain had compelled the duke to seek reprisal. She, too, would have taken any opportunity to avenge her kin. It was a brutal cycle, retribution. It would wind endlessly if it could. But it would come to a stop this very night.

"The point is," she resumed, "Damian longed for justice, and he thought he had found it when he'd captured the four of you. But he realized he was wrong. He isn't mad. And he isn't dangerous. He's hurt, and I'm not going anywhere until he's well, is that clear?"

"Belle," came a growl from the darkness, "it sounds like you care for the bounder. Are you telling me you *didn't* stay away from him like I ordered you to?"

She hesitated, then said, "Would you be furious if I said yes, James?"

Something crashed into the wall of the oubliette. It sounded suspiciously like a fist.

"I *knew* something was going on between the two of you!" James growled, "I should have chained you to your bed, Belle."

She made a wry face.

"Damian is dead," vowed the captain.

Her heart fluttered. "James, you promised!"

"I don't care what I said!" the captain blasted, then paused to ask, "Did he ask for your hand?"

"He's a duke!" she cried. "He's not going to marry a pirate."

"I don't care if he's a bloody king, the scoundrel! How could he disgrace and then abandon you?"

"I would hardly call it a disgrace," she said quietly to herself, remembering the torrid nights she had spent in Damian's arms. Nights *she* had wanted as much as the duke.

"Forget about it, Belle."

A bit dazed, she wondered, "Forget about what, James?"

"What I said about you marrying the duke. I forbid it."

She gnashed her teeth. "Damian isn't going to ask me, James." Then quietly, so he could not hear, "Not that you'd have a bloody say in it if he did."

"Good."

Exasperated, she demanded, "Why good? A second ago you wanted the duke's head on a pike for abandoning me in 'disgrace.'"

"Because he's a madman," said James, "and I won't leave you in the castle alone with him."

"He's *not* mad!" She let out a noisy exhale. "I have to get back to Damian."

"Forget it, Belle," James barked. "You're coming home with us!"

Mirabelle let go of the ladder.

An "ouch" from Quincy had her flinching, but just as swiftly, she was on her feet and hurrying to get out of there.

Leaving behind the tumult of four brothers, each

struggling to be the *first* one out the hole, she mounted the steps, and dashed back up to the ground floor and then on to the second level.

Inside Damian's room, Mirabelle found the duchess dabbing a moist cloth over her son's brow, a harried look on her face.

And Mirabelle could understand the woman's concern. Hell's fire, but the duke looked wretched. Bandaged and blanketed and struggling for breath.

Sickness roiled in her belly. A terrible fright and sense of panic. Oh God, she loved him! She couldn't deny it anymore. The truth pounded in her heart, clamored in her head.

Overcome by the fervid realization, Mirabelle needed a few measured breaths before she could find her voice again, shaky at that. "How is he?"

"I don't know," said the duchess, still nursing her son.

A quick spring to her step, Mirabelle skirted around the bed. Restless, she yearned to touch the duke, to curl up beside him and never let him go. If she could just feel the warmth of his skin, press her palm over his still beating heart, it would soothe her jitters. But out of respect for the duchess, she remained stationed by the bedside—though it hurt like hell to keep her hands off Damian.

"Well, where's the doctor?" demanded Mirabelle.

"There's nothing more he can do for the duke."

"He left?!"

"No, he retired for the night. He'll stay at the castle for the next few days to observe the duke's recovery." Features aglow under the fiery lamplight, the duchess glanced up to say, "You care a great deal for my son, don't you?"

"I do," Mirabelle whispered, a terrible ache in her breast. "You find that hard to believe?"

The baffled look in the woman's eyes shifted to one of chagrin. "He is not an easy man to love. I know of few who have ever cared for him."

"Do you care for him?"

The duchess seemed startled by the blunt query, but then she made a sad smile. "I loved him a long time ago. I suppose I still do. But when he turned out to be just like his father, I was devastated."

"He's not like that anymore," said Mirabelle, adamant. Damian had said so himself, he was a reformed rogue. She hadn't believed him then, but she believed him now. He had spared her brothers' lives tonight. He had saved her from Adam. Despite all he had suffered, great torment and loneliness, goodness still dwelled in his heart.

There was a long pause before the duchess said quietly, her lips sagging, "I lost Damian to his father long ago. I would hate to lose him again, only to . . ."

"Adam?"

She took in a sharp breath. "Yes, to Adam . . . my son . . . alive."

Mirabelle studied the older woman. She looked battered with age and woe. Such pain she must have endured at the hands of her husband. Such pain at the loss of *both* her sons. One from drowning, the other from debauchery. But now her sons were resurrected. Now she had a chance to make a good life with both. Hopefully.

The duchess swallowed her grief, casting Mirabelle a thoughtful look. "You never did tell me your name."

She hesitated. "My name is Mirabelle."

"I see." Her melancholy smile turned almost pleasant. "And how did you meet my son?"

"Aboard a ship. My brother was the captain."

The duchess nodded, then stared hard at Mirabelle's belly. "I'm going to have to find you some fresh clothes, my dear."

Mirabelle glanced down at the blood stain across her midriff. Her heart pinched at the gruesome sight. "Thank you."

She suddenly wondered why the duchess was being so kind, but then she remembered, she was still wearing Henrietta's ball gown. The duchess must think her a noble lady. And Mirabelle wouldn't disabuse her of that belief. She didn't want to be run off the estate should her true identity be revealed. She wanted to stay by Damian's side, to see him recovered. Then she would leave.

Her attention back on her son, the duchess pressed her palm to Damian's brow in a tender gesture. But right away, her features fell.

"What's wrong?" Mirabelle crawled over top of the covers, to hell with propriety. Close to Damian, she placed a hand on his chest and took in a sharp breath. "He's warm."

"I know." The duchess dipped the cloth in a nearby basin and squeezed the excess water. "I think I'll go and wake the doctor."

Handing the washcloth to Mirabelle, she quickly left the room.

Fingers trembling, Mirabelle wiped the compress over Damian's brow and cheek and neck and chest. Tears pooled in her eyes. Tears of fright. He had to live. Her heart would simply shatter without him. He needn't marry her or be with her. He just had to wake up. To live and breathe and walk the earth. She could endure anything then.

Mirabelle gulped back a shuddering sob. Here she was, just like her mother, her very happiness resting on a man's every breath. And just like her mother, she might lose the man she loved. Only she would lose him forever. Damian would not come back from the grave the way her father had returned from the sea. And that was more than she could bear.

Mirabelle closed her wet eyes and pressed her lips to Damian's in a tender kiss.

"Just live," she breathed.

Chapter 30

Mirabelle inhaled the dewy morning air.
Gripping the balcony ledge, she overlooked
the well-manicured estate, peppered with trees and
shrubs. Her eyes then roamed along the dusky horizon, as the first rays of sunlight peeked over the distant hills.

Damian was still asleep. A shadow of death hovered over him. For two days now, he had battled fever and chest injury alike. But would he come out the
victor? She had yet to determine that.

Fear ridden, she prowled the bedchamber most
nights. If she closed her eyes, terrible thoughts of
death and despair swarmed her mind. On occasion,
though, exhaustion overtook her, and she collapsed
into a nearby chair or napped next to Damian on the

bed. But most of her time was spent fretting and nursing and praying.

"How's he doing?"

Mirabelle glanced over her shoulder. Quincy filled the doorway. The rest of her kin were still hiding somewhere in the castle, waiting to take her home.

"Breathing," she said in reference to Damian's condition. It was the only optimistic thing she could say about the duke.

Quincy stepped onto the balcony. "And how are you doing?"

Barely breathing.

"I'll be fine," she said quietly. "How did you get up here?"

"I had this whole spectacular invasion planned in my head. Scaling walls, and all." He sighed heavily. "But I didn't need to do a single thing but walk up. Really, Belle, this place is like a tomb. The servants more like ghosts than flesh and blood folks. No one said a word to me as I passed through the corridors."

She stared at the glorious sunrise. "Years of dwelling in fear have dampened their spirits."

Quincy settled beside her on the balcony and propped a hip against the ledge. "I'm to deliver a message."

"What is it?"

"Come away with us and James will let you serve aboard the *Bonny Meg.*"

She glanced at her brother askance. "Bribery?"

"A promise."

She snorted. "A desperate promise." James had

already tried to steal her away, but she had locked the door on him. Barred from the bedchamber, the captain had grudgingly retreated, though he and the rest of her kin still lingered in the shadows of the keep, waiting for her. But James was weary of waiting, it seemed, for he had sent the baby of the family to try and coax her away from the duke.

"I don't think so, Quincy."

"But Belle." He took her by the arm, a beseeching look in his delft blue eyes. "You've always wanted to be a pirate."

And so she had. Ever since the death of her father, she had yearned to sail the *Bonny Meg*. It had always been a liberating experience, tending to the sails and gaffs high above deck, the wind whipping through her hair, the sun kissing her cheeks and tickling her skin. Such peace it had brought her. But now . . .

Mirabelle scrunched her brow. Now the ship seemed rather lonely. A lost body adrift on the waves without a soul. Without Damian.

And she wasn't going back to that hollow ship. Even the gentle swell of the water beneath the hull would not bring her comfort anymore. She was sure. Thoughts of her parents aboard ship would not console her any longer. She was sure. Nothing could take the place of Damian in her heart. Not even the sea.

"I'm retiring from piracy, Quincy."

But she wasn't going home, either. Not now. Not for a long time. She would wait to see Damian well and then she would leave. Go on a sojourn. She wasn't sure where, though. Scotland perhaps. She'd heard childhood tales of Scottish ancestors. She might go in search of them. But she wasn't going home to an empty house, that much was for certain.

"Oh, blast it!" He folded his arms across his chest. "Do you really care that much for the bloke?"

"Yes, Quincy, I do." She took a deep breath, quelling the fluttering beats of her heart. "I love him."

"Love?" He said the word like it was a foreign sound, something akin to Turkish. "Why?"

"Because . . ." Because she had never felt such a sense of belonging as when she was with the duke. And peace. And passion. All interwoven as one. She had never wept for anyone as she had wept for Damian, not even for her parents. She had never felt such pressing despair at the thought of losing the duke. It overwhelmed her, the fear . . . "Because I just do, Quincy."

He sighed in defeat. "You're bloody stubborn, you know that?"

"I have to be, with so many disagreeable men in my life."

"Fine." Quincy grumbled and scratched his head, locks disheveled. He really needed a bath. "I'll go back and inform James."

She nodded. "And tell James not to come up with any more offers. I won't accept them."

He muttered something about "pain" and "sister" and whatnot, but she didn't pay his ramblings much heed.

The glowing sun hovered above the hilltops, the dawn bright and welcoming, but even the warm and spectacular rays could not wash away the darkness staining her heart.

Mirabelle stepped off the balcony. She left the doors wide open, a soft breeze whistling through the room.

Tiptoeing to the bed, she slipped overtop the covers and nestled next to Damian. She liked curling up beside him, inhaling his heady scent, taking in his warmth, listening to his breathing, garbled as it was. It gave her hope that he would live.

Resting her head on Damian's shoulder, she bunched her fist against her lips and fought back the tears.

With a huff, she said, "You scoundrel! You had no right to make me fall in love with you. I was content to live out my life aboard the *Bonny Meg* until the day I met you. You ruined everything!" She spoke to him as though he could hear her, and she didn't care how ridiculous it seemed. She needed to talk to him. It made her feel better. Quietly, she said, "Too bad you're a duke. If you were a simple navigator, then we could be together."

Mirabelle sensed the tears leaking. Fright roiled in her belly. God, how she loved this man! It overwhelmed her, the emotion. Blanketed her in tranquil warmth. But it also allowed more sinister feelings to creep into her heart. Feelings of pain and loss.

She brushed away the moisture from her cheeks and gave Damian a peck on the lips.

When she pulled back and opened her eyes, she gasped.

Lids heavy with sleep, Damian peeped at her through the dark fringes of his faintly raised lashes. Though he couldn't get his eyes opened all the way, he still stared at her with indisputable scrutiny.

Her heart shuddered with bliss at the wonderful sight.

"Damian!" She kissed him again—hard. A little too hard perhaps.

He grunted, but otherwise didn't seem to mind. Slowly his eyes drifted down her frame, scorching the skin under her clothes, then lifted back up again. "All right?"

"I'm fine," she swiftly assured him, and reached across his chest to pick up the glass of water sitting on the nightstand. By the sound of his raspy voice, he really needed the refreshment.

Trembling hand tucked under his head—for she was giddy with delight; it was very nearly bursting from her—she held the glass to his lips so he could better drink the cool tonic.

Damian looked around the room. "Adam?"

"He's gone." She set the glass back on the stand. She almost missed the table, her fingers were shaking so hard. "But I'm sure he'll come home one day. He just needs some time to be alone."

Despair glimmered in the duke's eyes for a moment before he returned his smoldering gaze to her. Then warmth spread through the luminous orbs, and she thought her heart would shatter at the passion reflecting in the deep blue pools.

"I love you," she blurted out, then blushed at her outburst. But she was afraid he might fall back asleep—and never wake up—and then she would miss her chance to tell him what was truly in her heart.

"I heard," he croaked.

Her blush deepened. Her ramblings! And about all sorts of intimate things. "Um, about that . . ."

But her words trailed to a stop when she noticed his grieved expression. He wanted to tell her something. Something obviously unsavory.

"Oh," she said sheepishly and pushed away, a wicked wound on her heart. He didn't love her back. No wonder he looked so distressed. Here she was, revealing her adoration, and the man didn't return her affection.

A cumbersome pressure on her voice, she whispered, "I suppose it's time for me to go home."

"Belle—"

She scooted to the edge of the bed, "I understand, Damian. I'm a pirate. You can't have me about the castle."

He captured her wrist. "I love you, Belle."

Breath trapped in her throat. Her heart hammered in her breast, the beats deafening, ringing in her ears.

"But I . . . I can't be with you," he said softly.

The squeezing ache in her chest startled her for a moment. "It's the pirate thing again, isn't it?"

"No, it's not that."

Her brow wrinkled. "Then what?"

It was back in his eyes, that same forlorn, even hopeless, look. "I'll hurt you, Belle."

"Damian—"

"I will," he insisted. "It's in my blood. I'm just like my father. One day, I'll break your spirit and—"

Filled with comprehension, Mirabelle pressed her body next to his and kissed him for all she was worth.

She ravished him as he had ravished her so many times in the past.

Now that, surely, got some air into his ailing lungs!

"You are *not* your father," she said, breathless.

He was a bit breathless, too, and it took him a moment to say, "But I hurt your brothers, and one day ·I'll hurt you, too."

"You dropped my brothers into a pit, Damian. That's about all you did."

"The pit?" he rasped.

"Oh, I let them out, don't worry." Her hand flitted toward the door. "They're lurking about somewhere. But you see, Damian, you have a heart and a soul. I know you've kept both under lock and key for so long, and maybe you really think you've lost them, but you haven't. I believe in you, Damian. I trust you . . . I love you."

Arms clamped hard around her waist. Even with his ailment, the strength and brawn in Damian's embrace was still there. And she knew in that moment he would be all right.

"Don't go, Belle—ever."

She looked down at him, stunned. "What?"

"Marry me."

A little voice inside her hooted with joy.

"But I'm a pirate. What will the *ton* think?"

"The *ton* will think I've married a 'merchant's' daughter."

"But that's scandalous."

There was a dark glow in his charming gaze. "And I'm a rogue duke wont to scandal. I'd say it's fitting."

Mirabelle held her breath, as a flurry of sensations stormed her breast. But one sentiment prevailed . . .

She wanted to laugh. It tickled her throat, the merriment. Tears welled in her eyes, drenched her cheeks. Tears of delight this time. And of pleasure. Heavens, her whole body shuddered with glee. She wasn't afraid to give her heart away anymore. She understood her mother better now. It was worth the risk to love, she realized, for the joy was immeasurable.

Intent on a bit of mischief, she smiled and said, "And why should I consent to be your wife?"

"You'll have a castle, Belle."

Slowly, she shook her head. "Not good enough."

"A title, then."

Again, she shook her head. "Still not good enough."

"All the gold you could ever wish for."

She pretended to think about that, but then shook her head. "I still want more."

"How about a duke's heart?" he whispered, piercing her with a passionate stare. "It's yours, Belle. Forever if you want it."

Misty eyed, she pressed her lips to his in a tender kiss. "Now that, Your Grace, is a treasure too tempting to resist."

Epilogue

Damian waved his hand, clearing a path through the cloud of dust. The din of the workers around him was making his head hurt, and he headed for more clandestine shelter.

Winding through the castle causeways, he passed the sitting room. The door was ajar, and he could see his mother ensconced in a chair by the window.

Damian paused and stared at the woman thoughtfully. Macabre garb aside, she was arrayed in sapphire blue, lost to her thoughts and a letter in her hands.

Quietly, he closed the door of the parlor to give her peace. He was glad she had remained at the castle. After the wedding, the dowager duchess had resolved to return to London, claiming the newlywed couple needed their privacy. But Damian had asked the woman to stay. After so many years of separation, he wanted to get to know his mother better. And she wasn't opposed to the offer.

At the end of the corridor, the duke mounted the steps and headed for the west wing. The spring sunshine was pouring in through the unmasked windows, the heavy drapery dismantled and buried somewhere in the attic. It was tranquil, too, and he heaved a deep sigh to be away from all the commotion below stairs.

He soon reached the room. A smile on his lips, he stood under the door frame for a time.

Inside, his wife stood with a frilly cushion in each hand, her head whisking from one to the other as she tried to make a decorating decision.

His wife.

Damian loved the way the word sounded in his heart. It warmed his soul.

He stepped into the chamber and treaded softly toward her. She was bedecked in a resplendent gown of toffee brown, and when she moved, the morning light shimmered off the glossy fabric, making her glow and sparkle, taking his breath away. "Need some help?"

Mirabelle whirled around—and her belly nearly swiped him in the gut. "Yes!" She held out the pillows. "Look at the lilac drapes. Now which cushion is a better match? The powder blue or the mist green?"

Damian studied the two. "The mist green."

"Are you sure?"

"Positive."

"It's settled then." She tossed the blue one over his shoulder and huffed. "I'm so glad that's over with."

Withholding a grin, Damian wrapped his arms

around his pleasantly plump wife. "Why don't you let me hire—"

"No, Damian." Her amber eyes lighted with playful warning. "We've been through this already. I want to see to the nursery myself. But if you or your mother would like to help . . ."

This time he grinned. "How quaintly coaxed, Your Grace."

She fluttered her long flaxen lashes. "I'm well versed in manipulation, you know? I am a pirate, after all."

"A retired pirate, I should think."

She snuggled closer to him. "If you insist."

"I do insist." A quick peck on the lips. "And I'm afraid you'll have to be satisfied with my input for the nursery. Mother is secured below stairs."

"Is she feeling well?"

"Yes, she just needs a little solitude. She got another letter from Adam today."

Mirabelle hugged him tight. "I'm glad he writes to her."

"So am I."

It had been eight months since the night of the stabbing. Eight whirlwind months. Damian had recovered from most of his wounds. His body was sound, his soul at peace thanks to Belle. But his heart still ached for Adam.

Mirabelle wiggled in his embrace. "Something else came in the post today."

"Oh?" He quirked a brow, releasing his wife.

She shuffled over to the desk and picked up a little packet. "It's addressed to you."

Damian eyed the parcel, wrapped in brown paper

and secured with string. "Odd. Jenkins never mentioned a delivery."

"That's because I took the packet from Jenkins and made him promise not to tell you about it. I wanted to give it to you myself."

He grimaced. "It's not from your brothers, is it? A noose to hang myself with or some such rot?"

"No," she huffed and placed her arms akimbo. "Now are you going to open it or shall I?"

Damian cast his wife a curious eye, then loosened the knot of string. Peeling back the paper wrapping, he balked.

There in singed leather, the edges tattered and burned, was *Robinson Crusoe*, the very edition he'd believed lost to fire so many years ago.

Stunned, he looked to his wife. "But how did you—"

"Oh, it's not from me," she quipped.

"Then who?"

"Read the card, Damian."

The card? Damian glanced back at the book, heart throbbing, and noticed the scrap of paper peeking out from behind the front cover. He carefully opened the tome to the first page and scanned the missive:

> *To read to your children.*
> *Adam*

Damian didn't say anything for a time, a great welter of emotion ballooning in his chest. He just stared at the note, so simple and yet so full of promise.

"Adam must have saved the book from the fire," he

said quietly, still in awe, "and then hidden it, to keep it safe, all these years." He glanced up at his lovely wife to find her smiling. "You don't seem surprised by this, Belle."

She traced her fingers lightly over his. "Your mother and I might have written a few letters to Adam, encouraging a reconciliation."

Damian delved deep into his wife's golden eyes. Such lovely eyes, reflecting such warmth and love. "Oh, Belle." He kissed her then, a passionate kiss meant to sear her right down to her very toes. He couldn't find the words to express the joy rattling inside him. It was such an immense relief to know the brothers would be brothers again—one day.

When the kiss ended, Mirabelle smiled and twirled a lock of his hair around her finger. "Speaking of reunions and brothers . . ."

"No, Belle."

She sighed. "It's too late, Damian. I got a missive from James this morning. My brothers will be here on the morrow."

The merry moment was quickly tainted by the appalling news. "But I *just* got rid of them two months ago."

"Yes, well, they want to be here for the birthing."

Damian suppressed a growl. After the wedding announcement was made, the Hawkins brothers had moved into the castle. No one had invited them to stay; the brood had simply dug in their heels and set up shelter in some of the unoccupied rooms. And Damian had wanted to strangle the lot of them. The brothers had interfered in all aspects of keep life,

likely hoping to drive a wedge between Damian and
his intended bride. What the brothers didn't realize,
though, was that Damian would've tolerated the in-
cendiary brood for *life* in order to make Mirabelle his
bride. And so, having failed to convince their sister to
call off the engagement, the men had resigned themselves to the fate of brother-in-laws. *Six* bloody months
later, the troop had finally departed.

He grumbled, "I'll have Jenkins hide the silverware again."

She smacked his arm. "My brothers have retired
from piracy, you know that."

Aye, he did. It seemed one could not have a sister as
a duchess and still be a pirate, so the Hawkins brood
had declared retirement. Not from the sea—for such
men could not stay grounded for long; the call of the
water would always beckon—but from piracy. James
had resolved to turn the *Bonny Meg* into a respect-
able merchant ship. Damian wasn't so sure, though.

"I'll believe it, Belle, when I don't find any missing
silverware."

A loud crash boomed in the castle.

Mirabelle wrinkled her brow. "My brothers already?"

"I don't think so." Damian listened for a bit. "Must
be another gargoyle coming down."

"About bloody time," she huffed. "I hate those
fiendish things."

He nuzzled her brow. "I'm tearing the castle apart
for you. I hope you know how much I love you, Your
Grace."

She nuzzled back and whispered, "And I'm having

your child. I hope you know how much I love *you*, Your Grace."

He shuddered at her heartfelt words. A flurry of sensations stormed his breast at the delightful thought of their future together. He wasn't alone anymore. He wasn't in pain. He was at peace for the first time in his existence. And the gratitude inside him was overwhelming.

He couldn't wait to be a father. A good father. He couldn't wait for the laughter to start ringing throughout the castle. The patter of little feet in play. The merry cries of joy and shrieks of wonder as duke and duchess and children alike celebrated life together.

"I do know," he vowed, and took Belle's lips in his for a thorough kiss. "Most assuredly, my love."

Next month, don't miss these exciting new love stories only from Avon Books

Autumn in Scotland by Karen Ranney

An Avon Romantic Treasure

Charlotte MacKinnon will never get over being abandoned by her husband after just a week of marriage. Now he has returned, five years later, and he's far more handsome and charming than he ever was before. In fact, it's almost as if he's an entirely different person . . .

Passions of the Ghost by Sara Mackenzie

An Avon Contemporary Romance

In this conclusion to Sara Mackenzie's sexy Immortal Warriors trilogy, Reynald de Mortimer awakens from a centuries-long sleep to discover his castle has become a high society hotel. He finds himself strangely drawn to one of the hotel's guests—but will their love survive the demons that haunt them both?

For the Love of a Pirate by Edith Layton

An Avon Romance

The always-proper Lord Wylde is stunned to discover that he was betrothed at birth to the granddaughter of a pirate! True, Lisabeth is beautiful and intriguing, but she's the opposite of what he's always wanted . . . which may just make her the one thing he truly needs.

Confessions of a Viscount by Shirley Karr

An Avon Romance

Charlotte Parnell needs to prove her worth as a spy. When she meets Lord Moncreiffe, a man looking for a little excitement in his proper life, it's clear they make the perfect team. But will these spies-in-the-making really throw caution to the wind and unlock the secrets in their own hearts?

Avon Romantic Treasures

Unforgettable, enthralling love stories, sparkling with passion and adventure from Romance's bestselling authors

$\mathcal{A}$von $\mathcal{R}$omances
the best in
exceptional authors and unforgettable novels!